With one tapered finger he gently, but inexorably, raised her chin. "My beautiful Angel," he whispered, "Look at me."

For long moments, Cecilia's thick lashes hid her expression. Then, she raised her eyes to meet his.

Strangely, Cecilia felt as if she might willingly drown in the mist-grey depths before her; no longer did anger cause the opaque, metallic glitter that had earlier marred the surface of his eyes. Now their expression was smoke-soft, absorbing, ready to drink up her thoughts. Her hand seemed to lift of its own accord, wanting to reach up and brush the texture of his lips, the enticing fullness beguiling her.

None knew what might have occurred next, for the faint sound of the street knocker broke the spell.

OUT OF THE COMMON WAY

Melissa Lynn Jones

FAWCETT CREST • NEW YORK

A Fawcett Crest Book
Published by Ballantine Books
Copyright © 1993 by Melissa Lynn Jones

Library of Congress Catalog Card Number: 93-90196

ISBN 0-449-22236-5

Manufactured in the United States of America

First Edition: September 1993

CHAPTER ONE

PORTUGAL, 1812

". . . and *repiqued*, and *capotted*, by damn. I was warned you were a sharper!" The gruff-voiced speaker tossed down his playing cards and fixed his opponent with a fierce look, only to find a certain difficulty with maintaining his pose in the face of the trilling laughter which met his outburst.

"In that case," came the amused reply, "I suppose I must give you a chance to recoup your losses, Sergeant. Although for now I think it time you took your rest." The victor gathered up the scattered cards and tapped them on the tray top to even their edges. The cards were shuffled efficiently, then made to disappear into the capacious pocket of a crisply starched white apron.

"And here I thought meself a knowing 'un, wide awake on all suits," the old soldier grumbled, pushing back against the pillows as he tried to hide a smile.

Tiny gold flecks danced down from Miss Cecilia Linscombe's wide brown eyes. She regarded her playing partner pertly. "Oh, I'm sure you are a, um, *knowing 'un*, Sergeant, so perhaps by tomorrow your luck will be in. That's if," she teased, "you truly think you can best me so soon?" She then reached over to lay a gentle hand against Sergeant-Major Haskell's grizzle-whiskered cheek, ascertaining that there was no return of the fever which had kept him abed.

"Augh, miss. None of yer fussin' now," he ob-

1

jected crustily. "Me shoulder's gone almost well since that cursed French bayonet caught me; I'll be right as a trivet in no time. And ye can bet I will be having that game with ye tomorrow. I'll be a-winning it, too! Just see if I don't."

The old soldier leaned farther back against the linen-encased pillows piled up behind him. He considered his engaging young nurse; abruptly, he changed the subject. "So tell me, miss, how be it that a young lady like yerself is in this godforsaken country, anyways? Not that I'm complaining, mind, for I've been in field hospitals before this"—he looked around him at the sparkling windows and spotless floors—"but never did I see one near as fine. Never been around the Sisters afore, neither," he added, cocking his eye toward a modestly-gowned religious carrying a tray of medicants into the ward, "but they're good women, they are. Howsomever that may be, though, to my way of thinkin', ye don't belong here yerself. Ye should be back home, going to fancy parties and findin' yerself a young man. Just what's yer da thinking of to be keeping you here on the Peninsula?" He referred to her father, Major James Linscombe, quartered on this little town of Tôrres Vedras, a few miles from Lisbon.

"Father is not 'keeping' me here," she corrected firmly. "In fact, it was more in the way of being a rescue. You see, my mother died when I was quite young, at which time I was sent to live with Father's elder brother, who is a Sussex baronet. And to be entirely fair, I will have to own that Uncle Andrew and Aunt Margaret suffered at least as much from the association as I did."

"Whatcher be meanin' by that, miss? Didn't they take to ye?" The sergeant-major was puzzled by her admission.

Miss Linscombe shook her head, at the same time shrugging her slim shoulders. "No, I'm afraid we did not get on well together. It seems I had some difficulty in paying the proper obeisance to their notions of propriety."

2

"Sticklers, were they?" the old veteran sympathized. "I don't know too much about all them society manners. Nonetheless, I do know genteel young ladies shouldn't be tending common cannon-fodder like meself." He turned a reproving eye on the young beauty who sat in the slatted wooden chair alongside his cot. The late afternoon sun had burnished her short, dark-red curls to a fiery shade, and he decided that the color was quite unlike any he'd ever seen.

"Oh, good gracious, no," she interrupted his thoughts with droll tones. "Instead, I should be listening to lectures about how I must always give Lady Tra-la a respectful curtsy, yet must make only the barest of nods to the vicar who cares for the poor in the neighborhood. He is not well connected, you understand. I must never *ever* speak up when Aunt Margaret criticizes me for something I haven't done wrong, and must comply with all sorts of silly instructions without question. No, I thank you. It wasn't the life for me."

The old soldier digested this for a moment. "I suppose I see whatcher mean, miss. Wouldn't care for much of that, neither. At least yer here behind the lines and not traipsin' about with the troops."

"Oh, but I have been to Spain. Twice, in fact." Her eyes sparkled in remembrance. "The first time, I nearly became a bit of that cannon-fodder you spoke of, too. It was during my first year here, when I accompanied a few officers' wives who set up housekeeping in a tiny village just over the border. We were there for the whole of the summer—and, really, Sergeant, it seemed peaceful enough—until we received word that the French were taking up battle positions but a mile to the west."

"The de'il ye say!"

"Indeed, yes. The message was very specific."

"But your da was there to get you to safety, was he?"

"Unfortunately not, Sergeant. He happened to be out on patrol, so we had naught but a green lieu-

3

tenant left in charge at the village. Mercy! You have never seen such chaos, either. The lieutenant, I think his name was Blevins, shouted orders left and right, desperately trying to form a proper evacuation. Women were everywhere shrieking and flapping about, while oxen balked and carts overturned, jamming the streets with crates of household goods." Laughter came bubbling out at the memory. "It was truly the funniest sight!"

"Then, it was the lieutenant who saw everyone make it away?"

"Hmm? Not exactly," she answered slowly, a mischievous smile playing across the corners of her mouth. "You see, Sergeant, I left."

The sergeant-major's eyes nearly popped out of his head. "You . . . you did what? You don't mean to say, miss, that you went out all alone? By yerself? With no *escort!*"

"I'm afraid I did," came the answer. "I was assigned a darling little donkey who hitched to my cart without the least fuss, and, since it seemed we would be overrun before all the confusion was sorted out, I simply picked up the reins and started off on my own. All might have gone well, except that when I drove over a hilltop, I espied another contingent of French soldiers a hundred yards ahead of me."

Fond of a good yarn in the ordinary way, Sergeant Haskell silently admitted that this tale was becoming more nerve-shattering than most. The very idea of some gangling girl, riding unprotected into the hands of the enemy . . .

"Of course," she went on in a hushed voice, warming to her story, "I knew I had no hope of turning the cart around unobserved. I dropped the reins, slithered down, and began crawling away through a barley field off to one side. Soon enough, our cannon found the French and began firing round after mighty round, while I sat crouched in the middle of that field with my hands pressed over my ears. It's very peculiar, the things you recall,"

4

she next said musingly. "I remember peeking up through the pall of smoke, all thick and smelly, to see that my cart was still standing, much as I had left it. My little brown donkey stood placidly nibbling away at the grass by the side of the road. Only later did I learn that the beast was quite deaf, and thus unmoved by the horrendous noise."

"Yes, yes?" he urged her, impatient at the interruption.

"Well, the bombardment finally proved effective, but I wasn't certain it was really over until I saw the approach of our own grenadiers in their lovely red coats. Even at that I stood with care, for I was somewhat cramped after having sat curled up for so long."

At this point Miss Linscombe again paused, apparently mindful of her duties. "Am I tiring you, Sergeant? Perhaps I should finish tomorrow after you've rested."

The sergeant-major looked outraged that she should even think of denying him the details of the outcome. "Blast it, girl. Get to it, or I shan't get a wink of sleep!"

She picked up the tale, evidently not at all dissatisfied to have her audience so enthralled. "As you might expect, one of the men investigating the wagon recognized me. He immediately dispatched a message to my father; although, when the major came charging up to the scene, I could see that he was not in the slightest amused." She stifled a giggle at the recollection.

"I should think not!" the old soldier expostulated. "Tore into you, did he? And no more than you were deserving of, beggin' yer pardon, miss." The sergeant had no trouble imagining how Major Linscombe must have felt at such a moment. Why, if the chit was his daughter and had done such a stupid, totty-headed thing, well!

Miss Linscombe seemed to surmise the gist of these thoughts. "Quite so. Yes, Father came down from his horse faster than I have ever seen him do, shouting and stabbing his finger before my face. The platoon seemed to fall back, one by one, and several men turned absolutely scarlet." This time she laughed aloud and in earnest, a warm, rich sound that drew answering smiles from bunks up and down the ward. "Oh, my, yes, my father gave a masterful demonstration of military invective that day—legendary, in fact—for the men still talk of it. But the shame of it is, Sergeant, that with the roar of cannon fire still ringing through my ears, I could not hear a single word!"

Sergeant Haskell chuckled along with her. "Just as well you were spared, then," he agreed, considering that the language needed to redden grown men's faces, more especially amongst His Majesty's troopers, must have been colorful, indeed. The sergeant then thought to ask, "So, what happened to the lieutenant and the other civilians? Did they make it out a'right?"

"Afterward, we learned that all of the baggage had to be left behind in the village and was subsequently destroyed in the skirmish. The lieutenant did manage to lead everyone away to safety first, and was later commended, I think, while Father was so pleased that we ourselves had comfortable mattresses to sleep on, not to mention the supplies to make a good meal, that he soon enough forgave me.

"But that's quite enough for now," she said, rising gracefully. "I have a few tasks to finish before I go home for my supper, so I shall bid you *adieu*." With quick, sure motions she straightened the blankets and plumped up the pillows. "Sleep well, Sergeant, and I will look forward to having that game with you tomorrow." She tossed him a lively smile.

Watching her tall, slender figure move down the low rows of cots, the sergeant-major saw her take a minute to check a bandage here and adjust a screen there, once stopping to lift a man's shoulders so as to assist him with a drink of water.

6

Taller than most of the men in his regiment, Miss Linscombe would be noticed wherever she walked. Her elegant height was not really what commanded the old soldier's interest, though. She might be as pretty as could stare with her glossy, odd-colored hair and her huge brown eyes, but neither was it her unusual coloring nor her lovely face which made her so very notable. No. The sergeant marveled at the intrepid young lady with the infectiously undaunted spirit.

He had observed her closely during the two weeks of his convalescence and had seen how she encouraged the men with her complete assurance that all would soon be well. The ugliest wound left Miss Linscombe undismayed, and many a man found her easy acceptance of his disfigurement heartening. She seemed to have a way of making pain seem temporary and unimportant, her ready smile scattering the dark clouds of fear and uncertainty.

It was hardly the first time the old veteran had been carted behind the lines; scars of battles past proved it past any doubt. And yet, for once, he'd found the experience almost pleasant. Sergeant Haskell gave thanks that he had been brought under this young lady's care—even if the pert-eyed miss *would* outdo him at cards.

With a cheery parting wave, Cecilia left the wardroom and turned out of sight, pausing only for a quick glance at the small enameled watch-piece suspended from the delicate pinchbeck chain around her neck. It served to remind her that her escort would already be waiting below. She hastened down the hall to reach the narrow staircase, now sunk in late-afternoon shadows.

So intent was she while she skipped down the steeply pitched steps that she failed to note the man just ascending the cramped stairwell. Only his quick bracing prevented them both from tumbling to the bottom.

She felt herself thrown violently against a solid

7

and unyielding wall of densely muscled chest. Losing her single hold on the wooden side railing, she grabbed desperately at the obstacle before her, finding the board-stiff epaulets decorating an officer's tunic. The impact robbed her of her breath. She clutched at broad shoulders as she strained and fought to take in air.

"Steady there. Just take it slowly," instructed the man she held before her. He, at least, had managed to keep one hand on the rail, catching her waist securely with his other arm.

After regaining some measure of control, Cecilia finally found her voice. "Oh, I do beg your pardon," she gasped. "That *was* careless of me." She drew aside to let the man pass but found herself held fast by one long, unyielding arm. Uncertain how next to proceed, she pulled her hands away and leaned back to peer into the officer's face.

He was a big fellow with eyes of an indeterminate shade; his forehead was broad and smooth. Though the light was poor for its being so late in the day, she could also make out the shape of a clean, square jaw beneath handsomely carved cheekbones.

His eyes, much darkened by the dull light, seemed to study her face in return. "I would not care to think myself responsible for any accident to such a lovely ministering angel," he said softly in serious tones. "For only an angel could so fly into my arms from above, and I would dread causing harm to such a rare creature." A quick, abbreviated smile revealed white teeth through the enveloping gloom.

Cecilia chuckled, unable to resist the whimsy. "Well, I cannot think that I *flew* exactly. Especially since there is not sufficient room here to spread a set of wings. Be that as it may, sir, this so-called 'angel' was just leaving and is late in doing so. I am quite recovered now, I assure you, so if you will be good enough to permit me passage?" She gave a pointed look to his impeding arm. While not for the world would she have admitted it, her everyday work with the wounded had in no wise prepared her for the growing discomfort aroused by her prolonged contact with this obviously healthy specimen of young manhood. Truth be told, she felt rather eager to get herself gone.

"Ah, but how can we know for certain that you are uninjured?" the young officer questioned solemnly, his voice low in the afternoon quiet. "Is it not a fact that often the most serious wounds are those which do not reveal themselves to the eye?" A black, sharply defined eyebrow rose to a peak just above his own right eye.

At this sign of good humor, Cecilia forgot her unease. "That may well be, Colonel," she said, noting the gleam of the designating insignia attached to his jacket. "However, I do not believe I've sustained any damage. We ethereal sorts are not subject to the more mundane hurts, you understand. Now," she went on more briskly, "unless I can be of some service, you really must excuse me." Her brown eyes smiled politely in the dimness, though she held his gaze without wavering. The level tone of her voice showed she expected immediate compliance.

His hold on her waist did not relax in any measure. "Oh? And what sort of service is it you provide here?" His brow climbed to new heights, a soft, suggestive smile playing across his lips.

Unaware of any particular meaning to this question, Cecilia readily replied. "Certainly, I assist however I'm needed. There are so many men here, wounded and friendless, that I am glad to do whatever I can. Why? Do you require something I can perhaps help you with?"

The colonel reviewed the young woman's words . . . and the offer thereby implied. He had no doubts about the type of service she meant, for the class of women who toiled in her capacity were known to be accommodating, often *most* accommodating. And if the shadows prevented his precise inspection, he could still see enough to know that she was far more appealing than the usual of her sort: those enterprising women who thronged to any area where the military congregated. This young woman boasted a slim waist and firm bosom—attributes much to his taste—while the fair, smooth skin of her face presented a perfect oval in the dim confines of the stairwell.

Not one to lose an opportunity while wasting time over making a decision, he gave a brief nod of assent. "Yes, very well," he said crisply. "I am here to see to one of my men, but after that I had planned to take supper at my hotel. I would enjoy having female companionship with my meal. And afterward? Well, that will be up to you. However, should you decide in my favor and permit me your company through the night, you may be certain that it will be a pleasure to us both, and one that I will gladly afford."

Cecilia's mouth gaped open. She stared stupidly at the meaningless invitation, her eyes darting across those handsome, masculine features still so near to her own. Why should he wish for her to stay with him all night? Whatever could he mean?

Then, as comprehension dawned, her eyes slitted in anger as her mind raced for the words to bring this presumptuous, oh-so-superior officer into the right of it. Just because she served in a hospital, it did not mean she was *loose*.

But before she could bring any denial to her lips, a better answer leapt to mind. The frown just forming relaxed, and a devilish spark of mischief took its place. She knew that a single cry would empty the ward and bring any number of men swarming to her defense, able-bodied or not. The four good Sisters who shared nursing duties would all come on the run, not to mention the escort patiently awaiting her below. No, there was no real cause to feel concern.

This very surety now made her bold. She lowered her eyes lest he guess her intentions. "Pray, sir, at

10

which hotel shall you be found?" she asked in a coy voice, unlike her own. Trying her best to appear alluring, she offered up what she imagined would pass for a seductive smile. "And, please, exactly who is it that I should ask for?"

Thus assured that he had correctly taken her measure, the officer prudently bethought his own reasons for being in Tôrres Vedras. He answered her with a measure of caution. "Inquire at the Hôtel Quieroz for Colonel Trelwyn." Then, with greater warmth, "And you may trust me not to keep you waiting."

Cecilia noted his air of masculine confidence and had to work to keep her smile from stretching itself too widely. "Oh, I am sure you will not, Colonel. The Quieroz it shall be. Shall we say, at nine of the clock?"

The time and ground for battle established, she then acted to increase her advantage by a clever feinting tactic. Instinctively, she employed a previously unused weapon in her arsenal, one she trusted would mislead him further. Arching her brows in a way she hoped he would find coquettish, she deliberately fluttered luxuriant eyelashes in a most enticing manner.

Later, Cecilia had to deduce that she must be more skilled at flirtation than she had ever supposed, for no sooner did she fan her lashes than the colonel snugged her tighter against his deep chest, closing the small distance between them. The cushiony-soft pressure of his mouth upon her own was wholly unexpected, warm, and instantly beguiling to her senses. She stilled in curious wonder as he applied a kiss to her upturned lips; without conscious thought, her eyes closed and she raised her hands to rest upon his shoulders once more.

Delighted by the enthusiastic response to his advances, Colonel Trelwyn moved to support the back of her neck, tangling his long fingers in the short, satiny curls at her nape. He plied his mouth skillfully across her own, gently flicking his tongue

11

across her lips with feather-light touches, just barely felt.

For long seconds Cecilia forgot her purpose. She became absorbed in the newness of the experience, all the while a tingly soft, answering warmth stole through her. Accustomed to the hearty hugs and brusque kisses of her father, she had never suspected that the kiss between a man and a woman might hold so much more. Oh, she knew about the camp followers, for who could live among soldiers and not be aware of their casual relations? And she knew about the romantic attachments young men formed, since she had often penned the letters sent by the wounded to their sweethearts back home. But she had never particularly appreciated the bawdy drivings of the one, nor the earnest yearnings of the other.

A glimmer of understanding formed in her mind, and with it, a burgeoning awareness of what she was about! With exercised strength she pushed herself back in panic.

Somewhat lost in his own enjoyment, Colonel Trelwyn failed to note her fright or the stiff embarrassment that followed when he carefully loosed his hold. He regained his composure, his lips spreading in a slow, knowing half smile. "Until nine o'clock, then?" he questioned softly. At Cecilia's still-shocked nod, he eased to one side of the narrow stairwell, allowing her room to pass by unhindered.

On legs unaccountably shaky, Cecilia clung to the railing and cautiously made her way to street level before turning to look back up the steps. The officer had already moved down the hall and was, thankfully, out of sight. As she stood there and stared upward, a cool, damp nose pushed its way into her hand, recalling her to her surroundings.

She bent with relief to greet her escort. "Oh, Marpessa, forgive me," she apologized, albeit in a voice none too steady. "I didn't mean to make you wait so long. How is my good girl today?"

The slow-waving tail of an immense black French

12

Briard answered her words. Cecilia stroked the strong, thick coat beneath her fingers, deliberately relaxing the tension built up within her. When she ceased her attentions and straightened, the heavily built canine looked toward the stairs, then back at her mistress, as if requesting permission.

On most days the dog was allowed to go up to the ward for a visit before their leaving. There, she would weave in and out between the beds in her own prescribed course, letting no one ignore her presence. Marpessa could charm even the crankiest invalid with her bids for affection, her expectant black eyes and swishing plumed tail proving more than a match for anyone's crotchets. The quiet ones, the men in the greatest pain, would find her fine head laid upon their cots while she patiently awaited their notice. Soon, a hand would steal out from under the covers, reaching for the comfort she offered. The Briard, bred to herd and guard in splendid isolation, seemed to sense any loneliness, while she had the certain knack of dispelling its worst effects. Marpessa would absorb any confidence with sympathy, and a man whispering into her upright ears was a familiar sight at Santa Clara Infirmary.

"Nooo, I think the men can spare you today." Cecilia shied from the notion of a repeated encounter with the too-assuming young colonel. And despite her stalwart protector, she felt an unaccustomed shudder of what?—fear?—at the idea of another meeting with the wide-shouldered officer. She thought she might sooner prefer to face Napoleon himself!

She quickly untied the sash of her bib-front apron and hung the crisp white covering on a peg in a side closet, at the same time taking out a shawl of local weave from a second peg, discreetly wrapping it about herself in the Portuguese fashion. She straightened her posture and squared her shoulders.

"Come, 'Pessa." She spoke more incisively. "We

13

have a mission to accomplish, and less than two hours to prepare."

Giving a quick glance to be sure that the colonel was still above stairs, her legs once again firm beneath her, Cecilia stepped out into the orangy glow of the late August evening.

CHAPTER TWO

The way home sloped downward and the hurrying pair moved in practiced unison through the narrow, winding streets. Maintaining a position just slightly behind Cecilia, the dog followed in alert silence, casting her black eyes and ears with intent awareness. The sturdy Briard knew her duties, and she gave her total attention to safeguarding the way. Though she had once been the property of a vanquished French officer, Marpessa had served Cecilia loyally since she was little more than a squirmy, fat-pawed puppy. Now, every day after lunchtime, the Briard came with her mistress up the hill and, unless bidden to stay, returned to shepherd Cecilia home each afternoon. The years of association had made her sensitive to her owner's desires, so she willingly lengthened her stride as the tall young woman moved swiftly down the incline.

Despite the simple cut of Cecilia's serge cotton dress, passersby acknowledged the upright, gliding carriage of a lady of quality. Had the young colonel earlier seen her smooth gait, or had the light in the stairwell been strong enough for him to more clearly discern her fine, proud features, he surely would not have so badly mistaken her status. As the daughter of the second son of a baronet, Miss Linscombe bore no noble rank, of course, but it was indisputably evident that she had the advantage of gentle birth.

Cecilia had, in fact, endured the usual privileges of her class for her first fifteen years, acquiring the skills customary for a young lady of breeding. But for her, those had been years of infinite boredom, scarcely relieved by irritation. Sharing the schoolroom with her two older cousins, she had been pinched and teased by the two nasty girls whenever Miss Sheldon let pass a moment of inattention. "Sneaky little prunes," Cecilia had once heard Miss Sheldon say when the long-suffering governess had thought no one around to overhear. But Cecilia had applied herself to her own studies as needful and had mostly managed to avoid her cousins and their irksome ways. She had, however, found it somewhat more difficult to ignore her guardians' constant strictures.

Her uncle, Sir Andrew Linscombe, was the head of the family. Ever conscious of this elevated position, he frequently resorted to petty tyranny to bolster his own good opinion of himself. He was not the man to appreciate a child who dared question his dictates, more especially since he rarely managed to prevail over his young niece or extract her promise of future conformity. It must not be supposed that Miss Cecilia was rude or rebellious exactly; it was more that she seemed unable to accept what she could not quite understand. There were, unfortunately, all too many rules which she failed to see reason for, thus constantly landing her in the briars.

Lady Linscombe had proved rather better at plaguing her niece, holding out the two sly daughters of the house for good example. Cecilia had grown to dread hearing that "young ladies do not behave in such a manner" or how "Theresa would never soil her dress so!" when it was her cousins who had deliberately pushed her into the puddle which muddied her skirts in the first place. Both Theresa and her younger sister, Sibyl, had been cunningly skilled at presenting the proper outward appearances. And while Cecilia had *tried* to comport herself within the bounds specified, her endeavors had not always met with success.

16

"So you want to follow the drum?" her father had asked on that happy, happy day, four years before. The budding red-haired beauty of his long-dead wife and the forthright posture so much like his own had intrigued and delighted him. "Well, m'dear," he'd agreed, "from what I hear, you're not likely to fly up into the boughs over every least thing, and 'tis time and past we came to know one another better."

To Cecilia's intense pleasure, he had then acceded to her request and had taken her with him, dismissing the notably insincere protests of his brother and sister-in-law.

Major Linscombe viewed his daughter's aberrations with a far more tolerant eye than had his kinsmen. He never restrained Cecilia with meaningless conventions; he even applauded her ability to adjust to the fortunes of war without being easily thrown into a pelt. Whereas, particularly after the incident at a certain Spanish village, he should have suspected that such uncritical approbation would lead to a day of further independences.

And today was just such a day!

The decided glint in Cecilia's eye might not have warned a fond parent, but it would have filled her old governess with the greatest dread for her favorite charge. Miss Sheldon would have recognized the flinty look as the resolute young lady entered the unlocked iron gate to the tiny walled courtyard leading up to the house. She would have known that the determined young miss was bent on having her way and the consequences be damned. But Miss Sheldon was hundreds of miles away in England.

Late-blooming roses of exotic color rioted against the high sides of the stuccoed walls surrounding the house, yet Cecilia did not spare them a glance when she hurried through the courtyard and on into the small rented cottage she shared with her father. "Maria, *chegamos en casa*," she sang out, stepping into the cooler air of the vestibule.

In the sparse light of the entry, Cecilia then spot-

17

ted a hoped-for note on the front hall table. She snatched up the paper to read its message. More often than not she came home to find that the major's duties had kept him away, and today of all days she had prayed for just such a reception.

"Outstanding!" she murmured under her breath as she scanned the lines. It seemed that Major Linscombe had gone to report to regimental staff, and had left his regrets that his return home would likely be late. The note was written in his usual terse style, bearing a lightly sketched picture of a snarling dog penned in the customary place of a signature.

Cecilia breathed a sigh of relief that the first hurdle was so easily overcome. " 'Pessa, my pet, tonight I call up the reserves," she said gleefully, eyeing the odd little drawing. "Father intended that you be my protector, and we are about to test your value in the field!"

The dog thumped her long tail in apparently pleased agreement.

"I have the dinner now prepared, *Senhorita*." The interruption came in Portuguese in answer to Cecilia's call. A birdlike crone appeared from the kitchen, her button-black eyes on the big Briard as she welcomed her young mistress home. Maria had never become reconciled to having an animal, especially such a large one, living inside the house. But the payment for her services was good and the duties were light, so she merely kept her distance from the dog, saying, "The major he tells me that you will dine without waiting for him, please. I think he eats with the other *soldados* tonight, so you want the dinner for yourself now, yes?"

"Yes, thank you, Maria," Cecilia replied in the same language. "I will wash and be ready shortly." She was grateful that the servant could not have understood the words spoken in English just moments before. She turned to go to her room, Marpessa a few steps behind.

Marpessa. Named for that faithful maiden so beloved of Apollo, the dog was trusted to protect Cecilia against all aggressors. Major Linscombe knew that in defense of her mistress, the Briard would readily give her life if needed. Exceptionally intelligent, the Briard could follow as many as three sets of instructions in sequence without faltering. Her ancestors were well known for this ability, and they would have been proud to count Marpessa in their number. The major thus depended on the dog to keep his daughter safe, not realizing that Cecilia might use her four-legged guardian for an attack of her own.

So, with no prudent voice to say her nay, Cecilia went to her room and opened the lid to her scuffed writing case. The plan half formed by the afternoon's confrontation began to take shape in her mind. Years of slights and tricks by her cousins had never once moved her to retaliate—she had long ago understood that the effort was hardly worthwhile—yet somehow, revenge seemed very natural in this instance.

Just who *does that audacious colonel think he is, anyway?* Cecilia closed her eyes, visualizing the events to come.

After a few minutes of frowning concentration, she selected her favorite quill pen, dipped it into the inkwell, and applied it to a clean square of paper. Jotting down a few lines, she sanded the sheet neatly, then formed the paper into a screw with a certain colonel's name showing plainly on the outer edge. Not finished, she took up another sheet from the box and scribbled rapidly across its width, preparing another, similar scroll.

She finished the task and washed her hands and face before going to take her meal at the kitchen table: plain fare provided by the simple peasant woman who kept their house. Before being seated, Cecilia prepared a bowl with Marpessa's dinner, while the dog's toenails clicked impatiently against the white floor tiles with their glazed blue-and-yellow patterns. "Greedy beast," she admonished the dog affectionately. "But it shan't be said that I sent a soldier into battle on an empty stomach. Eat hearty, my 'Pessa!" she urged.

Cecilia was herself too excited to eat very much, so as soon as Marpessa finished, she called her onto the back patio, where the fading light was just sufficient to see. Taking up a snaggle-toothed comb and a stiff brush that were set aside for the purpose, she began vigorously grooming her pet's glossy coat until satisfied that the Briard looked her best. Cecilia grinned with positive wickedness at the thought of the scheme she had in mind.

Maria came to peer out from the doorway. "You are needing me for something else, *Senhorita?*" It was half past eight of the clock, the usual time when the servant retired to her room.

"I cannot think of anything more for tonight, but thank you," Cecilia responded, holding her excitement in check as she rose to bring Marpessa back inside. She watched Maria slide the wooden bar into place, securing the outside patio door. "*Boa-noite*, Maria," she said while the servant made for her little room at the back of the house. "We'll see you in the morning."

Done. There would be no hindrance from that quarter.

Swiftly going to her own room now that privacy was assured, Cecilia dug out a string-tied parcel from the back of her wardrobe. Stripping out of her unadorned dress, she carefully unwrapped the package which contained her costume for the evening. Each item was laid out in readiness: kerseymere breeches and a full-sleeved shirt, followed by a short, well-tailored jacket of unusually fine material. A waistcoat of beautifully figured brocade was produced and deposited alongside a narrow length of lightly starched white cambric.

A skilled needlewoman, Cecilia had bought the clothes second-hand on a whim and had altered the lines to disguise her sex. The markets were full of such rich items for sale, Napoleon's ambitions hav-

20

ing caused serious upheavals in almost every household on the Peninsula. She hadn't had any particular use in mind when she'd brought home her purchases, unless, just possibly, she had felt a tiny yen for the freedom to be found in a man's world. It was a freedom she had enjoyed once before.

The bedridden sergeant-major had been given the tale of Cecilia's first venture into Spanish territory. But her second trip to that country had ended in an even hastier exit, when the British were compelled to make a precipitous retreat from Marshal Soult's forces. Major Linscombe had suggested to the then-sixteen-year-old that she could travel faster and with more safety if she donned a soldier's uniform; he was pleased at the time by his daughter's enthusiastic and sensible compliance. "Pluck to the backbone!" he had commended her.

So it was this memory of disguise in the face of danger which had flitted into Cecilia's mind when the bold colonel had held her against him in the stairwell. However, on this occasion she would not be concealing her sex to run from danger. She intended, instead, to be right in the thick of it.

Boots with their toes stuffed with cotton wool to make them fit, and a postillion-shaped hat of brushed beaver completed the ensemble. Donning all, including this last, Cecilia noiselessly went to the front of the house and checked to be sure she carried her house key. She lit a candle by the door against her return, then knelt at Marpessa's side to secure a length of red ribbon around her pet's neck.

Quietly, they exited the little rented cottage: a fine young gentleman and a beribboned black dog, weaving their way purposefully through the darkened streets. No second thoughts—nary a one!—marred Cecilia's proposed enjoyment of the evening.

21

CHAPTER THREE

When Colonel Lord Trelwyn had so fortuitously aided the curly-haired nurse in the stairwell, he'd been on his way up to visit his regiment's sergeant-major. He had heard that the old trooper's wounds were not too serious, and, if that were so, it was imperative that the sergeant be told of the urgency of returning to the field as soon as possible.

"Mustered out with the 'walking wounded,' Colonel, or just come to gloat over an old man's travails?" the young officer heard himself greeted when he entered the wardroom.

Sergeant Haskell's bed lay in the afternoon's light amid long, neat rows of identical cots in the high-ceilinged room. The colonel was relieved to see the object of his visit so improved, for the two men had shared much over the years, and the young colonel had feared what he might find. Many were killed outright during a battle, but at least that many more were lost trying to survive the horrors of field hospitals. Neglect by overworked surgeons and cramped facilities, rampant with infectious disease, were nothing unusual; often, injured men even concealed their hurts so as to avoid the nightmares of amputation, further compounding the problem.

The corners of the younger man's eyes crinkled in pleasure as he gripped his old friend's hand. "I wish that was all the need for my coming here, Sergeant. Although, I must say, you are looking quite the thing—far better than I had expected." Colonel Trelwyn swung the sabre on his hip out of the way with practiced ease, making himself comfortable in a nearby straight-backed chair.

"Oh, I'm near fit as a fiddle, sir," the sergeant-major said with confidence. "Feeling better and better by the hour. Why, I'll be out o' here in another day or two, and you can mark my words on that."

"I'm very glad to hear it, especially since there is another reason for my stopping in to see you," the colonel said quietly, resting his hands on his knees. He fixed Sergeant Haskell with an earnest eye. "I have come to tell you that I am on my way out, Sergeant. You see, I've been called home."

The old trooper looked openly aghast at this disclosure. "Called *home*? You ain't serious, sir? Ye'll not be meanin' to sell out while we've got them Frenchies on the run!" Disregarding his bandages, the sergeant sat straight up in his bed, grizzled eyebrows shooting upward in disbelief. He was incredulous that anything could induce his commander to leave their unit, particularly now, when the far-outnumbered British Army was finally proving itself superior in the war. The casualty list was appallingly long, as the old campaigner knew, making every man needed to keep the tide turned in their favor.

"I am afraid I must," Colonel Trelwyn replied. "It seems that my father died in April, though I learned of it only last month. Just before Salamanca, in fact."

Neither man was greatly surprised that the message had been so delayed in reaching its destination. Over the spring and summer there had been constant skirmishes and troop movements which had made the mail more than ordinarily unreliable. It was a matter of common knowledge that many communications were misdirected long before they made it into Spain; from an April posting to a late-summer receipt was nothing extraordinary in wartime.

The sergeant could see the pain that darkened

the younger man's eyes at the mention of his loss, but before he could express his regrets, the colonel continued. "I am set to sail from Lisbon tomorrow. Is there anything you need before I go? I've time to run whatever errands you request, and would be pleased if I could do you a service."

" 'Preciate yer thinkin' of me, Colonel, but I don't be needin' a thing. As you can see for yerself, I'm comin' along just fine. But hold!" he exclaimed, struck by a thought. "Do we know yet who's takin' over yer spot?"

"Yes, of course. Wellington has approved my recommendation that Major Burton take command. He's still a shade raw to make it a permanent assignment, but we'll have to wait for no saying how long until Whitehall can send out a replacement. Never fear they won't name a good man, though. We can have only the finest for the 'Battling Ninth.' "

Sergeant Haskell grinned proudly at hearing the regimental nickname. "I'm as good as on my way, Colonel, and that ye can count on. Burton should do well enough, but it's *me* the rank and file will be needin'. I'll keep 'em so busy, they won't even have time so's to notice ye've gone. Can't have the men gettin' slack with them Froggies about. No, sir."

Colonel Trelwyn allowed himself to smile at the old soldier's pronouncement. He felt better about abandoning the front, knowing that Sergeant Haskell would be there to keep order. In war, it was the disciplined troops who fared the best, and the competent sergeant-major could be relied on to see to it that the men were drilled regularly. The regiment had earned its nickname when the Ninth Light was noted with envy for its snappy preparation and readiness to do battle, while other regiments were more used to the provost marshall's lash for their discipline. "You're a good man," he said approvingly. "But you are not to consider leaving here till you're quite sure you are well enough."

"Quick as the cat kin lick 'er ear." Sergeant Haskell cackled. "Just you leave our Johnnies to me, Colonel, or should I now say 'Your Grace'?"

" 'Colonel,' if you please. I am still your commander, or, at least, I am until the War Office declares otherwise." The younger man affected a look of great sternness. "And I expect you to see to it that every rifle is cleaned and every bayonet honed to perfection whilst I'm gone."

"Yes, sir, Colonel Lord, *sir!*" The sergeant saluted spiritedly from his sitting position. Then, more solemnly, he added, "But we'll all be sorry to see yer going, that we will, Colonel. I'll admit to having had my doubts when ye first took over a couple o' years back—thought ye was mighty young for the post—s'truth. But I don't mind sayin' how I was wrong. Yer as canny a man on a battlefield as ever I've had privilege to serve. The Ninth won't forget ye, be sure o' that."

"Thank you, Sergeant," the young officer responded on a somewhat husky note. "Just see to the men . . . and to yourself." The colonel again shook the old soldier's hand. He made his farewells with strong regret, at the same time feeling much easier about relinquishing his post with the competent sergeant-major soon back on the line.

Colonel Lord Trelwyn returned to his lodgings while dusk settled over Tôrres Vedras. Tangy salt breezes sprang up from the darkened sea just a few miles distant, adding their spice to the other savory smells wafting in through his opened bedchamber window. Tantalizing aromas drifted up from the kitchen, tickling his nostrils and stimulating his appetite to a fine pitch of anticipation.

Like so many of his meals over the past few weeks, the previous night's dinner had been taken in the open air along the roadside. Nothing unusual in that. The regiment continuously moved from pillar to post, chasing the French all across the Peninsula, and leaving him accustomed to taking sustenance wherever and whenever he could. Tonight he looked forward to sitting at a well-lit table with freshly prepared food and newly laundered linen cloths.

Completing his pre-dinner ablutions, the young officer disposed his large frame in a stuffed chair while he sipped contentedly from a glass containing a sparkling burgundy he'd had brought to his room. He was so pleased with the quality of the beverage that he bethought himself to purchase more on the morrow to take up to his sergeant; that is, if he could slip it past the white-gowned religious he'd seen attending the ward.

That thought put the colonel in mind of a somewhat less virtuous attendant. The pretty little miss he'd met at the infirmary was just what he needed to see him on his way. Well, perhaps not so *little*, he amended. With a slight smile softening his mouth, he recalled that in standing on the step just below her, he had stood no taller than she. Besides being a comely armful, it meant that on level ground she would come up to his shoulder at the least. The colonel had many times been aware of some awkwardness with those *petites amies* who scarcely reached his elbow; in consequence, he felt a pleasant stirring of desire for a woman who would better compliment his size.

Colonel Trelwyn paused to wonder what, really, had caused him to engage the young woman for the evening. Such invitations were not in his usual style. But he was on his way home to England, and tonight was his final farewell to the harsh realities of war.

I should have asked her name, he suddenly thought with surprise. Then he relaxed, realizing that he would know more than the young woman's name soon enough.

The sound of a knock brought him smoothly to his feet. As he opened the door, the concierge bowed low before handing him a small, rolled piece of paper. The colonel read the scant lines, a slight furrow forming itself across his fine, wide brow.

In a deserted side street outside the common room of the Hôtel Quieroz, a slender figure stood in the nighttime shadows facing the golden light extruded from the lower floor windows, each one thrown open to receive cooling drafts of evening air. Beneath a gentleman's modish chapeau, the erect posture seemed expectant, as though the watcher were waiting for something . . . or someone. The feeling of tension seemed to grow as, unmoving, the face beneath the narrow hat brim remained in unblinking survey of the four wide openings in the plaster-covered walls.

At last the watcher's patience was rewarded. A tall, trim-waisted man in a well-fitted military uniform entered the candlelit dining room to take up a seat at a separate table. The watcher shifted position and gazed on the officer, then whistled softly off to the side.

An inky-black shape came forward with liquid grace. At a low-voiced command, the beast promptly moved to the window pointed out and silently bounded over the sill. Finding the table as instructed, it moved easily to the specified objective, lifting one paw to gain attention.

"*What* the bloody—" Colonel Trelwyn nearly knocked over his chair in his haste to rise. Battle-honed reflexes compelled him into motion before his other senses could identify the source of the intrusion. With startled eyes, he looked down to see a very large, very black dog staring back at him with seeming rebuke for his overreaction. Around its neck was tied a red ribbon with a scrolled paper tucked within, similar to the one brought up to his room a few minutes earlier.

The first note had simply told him that he should await his guest in the dining hall, since she was reluctant to be so brazen as to come directly to a private room. That message was unsigned. Now he was confronted with this massive dog—looking for all the world as if it knew just what was going on—and bearing a second note!

Irritated to have been caught so unawares, Colonel Trelwyn nonetheless offered his knuckle to the Briard for a polite smell. After this courtesy was received, he removed the latest communication from the ribbon around the dog's neck, unfurling it to read the message therein contained. It was written in a by-now-familiar hand.

My dear Colonel,

As you requested Suitable Female Companionship for this Evening, please accept the Appropriate Company. Her name is Marpessa and her Manners are, I am sure you will Agree, at least as Refined as your Own.

P.S. Marpessa will do Anything for a Fresh Fish or a Rare Steak. I Regretfully Inform you that Not All Females are the same in this Respect.

A look of sheer incredulity was followed by one of pure, blazing fury as the colonel crushed the note in his hand. Dark gray eyes turned silver, glittering angrily like perfect twin mirrors.

Some dozen yards away, deep in the shadows of the alleyway, Cecilia assessed the young officer's enraged demeanor and knew a moment of dread. She feared that Colonel Trelwyn might somehow fathom her presence and come vaulting out of the window to inflict an awful revenge! She was glad to be unhampered by skirts; she stood at the ready to beat a quick retreat.

Before she could decide quite what to do, though, deep booming laughter abruptly replaced the officer's fierce scowl. The colonel had already drawn disapproving stares from the few occupied tables, for his sudden leap to his feet had startled more than just one of his audience, but so contagious was the unexpected sound of his laughter, that soon matching chuckles were heard to mingle and grow around the room. Apart in the shadows, even Cecilia's cheeks began to twitch. She anxiously clapped her hand over her mouth as the giggles sought escape. *Really,* she thought, the young man had quite the nicest laugh.

All sense of amusement fled in a trice, however, when she saw what next occurred. With a complete disregard for his observers, Colonel Trelwyn moved to the other side of the table and pulled out the empty chair, directing Marpessa onto the seat. Apparently nothing loath, the Briard hopped up and sat quietly while the red-coated officer regained his own place. The colonel then signaled to gain the attention of the confused waiter hovering nearby. To Cecilia's total bewilderment, Colonel Trelwyn proceeded to give the hotel servant some sort of instruction.

What was happening here? Cecilia's plan called for the overbold colonel to leave the room in disgraced disarray! But when steaming dishes of various foods began to make their arrival, she knew what it was that he intended to do. He was taking her at her word and sitting down to dine with her pet.

Colonel Trelwyn's lips continued to move while Marpessa's ears pricked forward with attention. As steaming dishes of various foods began to make their arrival, the dog daintily licked her chops in obvious anticipation, though she obediently kept to her seat. The colonel took a plate and served up a generous portion of what appeared to be poached sole, which he deftly chopped before passing it across the table. Marpessa sat patiently while he filled another plate for himself, cocking her head as if in inquiry. He was seen to say something that must have satisfied the Briard, for she then delicately dipped her head to her plate. If the officer was surprised by the dog's mannerly compliance, he did not let it show.

Not so the other diners. Twice the harassed

29

waiter had to retrieve someone's dropped fork and replace it with clean silver. Glasses of both water and wine toppled intermittently across white linens as curious hotel guests tried to eat their dinners, at the same time gawking at the very odd pair. The Briard sat quite as tall as the colonel, and like true aristocrats both, neither gave notice to the periodic lapses of their fellows.

The major's daughter stood watching in patent disbelief as her pet's plate was twice refilled: once with roasted beef, and later with more fish. The officer seemed to question his dinner partner before each change, and Cecilia barely made out a soft "woof" each time.

This was not going at all according to plan. She had meant for the colonel to read her note and take her meaning. Instead, the arrogant man had neatly turned the tables.

Something akin to envy, or perhaps jealousy, sharply pricked at her. Standing alone outside, she watched the meal progress even as delicious, mouth-watering smells floated out through the window to assault her senses. Worse, Colonel Trelwyn kept his undivided attention on his dinner partner, leaving Cecilia feeling vaguely deprived of something more than the sumptuous meal. With each attention paid to her pet, she felt herself become more and yet more put out.

She knew it was irrational to blame Marpessa. The dog had gone to the officer's table exactly as instructed; obviously, the Briard thought herself under the man's orders by her mistress's wish. But if it was nonsensical to blame the dog for this rather bitter, left-out feeling she now suffered, then it must be the overbearing colonel who was at fault. Ooo! How she longed to march up to the table and give that colonel a piece of her mind.

For his part, Colonel Trelwyn had overcome his initial anger and was thoroughly enjoying the novelty of the situation. With perceptions sharpened in combat, he'd spotted the figure in the shadows before regaining his seat. Without giving away his awareness, he found a certain perverse pleasure in playing out the charade, knowing that he remained under observation. Marpessa's entry had been no small surprise, but it did explain the watcher's vigil and confirmed that there was no immediate threat.

Colonel Trelwyn assumed that the nurse from Santa Clara Infirmary had sent some particular gentleman friend to oversee the ruse, although he could not for the life of him comprehend why she had not just refused his dinner invitation if she'd had no interest. And if she had changed her mind about meeting him, why not simply say so in her first note? Instead, he was given the company of this oversize dog, bearing a missive that could only be called insulting. *Why* ever was it that the young nurse with the wide eyes and cropped curls had felt it necessary to go to these extraordinary lengths?

The colonel had never had cause to doubt that he was attractive to the ladies before. He'd enjoyed success with the gentler sex since he was in his teens. And, while his involvements had mostly been rather casual and of short duration, due to the exigencies of his being a soldier, he was reasonably sure that he had never before given any real offence. What was there to have put *this* young woman into such high dudgeon?

Colonel Trelwyn forked up a flaky bit of fish and considered his dinner partner. He thought he might leash the dog until someone came for her; she was too valuable an animal to be abandoned lightly. That way, whoever came to claim her—likely the watcher beyond the window—could be held to account. However, since his ship was set to sail the following day with the last tide, what if no one came soon enough?

Well, perhaps there was another way. Sergeant Haskell was a wily old bird who always knew the ins and outs of a thing, so early tomorrow he would go back to the infirmary and put his questions to the sergeant-major. This solution settling his

31

mind, Colonel Trelwyn relaxed as he made his meal.

He was much diverted by Marpessa's efforts to please, for indeed, she seemed to watch for his approval as carefully as any debutante at Almack's Assembly Rooms, where young ladies from the highest circles socialized under the watchful eyes of the *haut ton*. Ensconced in the chair across the table, the sagacious canine cocked her head intelligently each time he spoke, causing him a moment of envy for the man who had charge of this magnificent beast.

Draining the last of his wine, the colonel signaled for the waiter and requested a paper and pen. When these items were brought, he quickly inscribed a message which he rolled up and tucked snugly into the ribbon still encircling the Briard's neck. Ruffling the dog's pricked ears, the colonel then strolled insouciantly out of the dining room without a glance for the watcher at the window.

When she saw the officer quit the room, Cecilia snapped her fingers sharply in the darkness. Not looking to see what effect this had, she broke into a soft-footed trot down the alley and away out of sight. Alert to the signal, Marpessa dropped from her chair to slip out of the dining room window, her keen nose telling her the way as she followed her mistress forthwith.

" 'Pessa, you rascal," Cecilia whispered between strides when the Briard caught up and matched her pace. "I fed you an honest dinner before we left home. How could you possibly have eaten again, and so well, too? You made an utter and complete pig of yourself, you wretched, wretched girl." Cecilia thought of her own modest dinner with regret. "And did you have to look like you were enjoying yourself so much?" she added on a plaintive note.

A low whine answered her. Cecilia looked down, filled with remorse that she'd taken out her ire on her pet. But she was reminded of the colonel's last deed as a glimmer of white peeked from her dog's ruff. Halting their progress, she knelt on the graveled pathway to remove the paper and open it. She tried her best to make out the bold handwriting, but since the moon was not yet out, she could not decipher the words. The major's *favorite* expression of disgust was heard in the darkness.

"Well, I just hope we make it home before Father returns, or we'll both be in the basket," she murmured, rising to her feet. At the reminder of this last, she speeded her steps homeward, the black dog trotting silently at her heels.

When they skidded to a stop at the stuccoed cottage, Cecilia was glad to see that the single candle she'd left burning still showed as the only light inside. She didn't think she wanted to have to explain her late arrival—or her outré manner of dress—to even the most indulgent of parents. A lurking feeling of guilt told her that she might have gone too far in her quest for vengeance. The major might not be best pleased if he knew what she'd done this night; Cecilia wasn't altogether sure how she felt about her little sortie, either.

She forgot her discomfort, however, as she bethought the note in her hand. She hurried to the light to read the colonel's reply.

Dear Angel,
How Perceptive of you to Understand that a Man would prefer a Flesh and Blood creature for Company to any Celestial Being, no matter how Divine. I neglected to realize that the Earthly Delights are not for one of the Spirit World.
P.S. I must Confess, I do Prefer to share my time with a Well-mannered Dog.

The letter was signed with a bold flourish that made Cecilia's blood boil. Crunching the note with a gesture similar to one seen earlier that evening, she crammed it into the side pocket of her jacket while she marched through the hall to her bedchamber, her heels sounding smartly on the tiles.

But after only a few steps, she remembered the sleeping maidservant and modified her walk in due heed.

In her room Cecilia stripped out of her boots and breeches. Rapidly refolding her disguise and tucking it back into the recesses of her wardrobe, she put on her bedgown and wrapper, then went to the kitchen to refill Marpessa's water crock. She allowed her pet onto the back patio, muttering imprecations under her breath all the while.

". . . deuced loose fish. Cavalry cavalier. The man's a chartered libertine, yet calmly sits at a table, sharing his dinner with a *dog*." There was something prodigiously aggravating about a man who would not permit her the last word.

When Marpessa scratched at the door to be let back inside, she whiffed her mistress's mood. Being a sensitive creature, she slunk out of sight beneath the kitchen table.

Hungry from the evening's ordeals, Cecilia rummaged in the pantry, found a loaf end, and bit into it angrily. She thought of the feast the colonel had shared with her pet and of plans gone all awry. She never stopped to ponder over why she had gone to so much trouble or taken such a horrendous risk of discovery. She concluded that her current unpleasant emotions were caused merely by disappointment that the object of her wrath had not suffered the embarrassment she felt he deserved at her hands.

"Calls me an 'angel,' does he? The unprincipled dastard." After wiping the scattered crumbs from the tabletop, Cecilia took herself off to bed, shaking her head at the day's absurdities.

Much later, her father tiptoed into her room. He gazed down in fond silence upon his peacefully sleeping daughter; the faithful French Briard, one eye opened at the intrusion, lay curled up on the rug by the bedside. Major Linscombe felt a surge of affection swell within his breast for this straightforward, uncomplicated young miss . . . as beautiful

34

When Major Linscombe had been assigned to one such reconnaissance unit, no premonition of disaster had warned Cecilia of what was to come. The subsequent report stated that the major's detachment had met up with a large party of French soldiers bent upon a similar mission, resulting in a particularly vicious skirmish. Major James Carlisle Linscombe had been later identified among the casualties, his daughter learning the details from her father's most trusted and much-saddened subaltern, who had been a witness to the fray.

Cecilia had felt the blow keenly. Although knowing that her father had died just as he would have wished, she did sorely miss his love. But she'd let the tears flow as needed and had kept herself busy at the infirmary, allowing the pain to wash over and through her while gradually reconciling herself to her loss. She had thus advanced the process of healing, letting herself repair from the inside outward.

When Sir Andrew had received the news of his brother's death, he had written his dry condolences along with instructions for his niece to return immediately to the family seat in Sussex. Cecilia had nowhere else to go, there being none left of her mother's family; perforce, her father had named her uncle as guardian. Despite the baronet's express wishes, however, several weeks were to pass before a respectable party could be found to conduct Cecilia back to England.

Now, as the supper hour neared and the thin light faded from overcast skies, Cecilia turned away from the railing and moved to go below. Her chaperones for the journey, a certain Mrs. Perkins and her married daughter, would be waiting for Cecilia to join them.

The cinnamon-haired miss stopped by her own cabin first. Extracting a copper-framed hand mirror from her portmanteau, she employed a tailed comb to fluff out her short-clipped hair. *No great beauty*

37

here, she mused, however wrongly, as she pushed an errant curl back into place.

All through her youth Cecilia's aunt and two cousins had derided her hair color as freakish and its tendency to curl every which way as being mere foolishness. As Cecilia had continued to grow, they were equally at pains to deplore her increasingly unusual height. Now, standing at nine inches over five feet, and in spite of her father's many assurances to the contrary, Cecilia was of the opinion that her looks were not such as could please. Still, she accepted her detractions without resentment and continued to hold herself gracefully erect. After all, there was nothing to be done about these faults in her appearance.

Without further ado, Cecilia went to tap on the door of the neighboring cabin. "We are quite ready, Miss Linscombe," intoned Mrs. Perkins. "Let us proceed."

Honestly, Cecilia thought, *you would think we were about to make our entry into Carlton House.*

Mrs. Perkins and her daughter, Catherine, had themselves been on the Continent only long enough to accomplish a wedding, but Cecilia had since learned that the pair was quite satisfied to leave the new groom behind. As a viscount's elder son, serving with Wellington's forces, his primary value to the two women was, apparently, dependent upon the fact that Catherine could now add "the Honorable" to her name.

When they entered the dining area, the captain and first officer were already waiting. The ship's other passengers of note were absent, laid low by the inclement weather. In unison, the gentlemen arose as the women made their entrance and seated the ladies with a minimum of ceremony.

"The Honorable" began speaking as soon as the wine was poured, relating detailed anecdotes about their connections and neighbors in Herefordshire. The taciturn captain and his mate strictly minded

38

their own plates and, as usual, without adding comment.

After tonight's meal, however, the captain spoke. Clearing his throat, but without further preamble, he addressed his undemanding guest. "Heard you met the hero of the Peninsula, Miss Linscombe. *Haa-ruum.* Do tell us about it, if you would."

Mrs. Perkins and her look-alike daughter glared around the table, then glued their eyes on their charge. Ignoring them, and not at all put out of countenance, Cecilia was happy to satisfy the captain's interest. "Indeed, yes, Captain Melbanks. I was introduced to General Lord Wellington first in the spring of '10, and he has seemed pleased to remember me ever since. He often came through Tôrres Vedras and would visit our wounded to offer a word of encouragement. He is a most impressive figure, as everyone who sees him must agree. Matching my inches"—she smiled without deprecation—"yet towering above us all. Truly, sir, I can tell you that we, each and every one of us, stand within his long shadow. The general is a great man for England," she affirmed with quiet pride.

"So he is," promptly agreed Captain Melbanks. "So he is, *haa-ruum.*" He then folded his napkin beside his plate, adding almost shyly, "Sorry to hear about your bereavement, miss. M' deepest regrets."

With these short concluding words, the captain and his mate pushed back their chairs. Bowing abruptly, first one, then the other, they left the table to return to their duties.

Mrs. Perkins gasped when the door closed behind them, her thin bosom heaving with indignation. "Rag-mannered, *I* call it." She sputtered and choked, an unbecoming shade of red splotching her normally sallow complexion. "It must revolt every feeling that he should address you so, Miss Linscombe. Oh, I am very sorry for it." She reached down the table to pat Cecilia's hand.

"But—but why is that, ma'am?" Cecilia questioned in some amazement. "Should the captain not have inquired after Wellington or offered me his sympathies?" Her finely shaped brows rose in puzzlement.

Mrs. Perkins jerked her hand back to her own place as if scorched. She seemed bereft of speech. She stared hard at Cecilia for several moments before turning to her haughty daughter for assistance.

"What Mama means," obediently entered the Honorable, "is that the captain should not have spoken to you at all and, certainly, not before according me his first attention." She twitched her nose disdainfully. "And as for his leaving the table ahead of us, well! Every feeling must revolt at such uncivil conduct."

With rising contempt, Cecilia fell back on a trick learned from childhood, allowing her eyes to fall demurely to her lap. She had no wish to prolong the time at table, so she employed the knack of appearing to give in before pressed too hard for retreat. It was pointless to make a stand on such a ridiculous issue; moreover, she needed to hide the all-too-knowing smile which threatened.

Fortunately, before her impertinence could be discovered, the steward knocked and offered Miss Linscombe his escort to the cargo area below. Managing to say all that was proper, Cecilia gratefully took leave of the two supercilious women before she could disgrace herself.

"Heavy weather tonight," the wiry-built steward cautioned as he led their way down into the ship's hold. "There'll be ice in the riggin' come morning. Be you sure you're wantin' to bring up the hound?"

"Oh, I don't think Marpessa will mind overmuch, for she will need the fresh air after being penned so long. But I do thank you for your concern, Mr. Leeks."

By the light from the lantern the steward held high for her, Cecilia gingerly picked her way through the cargo-cluttered storage area. She wrinkled her nose at the vile odors surrounding her and moved quickly to the Briard's crate. Fastening a leash to the wide leather collar encircling Marpessa's neck, she directed her pet topside.

The steward followed warily at a distance. Three nights before, he had inadvertently stepped too close to Miss Linscombe when they had set out for their walk, and he had been privileged to see the terrible length of the Briard's teeth! The silent warning had not been missed, and Mr. Leeks was careful to give no further offense. "Tomorrow should see us docking at Portsmouth," he now offered, "be you eager to get to your kin, miss?"

"Why, yes. I rather think that I shall like to be back in England," she answered thoughtfully. And although she didn't say so, she thought that the only person she was really anxious to see was dear Miss Sheldon. Her old teacher was the only one, in fact, who had readily returned Cecilia's correspondence in all the years she'd been away. Now the dear spinster lived in a neighboring parish, and Cecilia especially looked forward to that reunion.

Stepping out onto the deck, she shivered in earnest as the wind whipped about them. Mr. Leeks raised the high collar of his coat against the cold, taking shelter in the hatchway while the girl and her dog went about their exercise. As she walked up and down with the Briard's leash in hand, Cecilia considered just what her return would mean.

Her nineteenth birthday had passed in November. It would be more than a year before she reached her majority, and until that time, her uncle stood as her guardian and would have control of her affairs. Such as they were, that is. Cecilia had long been privy to her father's finances, so it was no secret to her that the major had been unable to set much aside on a soldier's pay. She knew that when she attained her twenty-first birthday and finally did come of age, she couldn't hope to claim independence on the small amount remaining. With no wish to forever make a part of her uncle's household—even supposing it would be permitted—Cecilia accepted that she must soon seek out a paying position.

Truth to tell, she quite enjoyed the prospect of providing for herself. She had never cared to be overly dependent upon others, and she rather liked the idea of shaping her own future.

Not for a moment did she give marriage a thought. Without a proper dowry, she accepted that it was out of the question. Uncle Andrew could not be counted on to increase her portion so as to attract a suitor to her hand, neither had she sufficient beauty to tempt a gentleman into foregoing the customary financial considerations. Of a surety, her one attempt at flirtation had gone off like a faulty cannon, leaving her with soot on her face!

The dark-haired young colonel she had encountered at Santa Clara *had* been intriguingly handsome, though. He had the well-muscled, graceful build of an athlete and the forceful, confident bearing of a good commanding officer. Of course, she had not totally forgiven him his insult in assuming her a light woman, but he certainly knew how to turn a prank to his advantage, and so she must admit. Cecilia smiled and paced the deck in dreamy reminiscence.

A faint whine put a stop to this moonraking when Marpessa decided they had been out long enough. In no wise reluctant, Mr. Leeks led the way back down to the cargo area, waiting while Miss Linscombe replenished the dog's provisions and straightened the wad of bedding inside the wooden crate.

Tomorrow would see them in Portsmouth, where the future awaited.

CHAPTER FIVE

Dawn broke miraculously bright and clear. The prophesied ice shimmered and glittered from the shrouds strung high overhead, but chilled winds abruptly stilled as the packet ship slid smoothly into the busy harbor. Pigtailed sailors rushed about while last-minute orders were shouted from the bridge, and heretofore-hidden passengers in gaily colored wools suddenly appeared out on deck. Mrs. Perkins busily directed her maidservant regarding the details of final packing, and the major's daughter readied her own single trunk and portmanteau for departure. The rigorous journey was at last at an end.

The south-England harbor was unusually crowded. So many ships had sailed in the same week that there was hardly mooring space for another. All of the dockside berths were taken, leaving Captain Melbanks to lower his anchor several ship's-lengths away from the pier, an inconvenience to passenger and crewman alike.

As the three women disembarked and were rowed across to the landing, Cecilia felt a quick bubble of excitement rise in her breast. She had no idea of what might await her, but she felt herself expanding with optimism on this brilliant new day. In the crisp, early air, sound was sharper and colors brighter, shinier, than they had seemed only one day before.

When the dory used to ferry in the first set of passengers was brought along dockside, Cecilia scarcely waited long enough for the lines to be se-

43

cured. Mr. Leeks had promised to see to it that Marpessa was carried safely to shore ahead of them, and on the instant the small craft touched upon the pier-post, Cecilia bounded from the boat to make a quick survey of the littered quay. Locating the familiar crate amid the clutter of the ship's unloading, she disregarded her chaperone's strident calls and deftly made her way through to the recognized container. In a matter of moments, she had the crate unlatched and her pet freed.

The huge dog, ecstatic to find herself released, bounced around her mistress with glad barks and high, acrobatic leaps. Her tongue lolling out in excitement, Marpessa sounded her pleasure while sailors paused in their labors to laugh aloud at the happy display.

Within moments, however, censorious tones issued from behind Cecilia as Mrs. Perkins bustled up to the scene. From beneath the trembling brim of an elaborately decorated poke bonnet, accented by dark green cock-feather trim, the outraged matron bristled with disapproval. "Miss Linscombe, *if* you please." Thin fingers reached over and grabbed hurtfully at Cecilia's arm. "This disgraceful exhibition must cease at once, I say. You are become the center of low attention."

The big Briard immediately stilled her antics and emitted a low warning growl. Her eyes narrowed to merest slits as they leveled on the woman who presumed to chastise her mistress.

Disregarding the dog's defiance, Mrs. Perkins continued with sharp instruction. "You will come with me while I procure your ticket to Hazelmere. That *is* where your uncle awaits you?"

Calmed by a discreet hand gesture, the dog quieted and Cecilia nodded in a rather ambiguous manner. Uncle Andrew's acres were only a short distance from the modest-size town of Hazelmere, so she actually had intended to send word to her uncle from there. But she thought it might be unwise to explain at this particular time, hoping that the dissembling in her unspoken acquiescence would not be noted.

Apparently it was not, for Mrs. Perkins turned her attention to another matter. "You will oblige me by locking that animal back in its cage," she snapped. "You can hardly mean to travel with such a creature on the loose, and the mail will never take up such a large crate. I suppose we must find a carter willing to carry it on to Sir Andrew's. Now then, miss, you have only a three-hour journey ahead of you, but we must hurry if we are to book passage on today's coach. I am informed that it leaves at ten sharp."

"Please do forgive me, ma'am," Cecilia broke in, "but those arrangements are not entirely adequate. In fact, they will not do at all. I cannot leave Marpessa to travel alone; you must not think I will treat her so shabbily." Said with no hint of insolence, Cecilia nevertheless spoke with strong resolve.

Mrs. Perkins looked shocked. Coming up beside them in time to overhear this last exchange, Catherine, too, seemed unable to speak in the face of Miss Linscombe's unexpected denial.

"Just how do you propose to travel, then?" Mrs. Perkins finally hissed. "You cannot mean to go on the common stage, and I doubt even *they* would take such a large beast aboard. Come, come, Miss Linscombe. Forget this nonsense and do as I say!"

Miss Linscombe took a single step back and faced her antagonist with steadfast calm, her composure clearly not in the least shaken. Then, for the first time in their acquaintance, Mrs. Perkins noticed the tiny golden glints in the tall young woman's widely spaced brown eyes.

Cecilia regarded her opponent for only a moment and then said quietly, "If the stage won't take me, then I shall hire a private carriage, ma'am. Marpessa is the only safeguard I need, though you must not think me ungrateful for your care. But it is not so very far, after all."

45

"Impossible," breathed Catherine, her small eyes round and disbelieving.

"Inconceivable!" spat out her mother, her long nose fairly quivering in outrage.

"Have you another suggestion, then, ma'am?" Cecilia looked squarely into Mrs. Perkins's upturned face. "For I have told you that I will not leave Marpessa."

Mrs. Perkins shrewdly changed tactics. "I cannot force you to follow wise counsel," she said leadingly, "but you may be certain that my letter detailing these events will go to your uncle as soon as may be. I am persuaded that he will be interested in knowing of these headstrong, ill-bred tendencies of yours."

When no sign was forthcoming that Cecilia would relent at this threat, Mrs. Perkins pinched in her lips. "Very well then, miss. Have it your own way. I wash my hands and have done with you." Mrs. Perkins whirled away, the long, iridescent-green cock feathers atop her large bonnet all atremble as she elbowed a path down the quay. She and her sycophantic daughter were soon lost from sight in the hurly-burly crowd on the pier.

Honestly regretting the contretemps, Cecilia couldn't help but feel relieved at being further spared Mrs. Perkins's company. Neither would she miss Catherine's stiff-rumped companionship; her previous endeavors to befriend that young lady had not fared well from the time she had discovered that the Honorable, like her mother, viewed the war as little more than an inconvenience. To them, Bony's incursions were merely bothersome!

Cecilia wondered briefly at what a fool Catherine's bridegroom must be to align himself with women who were obviously interested in nothing so much as their own elevation in Society. If *she* had been the one taken to wive, she would have made it her business to make a place beside her man, just as she had done with her father.

Shaking her head in dismissal, Cecilia pulled the

46

plain hood of her black cloak more warmly against her ears and set off with Marpessa. She needed to find a stable which would rent her the means to get to Linscombe Hall, and she didn't care to waste another minute of this brisk, lovely day. It was rather marvelous to be off on her own.

Long used to making such arrangements, Cecilia soon procured a suitable conveyance from an establishment offering rigs and drivers for hire. Because few travelers could manage with such a small vehicle as she requested, there was no delay in readying her chosen transport, and the stablekeeper helpfully gave her a voucher which would allow her to exchange the hack halfway through her journey.

The lanky stable lad assigned to accompany her gave assistance, as well. In exchange for three copper pennies, the boy brought up her much-battered trunk from the docks and loaded it behind the gig's seat. It remained cold, but spring seemed a not-too-distant prospect beneath the shining sun.

Fellow wayfarers regarded the girl swathed in black without any particular interest. Or, that is, unless they noticed the rather large dog up beside her in the gig. But the British were ever fond of their pets, and so, while many may have found the sight somewhat odd, none saw cause to interfere. When Cecilia stopped to change the hack and take herself an early lunch, the proprietor of the country inn even provided Marpessa with a welcome meal of her own.

"A reet fine dog tha' hast there, miss," the innkeeper commented in broad, south-country accents after Cecilia handed him the voucher from the Portsmouth stable. "I raise a few hounds for retrievin' meself, but she's a herdin' dog, ain't she? I canna' say as how I've ever seen her p'ticular like around these parts, howsomever. I'd na suppose tha'd be a-knowin' her blood, would ye?"

Rather than go into a long story about how she had come into the possession of a French shepherd, Cecilia merely smiled in a vague manner and agreed that Marpessa was some variety of herding dog and "possibly" of mixed heritage. She felt traitorous in denegating the Briard's ancient bloodlines thus, but with England so long at war with France, she thought it politic to make no further explanation.

After a light refreshment, the stable boy resumed his position, and they recommenced their journey northward. Cecilia let her mind drift and wander at will, until she remembered her parting with Mrs. Perkins. *That* thought made her sit up straighter on the gig's bench seat.

There was no doubting that the irate chaperone would make good on her threat as soon as may be; the dreadful woman was not one to waste time in making her complaints known. No, there was no doubt at all about it: Sir Andrew would be vastly displeased with his niece, and soon.

But what Cecilia could not predict with any surety was what penalty might be in store. Tooling the light two-wheeled carriage along the road, she began to worry lest some measure of blame fall upon Marpessa. Unlike the interested innkeeper, her uncle was not a hunting man. He and Aunt Margaret had no use for dogs.

How could she have forgotten? They both *loathed* animals.

A flood of apprehension made Cecilia suddenly fearful of presenting herself at the Hall. The tattling letter might even now be on its way. She decided on the moment that instead of proceeding directly to Linscombe Hall, she would make a short detour to Wicksham Cross. There, she would see Miss Sheldon and beseech her advice on the matter. Her old friend from the schoolroom might well be able to serve her once again.

As Cecilia remembered it, the rather obscure village where the retired governess had taken up residence was a scant two or three miles off the Hazelmere road. And though she had never before seen the house, Cecilia had no difficulty in locating it, for the quaintly styled half-timbered dwelling was just as Miss Sheldon had so proudly described it in her many letters. Excepting two brief notes from her aunt Margaret, those letters were the only ones Cecilia had received from England in the four years of her absence.

The sparkle of diamond-paned, lead-glazed windows made the identification complete. Asking the stable lad to tie the hired hack to the front railing, and promising she would not be too long, Cecilia walked the few steps up the graveled path to knock on the door.

"As I live and breathe!" came the thrilled cry of recognition as a lady of uncertain years opened the door. "Miss Cecilia, you have come home at last!"

Cecilia was shocked to discover how far below her the neat little figure stood. She was aware she had grown an inch or two since leaving England, but that did not in itself account for the drastic change. She supposed it must be because she was so much older now that Miss Sheldon was perceived as smaller. The sky-blue eyes below the lace-edged cap were just as keen as remembered, though, and the pleasant scent of lavender water brought back a flood of schoolroom memories. Cecilia stooped to return the hug so generously offered.

"Miss Sheldon, I am so very happy to see you. It has been a good many years and . . . and I have just realized how terribly I have missed you." Tears leapt to stand in Cecilia's dark eyes, though a wide smile lit her face.

"Oh, my very dear, how kind of you to say so. And I must tell you, I am most truly sorry for your sad loss." The sensible spinster patted Cecilia's arm consolingly. "But do come in and let us make ourselves more comfortable. Would you like to go along upstairs and freshen up? I manage for myself here, so I'll be just a minute making us a nice pot of tea. Oh, and I can set the stable boy a place by the stove in the kitchen while we have our visit."

Just then the dog's presence was noticed and remarked. "And whom have we here?" Miss Sheldon cooed, reaching out to run her fingers through thick black fur. "My, you are the great beauty, aren't you! Marpessa, is it not?" The big dog did not flinch at the stranger's confident touch, reveling in the pleasurable sensations wrought by skilled fingers.

"Yes," Cecilia answered, "this is Marpessa. Actually, Miss Sheldon, you must know that she is the reason I came here first." Cecilia had the grace to look shamefaced at this admission. "Our ship docked only this morning, you see, but before I go up to the Hall, I wished to speak with you about my pet."

"Whatever can you mean, dear? Do not tell me that you have traveled all this way with only your dog as company!" Miss Sheldon's voice quite squeaked at the thought.

"Oh, I had a very respectable party with me on shipboard, but we disagreed at the last minute concerning further transportation for Marpessa. I could not go off in the mail coach, leaving her to be brought up later by some clumsy carter under who knows what sort of conditions." Cecilia's eyes begged her old friend for understanding.

Miss Sheldon studied her imploring face. "Well, run along for now, my dear. We can discuss it before a cozy fire when you come back down. I take it that Sir Andrew does not know precisely at what hour to expect you?" Seeing Cecilia's second guilty look, the old schoolroom mistress rolled her eyes and shooed her guest along with a look of exceeding forbearance.

When she entered the parlor a short time later, Cecilia found Marpessa complacently stretched out before the cheerily crackling fire. "Lazy girl," she said with affection, smiling at the ease with which her pet had made herself at home. While Miss Sheldon poured their tea, Cecilia described her parting with Mrs. Perkins.

Miss Sheldon tut-tutted as the story unfolded, her white brow crinkling lightly in all directions. Having been some years in the Linscombes' employ, she was well aware that Cecilia was right to fear the consequences of her actions; it was everything likely that Sir Andrew would see this as a golden opportunity to exert further authority over his niece. *But surely,* she thought as the creases in her forehead deepened, *there must be some way to get over this stretch of rough ground lightly.* . . .

"What do you think will happen to Marpessa, Miss Sheldon?" Cecilia's words interrupted the older woman's ruminations. "Will I be allowed to keep her, do you think? For now that Uncle Andrew is my legal guardian, why, he could even sell her away!"

At the anguished cry, Marpessa raised her head and whined softly. Her pitch-black eyes looked a question.

"There, there now, my dear," Miss Sheldon temporized, observing the scene. "No need to borrow trouble just yet, is there? Suppose, instead, you were to make Marpessa a gift to me—an old woman, living alone as I do, must appreciate the company. Then, after a week or so when you are established and the dust has had time to settle, I will come to say that she has missed you so much that I feel I must restore her to your care. By that time, Mrs. Perkins's letter will have already been forgotten and without Marpessa being involved at all. What say you to that idea?"

Cecilia considered the dog comfortably sprawled across the floor. The Briard *had* seemed to take to Miss Sheldon, and certainly no better alternative appeared to offer itself. Coming to a decision, she made a mock-solemn face before pointing to the black canine covering a large area in front of the hearth. "Dear ma'am." She spoke with exaggerated formality. "Will you do me the honor of accepting the present of this fine dog: loyal, obedient, and true?" She couldn't repress a short, relieved gurgle of laughter. A black tail swished across the floor in apparent agreement.

Miss Sheldon joined into the spirit and nobly affirmed her acceptance. "Well, that's all right and tight, then!" Light blue eyes twinkled as she gave a naughty grin. "Now, my dear, you must prepare a letter to send on to the manor house, saying that you have stopped here due to a *further* lack of escort. Let your uncle think what he may. I'll step next door and request young Johnny to deliver it, and we should see your uncle here within the hour."

"Oh! And we mustn't forget the gig out in front," Cecilia cried. "Uncle will know it all for a hum if he sees it. I'll send the boy back with it at once!" Wasting no time, she undertook arrangements for the vehicle to be returned to Portsmouth, quick as quick may be.

Confirmed in her faith that Miss Sheldon would untangle the coil that she'd got herself into, Cecilia soon sat down to the writing table to set careful words to paper.

CHAPTER SIX

Just as predicted, Sir Andrew Linscombe reached Wicksham Cross in something under an hour. He arrived in a stylish carriage painted in the darkest shade of red, with black spiral designs drawn across its sides. The wheel spokes were also picked out in black, the same design continuing right to the hubs. The carriage boasted door panels inescutcheoned with ornate coatings of lacquer and fine gold leaf, announcing to the world that Sir Andrew was a "1661 man."

Less impressively, however, instead of the prime goers which would have completed the imposing picture, two common dray horses pulled stolidly in harness. One a sorrel and the other a poorly marked dun, they could be considered to match only by virtue of their massive sizes and their equally shaggy, dull coats.

The baronet entered the cottage, wrapped in an air of considerable self-consequence. No matter the shortcomings of his equipage, he was himself attired in the latest kick of Town fashion, from the top of his steel-buckled shaved angora hat to the toes of his brilliantly polished and tightly fitted short-boots. He strode rather heavily into Miss Sheldon's little parlor, also bearing what was, unmistakably, a look of disapproval. That unfortunate expression did not seem to lighten when he met his niece's eye.

Dropping into a respectful curtsy, Cecilia gave him greeting.

But Sir Andrew barely glanced at the young

woman. His wife and daughters had so often assured him that his niece was unattractive that he now marked nothing more than an overtall young miss with garishly colored hair and an unbecoming dress. The harsh black of Cecilia's gown did most effectively drain her creamy skin of life, making her complexion appear wan.

"So then, niece," he opened sententiously, "you must be glad to be back in England, eh?" He gave Cecilia no chance to answer as he continued. "Too bad about James, but it's no more than I expected, still and all. Traipsing about in foreign parts is dangerous business, and so I warned him. And as for you, Cecilia, you might have returned here sooner. It has been what—three months? You could have saved us all a deal of trouble, a great deal of trouble, I say! Such inconsideration is not appreciated, and that I don't mind telling you."

How like Uncle Andrew to fix on the least aspect of a thing, Cecilia thought grimly. Just what he envisioned a soldier *should* do in wartime, she couldn't imagine. Was her father supposed to have ignored his sworn duty and finessed a way to remain safe in England? And if Uncle or Aunt Margaret truly cared a jot for her tardy return, it was for no cause that she could think of.

Miss Sheldon, shocked that the baronet should disregard his niece's grief in such a manner, managed to gather her wits and step into the breach before Cecilia could say something unwise. "Sir Andrew," she offered, "I am sure your niece came as soon as she could. As it is, she has had a very long and difficult journey." She gave Cecilia a stern look, warning her to silence.

Sir Andrew rocked up on his toes in a familiar, pompous movement. "Right you are, Miss Sheldon, quite right. We'll just be off, then. If you'll show Rob Coachman the baggage, he'll have us back home in no time, eh, eh? No sense in us standing about, is there?"

Cecilia bent and hugged her old teacher tightly.

"I thank you for everything, Miss Sheldon. You truly are the best of good friends." She then lowered her voice so her uncle couldn't hear. "Oh, I do so hate leaving you both, but you *will* send word if Marpessa is any trouble?"

The old woman's heart melted at the anxious note. She whispered back, "Yes, yes, dear, but you'll remember that years ago my father kept a fine pack of hounds, so I shall know just what to do. We'll get along quite famously, never fear."

Necessarily content with that, Cecilia took a place in her uncle's incongruous transport. Absorbed in her own worries, it was several minutes after they'd started off before her uncle's words penetrated. "So at first light tomorrow you'll be off for Nottingham, and high time, too," he was saying.

Trying to recall his preceding words, she asked, "Ah, Nottingham, Uncle? Isn't that where Cousin Theresa now lives?"

"Well, what have I just been saying? I know your aunt Margaret wrote you when each of our daughters married, and Theresa and her husband, Sir Rupert Whiting, are agreed upon having you. Sir Rupert was a widower with four young daughters by his first marriage, and, what with Theresa now expecting a happy event of her own, you can consider yourself fortunate to be so wanted."

Cecilia could feel only acute dismay at being shuttled off to her least favorite cousin's. Especially since she knew it would mean leaving Marpessa even farther behind, for she recalled that Theresa disliked dogs almost as much as her parents did. Still, if Cecilia were needed, she could at least put a good face on it. "If my presence will make things easier for Theresa during these coming weeks, I shall be glad for it, Uncle. I'll make ready to leave in the morning."

"Oh, but this is not just some temporary arrangement, Cecilia." He quickly disabused her of the notion. "No, no. You are to take over the schoolroom for your cousin. Why, your place there is assured for many years to come!" He then named a meager salary which made the amount she had paid old Maria for her simple services seem a fabulous sum.

"But, Uncle," she protested, "you must acknowledge that Theresa and I have never been on the best of terms. And while I had thought to take a situation of employment, I had hoped to employ the skills I learned at Santa Clara Infirmary."

Sir Andrew's eyes narrowed and he rounded on her at once. "We'll have no more of that kind of talk, miss! Whatever foolishness my brother allowed will not be permitted here. *I* speak for Linscombe Hall, and you will go precisely where you are told."

I speak for Linscombe Hall. Experience told Cecilia to believe it. She left off arguing, her eyes taking on a certain stillness as she reflected on her suddenly changed circumstances. Red-haired she might be, but she was rarely afflicted with the uncertain temper so often associated with that coloring. Hers was a more deliberate nature.

If only there was time to think the thing through.

An unanticipated form of relief was granted sometime during the night. Temperatures plummeted and the county awakened to a thick, sleeting rain which made travel of even the shortest distance unthinkable. The icy substance drummed against the windows of Linscombe Hall, blearing every surface and completely distorting the skeletal shapes of the linden trees lining the drive outside.

Using the unlooked-for reprieve to work out some solution to her problem, Cecilia spent most of the day in her old room at the Hall. She was determined to escape the drudgery her kinsmen had planned. Luckily, the means of her deliverance were immediately to hand. For along with a few gowns and other sundry keepsakes, her travel-scarred trunk held a particular paper-wrapped par-

56

cel—a parcel containing kerseymere breeches and a rich velvet coat of bottle green.

The last time she had worn these items was the occasion of her almost introduction to the arrogant Colonel Trelwyn. Diverted by the memory, Cecilia recalled a so-soft kiss in a dark stairwell, even while echoes of the young officer's shouts of laughter made her to chuckle outright.

I wonder whatever became of him? she mused.

She had learned the next day that he had come on a visit to Sergeant Haskell. But by the time she thought to ask for more particulars, the sergeant-major had been declared fit for duty and had been released to return to the field. She didn't even know if the big colonel was married—he could have a wife and six hopeful little Trelwyns, for all she knew. So, if she had kept her eyes open for his name on the casualty lists, or looked for the sight of a particular officer's uniform in following weeks, it was simply because she wished to avoid his notice. "And no other reason!" she said aloud.

Well. These kinds of thoughts were getting her nowhere in a hurry. She pulled her mind back to the problem at hand. The weather was not likely to last forever; it would be April in just a few days.

She had a disguise and she had funds. Her uncle would be shocked to learn that she had eighty-odd pounds safely sewn by her own hand into the quilted lining of her portmanteau; a goodly sum, it gave her a much-needed feeling of security. It was all that was left after paying for her passage from Portugal, money she would have given up to her guardian for safekeeping had things been otherwise.

The next item was to obtain a suitable employment. Oh, she was not such a fool as to suppose she could find another situation such as she'd had in Tôrres Vedras, but she was proud of the skills she had acquired there, and thought she might be of use in a private capacity to someone old or infirm. There must be many who would appreciate her particular abilities, for she knew herself gifted at giving others ease. Unlike the position outlined by her family, she wanted work that made her feel useful, not *used*.

Cecilia's bedroom window faced southwest, the direction of Wicksham Cross. And who better to ask for advice than dear Miss Sheldon? It was entirely possible that once again her old governess could furnish instruction on how she should proceed.

And what better time to put it to the test than this very night?

Once more the uncertain weather struck. As the Swiss case-clock in the hall chimed the hour of midnight, the cold winds sighed fitfully, then died altogether. The overcast skies cleared, and twinkling stars were unveiled overhead, one by single one. A new moon dispensed a ghostly light, and only the muted crunch of ice on the drive gave sound.

But there was no one left awake in Linscombe Hall to hear.

Carrying her carefully repacked portmanteau and a single bandbox, Miss Cecilia Linscombe stole away through the night, using the scant shadows of the ice-bedecked trees to disguise her progress down the drive. By tucking the hood of her long black cape inside her collar, her cloak was indistinguishable from a gentleman's outer garb. The postillion-style hat perched atop her short curls added authenticity to her disguise. The same fearless nature which had once sent her out alone into the war-torn Spanish countryside now determined her steps. Only when the manor house was well out of sight did she lengthen her stride, careful of the treacherous ice underfoot.

Cecilia walked through the chill, eerie darkness for one full hour, then yet another. Her exertions kept her in reasonable comfort, and she slung both bags over her back for economy. Wisely, she had not worn the fancy dress boots that completed her gentleman's ensemble, but instead chose the better-fitting hobnailed footwear her father had insisted

58

she have. The conscientious infantry major had also taught her a loose, swinging stride that did not tire; to be sure, she had marched over far rougher country than this.

Sometime later, a dog's excited barking drew a peacefully sleeping Miss Sheldon from her rest. The aged spinster could hardly trust her ears when she next identified an additional sound, the sound of Cecilia's calls for entry. Lighting a taper and scrambling into a wrapper, she hastened down to answer the door.

"My dear, what on earth . . . !" She goggled at Cecilia's costume.

Stepping inside with a wildly excited Marpessa hard by, Cecilia removed her high-crowned hat and followed Miss Sheldon into the parlor to explain.

"Help you?" her old governess exclaimed at the end of the telling. "Naturally, I will do so, dear. And I know just the person in London you should see." Fully awake by now, Miss Sheldon's brow puckered in consternation. "But, my dearest girl, have you honestly thought about what this step will mean to your future? I cannot like to see you giving up every prospect for a husband and a family of your own, which is what will happen if you proceed along this path. For what you intend means that you will lose the respectability of your name; make no mistake about that! You cannot hide yourself otherwise, and without a family to grant you protection, no honest man will consider you for an honorable estate."

"But, Miss Sheldon," came the anguished cry. "Who is it that you think will have me, anyway? Just look at me! Tall as a gatepost and poor as a church mouse. A whole *basket* of carrots could hide in my hair with no one ever the wiser!"

This last was not entirely true. Cecilia's shiny locks were of a far deeper red than the specified produce. Unaware of the inaccuracy, however, she slumped into a chair with unusual gracelessness, adding softly, "Is it not better to just forget about what cannot be and get on with my life as I may?"

Jane Sheldon understood to a nicety what had given the young woman such a false opinion of herself, but said merely, "You are very wrong, Cecilia, for you are a remarkably beautiful young woman—an Incomparable, whether you recognize it or not. But I don't suppose we've time to discuss it. Now. You say that you have the funds with which to travel, and I suppose I must approve of your disguise for safety's sake. Though for the love of heaven, do put those things away after this! You must pledge never to dress in such manner again." A stern look underscored her meaning.

"Yes, ma'am," Cecilia answered docilely.

"So. I will immediately write you an introduction to two dear friends of mine, Lawrence and Amelia Dockery. Mr. Dockery is a solicitor in the city, and his wife and I were schoolgirls together. You will go to their home straight away, but you will not disclose your real name or age, remember. Mr. Dockery's duty may otherwise compel him to notify your uncle, since you are underage. I will simply explain to my friends that you are the orphaned daughter of one of His Majesty's officers and left in need of support. Now then, my dear, you must decide upon the name you intend using, so that I may begin the letter to my friends."

But Cecilia was not quite done with her worries. "What, then, if my uncle comes here to question you about my disappearance? I won't have you taking the blame for my decampment," she said on a note of concern.

"Don't bother your head on that score, dear. Should they come to me with their questions, I can honestly answer that I've seen not a soul in skirts!"

CHAPTER SEVEN

So it was that "Cecil Langley," as those in the Reading Public Coach knew her, spent the next two days on the road. London was only one day's journey north from Hazelmere by way of Guildford, but Cecilia had chosen to start from Farnham, going thence through Reading to approach London from the west. Her disguise probably made such roundaboutations unnecessary, but she was determined to take every precaution to avoid discovery.

And by now, she thought, tugging at her hat to be sure it concealed the telltale color of her hair, Uncle Andrew would be castigating his ungrateful niece. He would have read the letter she had left atop her abandoned trunk, assuring him that she felt herself capable of securing her own future. Though not even after making a conscious search had Cecilia found words of real gratitude to include. A wry half-smile twisted its way across her face at this failure.

Her smile faded, however, at the thought of Marpessa. The Briard had seemed to understand that their parting was to be of some duration, for she had whined unremittingly when Cecilia had left her behind. Even under Miss Sheldon's encouraging pats she'd not subsided, and Cecilia had started for Farnham under a fading moon and with the dog's mournful notes in her ears. She could only trust that the separation would prove temporary.

Under cover of a pretended sneeze, Cecilia surreptitiously wiped a trickle of moisture from her eyes.

At the end of the second day of her journey, eight mud-bespattered horses were unhitched in the yard of the London coaching inn. The driver had to knock great chunks of accumulated mud and slush from the sides of the vehicle before he could force open the door to allow his passengers exit, but Cecilia's concern was limited to whether or not she might again obtain a private room. Her luck held, and she even managed the luxury of a hot bath.

When a tall, heavily veiled woman dressed in mourning weeds left the busy inn the next day, none gave it any particular notice. The disappearance of the young gentleman who had sought rooms the night before went unremarked, since Cecilia had cleverly paid her shot upon arrival. She signaled a hackney carriage to take her to the Dockerys' address near Kennington Oval.

Cecilia had not had occasion to visit England's capital before. Her travels on the Continent notwithstanding, she had never in her young life seen such sights as she found in London. Fishmongers, street singers, and scurrying apprentices filled the streets, and neat shops alternated with colorful stalls, selling every imaginable thing from buttons to harps. When the jarvey pulled in before a sizable half-bricked house, she felt a brief disappointment that the ride was over.

Paying out the sum requested by the driver, Cecilia stepped up to the knocker of the specified dwelling. It was a pleasant-looking residence among similar habitations in an area on the Surrey side of the Thames. The owners were evidently among the city's more prosperous; fresh paint glistened and lacy curtains showed in the windows of each address. She held her breath for the few seconds it took for the door to be answered. The uncertainty of what awaited made her feel tense and ill at ease.

A pretty blond housemaid came in answer to her knock. Astonishingly, she bade Cecilia enter without so much as asking for her name or purpose! Cecilia stepped inside and set her portmanteau and

62

the smaller bandbox down. She extracted the letter Miss Sheldon had prepared. Before she could present her credentials, however, a pillowy-plump woman of sixty or so years peeked over the top railing of the polished staircase.

"Who is it, Sally?" the woman called to the maidservant as she started down in a rush. Cecilia murmured her assumed name to the serving girl, who in turn repeated the information.

"Langley? How nice. Have we met? No, I do not believe that I know you, do I? I, of course, am Amelia Dockery." As she took the last step, Mrs. Dockery thanked Sally and shooed Cecilia ahead of her into a small salon.

Although the residence of a Cit, a professional man of the city, Cecilia noted that the room was furnished not only with comfort in mind, but in remarkably good taste as well. The decorations and kickshaws were well-chosen pieces without a hint of vulgar ostentation. Leaving her inspection for another time, Cecilia met the rounded little woman's open, guileless look. "Mrs. Dockery," she said, "we haven't before been introduced, but I am a friend of Miss Sheldon's, now of Wicksham Cross."

"Jane, of course!" Mrs. Dockery cried, a dazzlingly youthful smile wrapped across her face. "She always sends me the nicest people, oh, indeed, yes, she does! Do, please, sit down, Miss Langley. Sit down and I shall send for us some tea—you do drink tea, don't you?" Without waiting for a reply, she hopped over to the bell-pull, the skirts of her mulled primrose muslin fluttering about ridiculously tiny slippered feet. Nonstop, her words followed over her shoulder. "I have not seen Jane since she acquired that darling house she writes to me about. Is it as charming as she says? I am *so* glad that she no longer has to work for a living, though often and often I have tried to get her to join Mr. Dockery and me here. We have more than enough room, and it would be such fun to have her with me every day. It must have been just *awful* taking responsibility for other people's children all of these years and—"

The stream of words seemed capable of going on indefinitely if Cecilia did not stem the tide mid-flow. "Excuse me," she finally dropped in her oar, "but Miss Sheldon gave me a letter explaining why I have come. Perhaps you would care to read it?"

"Oh! Yes, indeed I shall; have I been running on too long? Mr. Dockery always tells me that I do—not that he ever fusses! He says that it is just my way, and he wouldn't change me for the world. *Isn't* that the sweetest man?"

Cecilia handed her the sealed packet, watching in disbelief as the artless chatter continued throughout the reading with never the slightest pause. She didn't learn the letter's exact contents, for Mrs. Dockery's comments did not enlarge upon the information that Miss Sheldon had already given Cecilia to know.

The tea tray was brought in before her hostess had finished with the letter, and Cecilia was requested to pour. She did so willingly, since she'd not dared break her fast before making her exit from the coaching inn that morning. The pastries were scrumptious. Fruit and nuts were baked into a variety of breads, with a crock of fresh yellow butter and another of honey set out to complete the repast. Cecilia fell to with a will; Mrs. Dockery not behindhand in diminishing the delectable contents of the tray.

After the last crumb was rinsed down with a fragrant hot drink, Mrs. Dockery surged from her chair and volunteered to show her visitor up to the guest chambers. "For you certainly must stay here for the nonce," the good woman said. "I'll send out inquiries at once, though it will likely be a few days before we hear of anything for you. Jane tells me that you are quite skilled in nursing, so it shouldn't be too difficult to find something unexceptionable. You won't mind being here with us, will you?" she rambled on. "Mr. Dockery and I will do our utmost *best* to make you comfortable, so when—"

Cecilia rushed in with the words to assure her hostess of her gratitude and said she would be honored to be counted their guest while a position of employment was sought. Whatever Miss Sheldon had written, plainly it had satisfied Mrs. Dockery sufficiently so that such questions as Cecilia had feared might be asked were already answered.

She was led up to a cheery room where she could unpack her few things: mainly three serviceable day dresses in the mandatory black. Mrs. Dockery left her alone to attend this chore, saying she should come down and join them for lunch later on. Mr. Dockery would make her acquaintance at that time.

As the door closed behind the gregarious goodwife, Cecilia shook her head in bemusement. She set about arranging her gowns in the clothes press, then began refolding the articles of male attire to tuck down into the bottom of her bag. While she was smoothing the nap of her green velvet coat, she noted a stiffness on one side of the garment. Searching through the pockets, she pulled out the note square written so many months ago.

The flowing signature was unfaded. It stood out on the paper as firm and black as originally written. *Ebon black. Like his hair,* she mused with unaccustomed poetry. Quixotically, she moved the note to the bottom of her writing box, where it would remain safe and unspoiled.

Completing the disposal of her clothing, Cecilia pushed the portmanteau with her gentleman's outfit out of sight in the wardrobe. Even if uncovered by one of the maids, she doubted that the items would be questioned. They would be assumed to have belonged to her father, things that she could not yet bring herself to part with.

At the thought of Major James Linscombe, killed in action, tears rushed up but did not quite spill over. Cecilia realized that the memory of her father's death was no longer accompanied by the acute, burning pain the news had first caused; now she was more aware of the close, secure love his nearness had always brought, a love that was not harsh in its judgment, only caring. She accepted that he was gone and that she always would miss him, but she also understood that he would forever be with her, an integral part of her mind.

When her pendant watch showed it about time for luncheon to be served, Cecilia ventured forth from her bedchamber, still wrapped in the warmth of remembrance. She met Sally in the hallway, arranging a mass of early daffodils, and the maidservant helpfully pointed Cecilia to the dining room. There, an oval table was set with plates for three.

Her hostess had not yet come down. Instead of Mrs. Dockery, Cecilia found herself met by a rotund little man wearing starched shirtpoints which reached all the way up to the tops of his ears. The rest of his dress was more restrained, even conservatively styled. It was only the altitude of his collar that marked him as a man moved by Fashion. Swallowing a smile at the incongruous picture, Cecilia accepted the introduction to her host: Lawrence T. Dockery, Esquire.

"Miss Langley, it is a pleasure to have you with us." The lawyer shook her hand with a firm, dry clasp. "My wife tells me that you are a friend of Miss Jane's, and as such you are most welcome. You will, I hope, allow me to express my regrets on your recent bereavement—that Corsican monster has much to answer for. Why, if we allowed him to have his way, the whole world would be under his thumb." He seemed to take Napoleon's aspirations as a personal affront. "Well, well." He bobbed his head more benignly. "My Amelia is a most resourceful woman and will soon find a pleasing situation for you. Please believe that you may trust us to look after your interests."

"Thank you, sir," Cecilia responded. "I have been

made to feel quite at home, and I will appreciate any help you can give me." Cecilia liked the funny little man every bit as much as she liked his wife. The frivolous collar did not take away from the genuine concern she heard in his voice.

"I must *beg* your pardon all for being so late!" Mrs. Dockery sailed into the room and fanned her fingers, motioning for them to sit down. A footman stood by to assist with their selections from the sideboard, arrayed as it was with an assortment of aromatic dishes.

An informal meal, Mr. Dockery pulled back each lady's chair in turn while his wife continued speaking. "I dare not tell you too much just yet," she said, "but I think I've come up with the *very* thing to meet dear Jane's requirements. I am happy to say that I enjoy a gratifyingly large circle of acquaintance—most agreeable!—and I'm sure I couldn't count how many of them number themselves as my friends. But I have an idea, Cecilia—I *may* call you by your given name, mayn't I?—an idea that I think will answer. Goodness! This will be so vastly diverting." Cecilia was left to wonder what exactly all of this meant, since the subject was promptly changed, leaving the better part of the meal to be taken up with a rather one-sided discussion of the latest topic explored in the *Ladies' Magazine*.

At the meal's end, Mrs. Dockery was still blithely prattling away. ". . . And the latest dress lines are so perfect for you, Cecilia, for you must have a new gown or two made up. Oh, my! To be blessed with such a splendid figure, such regal height—you must consider yourself fortunate. Why, these new styles are simply *made* for you, and I know the dearest seamstress who can outfit you in no time at all!"

"Amelia, please." The sprightly prattle of the voluble woman was interrupted by her spouse as, with a tolerant eye, Mr. Dockery called his wife to order. "Let us not forget, my dear, that Miss Langley is still in deep mourning. All this talk of fashion will have to wait, I think."

"Oh! Oh, how absolutely *callous* of me. Of course, you are in the right of it, Mr. Dockery." She turned abashed eyes to her guest. "Pray tell me that you will accept my apologies, dear girl! I daresay I have been very rude; I beg you will forgive me."

Before Cecilia could assure her hostess that no offense was taken, though, Mrs. Dockery was off and running again.

"But you must know, Cecilia, that I do have a lovely silver-gray fabric stored in the attic—more than a dress length, do I remember correctly—and some delicious lavender lawn that would look very well on you. Half-mourning, don't you know! I hope I am sensible of the respect that must be shown to the departed, but if you are to give cheer to the sick, isn't black just a trifle too *lowering?*"

Cecilia had to agree. The major would have been the first to see the sense in such a practical suggestion, so Cecilia immediately offered to purchase the materials needed. Since she knew herself skilled in any sort of handwork—she even cut and dressed her own hair—she informed her hostess that she could do the sewing herself quite easily.

But Mrs. Dockery overrode her with effusive protestations of friendship. It left the bewildered girl to think she must be the greatest beast in nature did she not allow Miss Sheldon's dearest friend to have the dressing of her. When appealed to, Mr. Dockery smiled helplessly and said that he thought that she would have to give in and put herself totally in his wife's hands. Cecilia was rather astonished by such generosity from people she scarcely knew.

Accordingly, the next morning saw Cecilia and Mrs. Dockery off to the mantuamaker, several large bolts of cloth protruding from the back of the carriage. But after they entered the shopping district, it quickly became obvious that dresses were not all that was needed.

"*Shoes*, dear Cecilia," Mrs. Dockery declared excitedly, adding another pair to the rising stack of sandals found to be in Cecilia's size. "You must have footwear that can pass silently around a sickbed. Oh, and see here," she crowed in triumph at yet another shop, "this darling pelisse will prevent your catching your death while out running errands for your employer. My, yes, we must have that," she said positively, motioning to the clerk to wrap up the purchase. "And *fans!*" she cried out in still another shop. "You can never know just when a nice fan will be needed for faintness, dear girl. And would you look at these?" she said, rushing over to another display table. "Certainly, one can never have sufficient stockings—the silk ones are so very comfortable, don't you agree? But they do tend to shred easily, so we must have plenty of them. Also, I think that you must have some of these lovely . . ."

And so it went. Hats were excused as being just the thing to brighten the day for some doddering old woman, gloves must be worn to uphold the reputation for refinement in any respectable house, special evening gowns would enable Cecilia to attend the select musical functions—"So restful for the infirm," according to Mrs. Dockery. And so on and on. Parcels were stacked upon parcels as the "necessary" accoutrements were added to the list.

For two whole years Cecilia had worked in a crowded wartime infirmary. She now began to wonder how her patients had managed to survive without her wearing the latest in bonnets and carrying a daintily embroidered reticule. To hold all of the medicinals, of course.

While Mrs. Dockery raved about Cecilia's elegant inches, and even the modiste and milliner gave praise, the younger woman was just glad that her height seemed to successfully disguise her age. People seemed to assume that she was older than her years merely because she stood somewhat taller than they. She had to concede, though, that the new high-waisted styles became her well enough—and that Mrs. Dockery was altogether too kind to be believed.

CHAPTER EIGHT

"Cecilia, dear girl, it has come." Mrs. Dockery flew into the breakfast room on tiny, sandaled feet, waving a letter which bore a mark that looked suspiciously like a lozenged crest. Cecilia had been with the Dockerys for just over a week, and she looked up from her plate as her hostess fairly bounced over to her side. "I told you that you could rely upon me, did I not?" Mrs. Dockery cried with glee. "I set to work immediately after Jane explained the matter, thinking that I might know just what would answer. Oh, this is such an opportunity for you. The very thing indeed! When I took up the mail this morning, I *knew* that today would be the day."

"What is it, ma'am? Have you found me a position?" The excitement was contagious.

"I have in my hand," the good woman announced, "the response to a letter I sent out to an acquaintance of mine on the selfsame day you arrived. Mind, I have met Her Grace only the one time, and that some years ago, but Mr. Dockery has been her business adviser for *ages*. She writes here that she does indeed have need of a companion, and that she thinks you may do for her quite nicely as—"

"Who is it you refer to, please, ma'am? And can you tell me the extent of her infirmity?" Cecilia had learned from the first day that the only way to progress was to jump right into the middle of Mrs. Dockery's outpourings.

"Oh, to be sure, dear Cecilia. And she is not exactly *infirm*, you know. But with most of eighty years in her dish, well, she's not likely able to manage a 'capriole, do you think? Such a distinguished family too, not like some I could name who go through money like there was no tomorrow. Oh, no. Her Grace is as sharp as can stare; she is what Mr. Dockery calls 'no one's fool with a golden boy.' "

"But if you please, ma'am, who exactly is 'Her Grace,' and where does she live?"

"The dowager Duchess of Kelthorpe. Did I not say? Although there is no duchess now, since the dowager's daughter-in-law has been gone any time these last twenty years or more. Now the only one left is—" Her words faltered and seemed to lose direction. "But you wanted to know where? Right here in town! She has a enormous pile of a house on Cavendish Square, at least thirty rooms. She must be quite lost rattling around all by herself, or so I should think. Why, the ballroom alone can comfortably entertain *hundreds* of guests—"

"And does Her Grace say when I may come?" Cecilia asked, thoroughly infected with her hostess's enthusiasm. She felt the greatest affection for this couple who had taken her in and made her feel so wanted, but she did not like to presume upon the Dockerys' hospitality too long. Privately, she permitted herself to envision a rosy future of quiet days spent dispensing medicines, ordering meals to tempt an invalid's appetite, exchanging pillows, and reading aloud to her patient.

"Why, today, dear girl, today! She writes that she will be ready to receive you any time after three of the clock. And when you have as little time remaining as she has, punctuality is most important. Yes, indeed, it is! We must be certain that you do not keep her waiting."

Mrs. Dockery then did something very strange. She looked seriously into Cecilia's eyes and spoke more slowly and in a tone Cecilia had never yet heard her use. "You must not feel that you have to stay there, dear. It's possible that you shan't like it," she said earnestly. "Her Grace is known to be something of a tartar, and you may find yourself unable to cope. Mr. Dockery and I would be more than pleased to have you here with us forever, come to that. You will keep it in mind?"

Cecilia was touched by such kind sincerity. She did not think that it was meant solely for Miss Sheldon's sake, either, but that a genuine affection had grown up between them. She, too, had enjoyed Amelia Dockery's support and friendly prattle, and the portly Mr. Dockery had more than once reminded her of her father by the way he so easily put her at her ease. *How very different from Uncle Andrew.*

That opinion was reinforced when the little lawyer joined them later for lunch. He congratulated his wife on her accomplishment, but also counseled Cecilia that while the remuneration mentioned was half again above the customary amount—seventy-five pounds per annum, no less—she should still feel herself free to return to them at any time, and welcome.

Cecilia dreaded losing contact with this wonderful couple. They assured her that it was to be no such thing, though, telling her that they expected her to visit them every week on her half-days.

Twenty minutes before the specified hour, the slender young woman set off in the Dockerys' smartly styled town carriage, bound for Kelthorpe House. And when they stopped before an exceedingly large house fronting the square, Cecilia scarcely had time to take in its stately exterior before an equally worthy-looking butler came to escort her inside. He ushered Cecilia across wide, smoothly polished floors of delicately veined pink and white marble.

She tried not to act the gapeseed as she was led into a magnificent withdrawing room with draperies of Lyons silk in a rich shade of rose. Large gilt-framed mirrors were strategically placed to lighten the room; set between them were paintings of different sizes and subjects.

Quite as soon as she was left alone, Cecilia strolled around the spacious room, examining the oils and watercolors displayed on the walls. Some of the pictures interested the viewer more for the artist's use of shadow or brilliant choice of color, but Cecilia was captivated by the method of presentation of one particular landscape.

Clearly drawn from imagination, she found herself looking down onto the crenelated parapets of a huge castle set amid the grandeur of high, rugged hills. A great, dark lake was just visible in the distance. The painting was almost somber in tone, but she admired the perspective of a bird's-eye view, never having seen such a splendid panorama. The mighty castle walls were of oddly colored, golden-gray stone, the same color as seen in the boulders scattered up the nearby hillsides. She chose a chair that let her keep the fascinating picture within sight as she waited.

Sitting patiently, her back away from the cushions, she wondered whether she would be taken up to the venerable old lady's room, or if Her Grace would be brought down in an invalid chair.

She was soon to learn that neither guess was correct. The black-suited butler reentered the room to bow in Her Grace, the dowager Duchess of Kelthorpe . . . with only a bejeweled, gold-topped cane to lend that lady support.

As Cecilia sank into a deep curtsy, she thought that this prospective employer looked to be in no need of nursing. Her lightly powdered face was seamed and lined with the years, it was true, and the curls at her temples were of a nearly transparent white, but there was none of the sagging flesh usually brought about by age. Spare of figure, fashionable of dress—the slender cane notwithstanding—Cecilia saw little of the slowing which was supposed to occur with time. Had Mrs. Dockery been misinformed? Dressed in a round gown of indigo-blue pongee silk, the dowager Duchess of Kelthorpe looked to be more of an age with Miss Sheldon.

"Miss Langley," the dowager opened after requesting Cecilia to be reseated, "you are highly recommended to me by one whose judgment I believe to be sound. It is most unusual that a genteel young woman has acquired your nursing experience, but it has been explained to me that nothing was done without your father's consent." There was no hint of question in the words; in fact, there might be heard a trace of admiration as Her Grace went on speaking. "So, miss, while you might prefer it if we not bandy your history about, *I* have no objections. And as for your discarding your blacks, I cannot disagree with that, either, considering that it would serve only to curtail the activities I regard as your duty to me. When my only son died a twelvemonth ago, I refused to don mourning colors. In my experience, gained many years earlier when my own lord died, such custom serves only to blight one's recall of the bright moments that should stay in the forefront of our memories."

"Thank you, Your Grace," Cecilia said. "I wasn't sure—"

"None will dare take exception to one whom I have approved," the dowager interrupted with absolute confidence. "Now, you will pay close attention while I outline your responsibilities, for I am not in the habit of repeating myself."

With no further ado, Cecilia was thence presented with a lengthy and detailed list recited in a no-nonsense tone. Every minute of her days was to be accounted for, and the particulars of her conduct in company were precisely specified. But as the rules were rapped out in the dry, though not unpleasant voice, Cecilia felt a spark of resolve ignite. It was the prohibition against using the front staircase which finally caused her to grit her teeth. She was not averse to using the servants' staircase when convenient, but supposing it was not?

75

She didn't think of the embarrassment she might cause the Dockerys, nor did she stop to consider her own financial needs. She thought only that she would be unable to submit to all of these despotic-sounding demands. While it was ever her way to be forbearing with those suffering from pain, she saw no reason to endure such constraints from someone who evidenced good health. Cecilia held to her patience. She sat quietly until Her Grace completed the statement of her requirements and seemed about to summon someone to show her up to her new quarters.

If the dowager duchess expected meek acquiescence from her petitioner, she was certainly in for a surprise. Cecilia rose from her seat to stand to her height and spoke down to the startled dowager. "I thank you for the time you have given for this meeting"—she had to discipline her voice not to show her irritation—"but I am afraid, Your Grace, that you and I would not suit."

A suggestion of dismay flitted across the dowager's face, prompting Cecilia to continue with a shade more kindness. "Please, understand me, Your Grace. I don't think you really have use for a trained nurse, and I would prefer to go where I am more needed. The tasks you have set forth would be better completed by someone else, for, soldier's daughter or no, I do not follow instructions at all well. We should forever be at odds, you see." Cecilia dipped a graceful curtsy and made to leave the room.

"Oh, do sit down, gel. Sit down I say," barked the elegant old lady. She rapped her cane against the hardwood floor. "Perhaps I haven't made myself clear. Please allow me an opportunity to do so!"

It was not the voice of command which impelled Cecilia to subside into her chair; she was more than capable of ignoring orders from any source. Rather, it was an additional note of something else that she discerned in the redoubtable old woman's voice. That something else, along with the sight of gnarled

76

fingers, whitening as they gripped the polished cane, indicated that the speaker was in some sort of distress.

"Miss Langley," the dowager said after Cecilia had returned to her seat, "I really must have someone to attend me. I am seventy-eight years old and have seen the friends of my youth dwindle to a very short list. True, I would never permit the cosseting and carryings-on I have seen among older persons who would be far better off with a bit of exercise instead of dosing themselves with possets and potions, but I would have someone about me who knows how to deal with the, ah, the physical impediments."

Cecilia recognized the thread of fear which forced such candor from one who was apparently unused to asking favors. She considered the effort Her Grace had made, and decided that she might have been too hasty in judging the dowager's condition. "Are you ill, then?" she asked tentatively.

"Certainly not!" The dowager challenged her with a haughty look. "There is nothing seriously wrong, nothing more than the natural limitations brought by time. I cannot make a pretty turn around the dance floor anymore, nor, I assure you, do I wish to." The old lady then paused and turned her eyes away to say, "Regrettably, Miss Langley, I'm afraid I can no longer hear."

Her words came so softly that at first Cecilia wondered if she had understood correctly. Yet the dowager duchess must be able to take in auditory messages to some extent—she had been quick enough to understand when Cecilia had tried to refuse her employment. Cecilia fixed steady brown eyes on those of the dowager duchess. "If that is so, Your Grace, how is it that we have been conversing?"

"Well, I have eyes, don't I?" the old lady snapped almost angrily. "Your lip movements are easily read by someone who has been an observer for many years. But there are worse difficulties which, as a nurse, you might understand. When people learn of a disorder like mine, they seem to assume that the mental faculties are likewise impaired. I would prefer to keep my affliction to myself. Thus far, when I fail to respond to a question or comment, people think me either snobbish or else eccentric. Oh, I considered using an ear trumpet," she said, frowning fiercely, "but decided that it simply would not do. Wouldn't the *ton* just love to know that I could no longer hear their slurs and gossip? Why, I would soon become the laughingstock of any gathering."

"But, surely, Your Grace—"

"You are thinking that I exaggerate, Miss Langley? Be assured that it is no such thing. The society of which I am a part enjoys nothing so much as tearing one of their fellows to shreds. I refuse to stay inside my doors and become some sort of recluse, but I can go out only if my secret remains unknown. And you must help me."

While the imperious tones had nothing of humility about them, Cecilia considered that a deal of courage had been needed for the proud old woman to make such an admission. And it was true that the world often looked upon the deaf as if they had their upper stories to let. The dowager's assessment was all too accurate. People, including those of the *beau monde*, were capable of cutting cruelty.

Cecilia's own brief episode of deafness in Spain— it was three full days before she regained her hearing after the cannonade over the barley field—had taught her something of the problems involved. It went against the grain to refuse assistance to a fellow in need, and especially now that she knew she could be useful. It must be horrid to feel alone and incapable. Her Grace was really not asking for so much; Cecilia found herself intrigued. Perhaps, with other ground rules, they might come to terms.

"Very well, Your Grace," she said finally. "I think I can manage to meet most of your conditions; I understand better now why you wish me to choose a seat facing you in company, for example. But I tell you to your head that I *will* use the front staircase if it proves quicker to hand, while as for your other strictures, I can only promise to try and comply if I can. I fear that I may have to be reminded to the submissive aspect you seem to prefer, though. Despite my time with the military, I have thus far been unable to acquire the regular use of that virtue."

"Ha! Gammon!" the old lady barked. "And I'll lay a monkey to a groat that you never do!" She scowled ferociously at the incorrigible young miss.

But Cecilia detected a twinkle lurking from the corners of the fine old eyes before her. "Well, you are probably right," she admitted, "so I shan't take up your bet." Her ready smile brought a still-deeper scowl to the old lady's face. Cecilia refused to be deceived.

Acknowledging that the girl had seen too much, the dowager duchess stood to signal an end to the interview. "So, miss," she said, "we are agreed. I will direct Iverson to send for your things. Oh, and by the bye," Her Grace then added innocently, "I don't suppose there is any chance that you *play*, is there?"

"Play, Your Grace?" Cecilia, in fact, had an absolute dread of musical instruments.

"Cards, Miss Langley. Do you ever care to sit to a hand of cards?"

"Oh, certainly, *cards*," she replied, suddenly realizing the unlikelihood of her first supposition. "Yes, that may be the one good thing I *did* learn from the army. I confess to an appreciation for a good game of piquet. Would Your Grace care to invite me to a round?" Neither one loath, it was decided there and then that the two would have a friendly game after supper, Her Grace being without other engagements that evening.

Much later, long after the day's last meal, the two women could be seen bending intently over a

79

worn pack of playing cards. Markers were distributed almost evenly in front of each; apparently there was not yet a clear winner. A postprandial refreshment tray rested untouched on a nearby table, and the ormolu-fitted Lépine clock on the mantel above their heads chimed the hour without being noticed.

A muted rap at the door was followed by the entry of Iverson, the stately head butler to Kelthorpe House. "Two o'clock, mum," he said, catching the dowager's eye.

"Oh, good gad, but we're dished!" Cecilia exclaimed. "A fine watchdog I've turned out to be . . . Eh-hem. That is, 'goodness,' I say . . . and, er, 'companion,' I meant." She then gave in to a grin. "But perhaps you should seriously reconsider my employment, ma'am." She laughed without apology. "For I've an unruly tongue, as you've just witnessed, and no sense of duty, besides."

"Bah! And discharge such a rarity?" the dowager grouched. She turned to her butler and said, "We thank you for the reminder, Iverson, but please remember that I haven't enjoyed a decent game since Lord Bemis laid down his knife and fork. With but just a little tutoring, I expect Miss Langley will make as fine a player as any." She arched one pencil-thin white eyebrow in cunning good humor.

Cecilia saw an answering sparkle in the imposing butler's eye. He said not a word, though, just tidied the tables while the ladies bade each other good night.

Nonetheless, Cecilia was completely nonplussed, when a few days later she was given leave to drop the formal "Your Grace," and encouraged to more intimate address as between friends. For a paid companion-*et*-nurse to be so honored, especially by one so notoriously high in the instep as the dowager duchess, was "beyond *anything*," as Mrs. Dockery later confided to her spouse.

CHAPTER NINE

In the following weeks Cecilia learned that her impressions of the dowager Duchess of Kelthorpe were accurate. Her Grace was indeed a haughty *grande dame* inclined to stand on her dignity; she would dice up an encroaching mushroom without remorse, allowing no one to infringe upon what she considered to be her prerogatives. She was also a woman capable of a marked degree of sensitivity, one who respected each person's position in life and did not stint in giving to each his or her due. Apparently, she assigned to Cecilia the exalted rank of friend—for so she considered *her* companion *must* be—and they managed to rub along comfortably together. This situation was not to prove as stable as one might have supposed, however.

The first indication of change came with a letter Cecilia's employer read aloud over the breakfast covers. An ordinary letter, it was from her grandson, the sixth duke. Short and succinct, he directed that his rooms be prepared for his immediate occupancy. He apprised the dowager duchess that while resident, he intended to seek him a wife, and that he expected to engage a suitable bride by July at the latest. Further, he assured her ladyship that he was well aware of what was owing to his name, and that he intended to make a review of the candidates himself. She should not feel it necessary to advise him in the matter.

Insult. *Outrage.* Cecilia felt her loyalty to the dowager aroused by the reading of each successive word. What manner of man wrote with such cold-blooded detachment, informing his only kin that she should immediately make ready for his coming, telling her that her advice on what was, after all, a family matter was not wanted?

Cecilia wished she could better see the salient handwriting from where she sat. No matter. Every sentence repeated from the detested letter showed one who held himself superior to his fellows—a man with an overweening awareness of his consequence such as made Cecilia want to shake him.

"What's amiss, gel?" the dowager asked, looking up to see the storm gathering in Cecilia's brown eyes. "You don't like the idea of Stephen joining us?"

"No. Yes! That is to say . . ." Cecilia began with confusion. She shook her short curls in dismay. "I mean, well, I must be glad if your grandson is coming to see you, although I admit that I cannot quite like the *style* of his communication. It all sounds rather horridly overbearing. He positively demands that you arrange all to his benefit, and then, ma'am, he tells you to stand clear!"

"Hmmm." Her Grace again ran her eyes over the boldly scripted words. "Perhaps you are right. However, he is a duke and may have something of his grandfather in him. Why, my lord could freeze a cobra with a single look if such a creature dared to get in *his* way. But, regrettably, I fear that my grandson is more like his father than like my lord. In point of fact, I've never understood how Stephen always received such favorable notice in the military dispatches sent up to the Lords. Oh, he is a good man, certainly, but sometimes almost maddeningly dull."

Cecilia didn't know whether this sixth duke was dull or not; instead, she found his words monumentally self-assured and wonderfully provoking. But she couldn't explain to Her Grace how it sounded so exactly like something her uncle Andrew might have written, nor about how the letter served to prove something she had learned to expect from most *soi-disant* grandees: They doted on any opportunity to puff themselves up. No, she could say none of these things, and so said only, "But to address you so coldly, and give so little notice of his plans, ma'am?"

"We won't be called upon to curtail our activities in the slightest, Cecilia. Is that what you are afraid of?" Her Grace flicked her fingers in unconcern. "I can think of no reason why Stephen's coming should make any change in our routine. While he goes on about his own business, you and I shall continue much as we have been doing."

Cecilia decided not to make an issue when she had so little to go on. Time would tell whether His Grace was actually the sort of man she supposed, and she sincerely hoped she was wrong. "You relieve my mind, ma'am," she said, then brightened. "And it has been everything marvelous to be here with you, seeing the new sights and meeting so many interesting people—many of whom have quite kindly accepted me. Why, I've been introduced to poets, diplomats, and I don't know what all. I must own I would hate to give up a single moment."

"And do not forget that we are become the terror of the cardrooms," the dowager duchess reminded slyly. "None can gainsay our several accomplishments, more especially did they realize my impairment. I'll warrant that I have you to thank for it, too." A look of pure mischief danced across the old lady's finely wrinkled face.

Cecilia had to smile. "Well, I shan't deny a certain enjoyment in fooling the world into thinking you immune to the march of time—and, yes, since you mention it, winning twenty pounds from that ghastly Lady Renport last week was most satisfying."

Both chuckled at the recollection. The viscountess Renport had tried to snub Cecilia when the dowager had offered her young companion as a partner in a game of lanter-loo. At Lady Renport's show of incivility, the dowager and Cecilia had then partnered each other, deriving great pleasure from trouncing their snobbish opposition.

But the momentary lightening of Cecilia's look was lost when she recalled herself to the purpose. "I suppose," she said next on a considering note, "that I've taken an absurd dislike to someone I have never met simply because he seems not to hold you in proper esteem." She looked sheepishly across the table. "Am I being very silly, ma'am?"

"Of course not," responded the dowager with decision. "However, this is his house, remember. Stephen is perfectly within his rights to come here whenever he pleases. You may even find that you two have a great deal in common when you meet, for he was with Wellington until eight or nine months ago. I think perhaps you misjudge him."

But Cecilia was not nearly so sanguine. *If this was his house—* "This property is entailed to the dukedom, then, and not your own?" she asked in some alarm.

"No, indeed. What an idea. Kelthorpe house belongs to the title, though I have resided here for almost sixty years. Just what is going on in that pretty red head of yours, anyway?"

Cecilia hesitated to answer. Her suspicions were too vile to speak of without adequate proof. Yet she was dismally afraid that once the vaunted wife was attached, it would be found that there was no more room at Kelthorpe House for the proud old woman who had forever made it her home. Anyone would wish to have charge of this marvelous house in Cavendish Square, especially someone with such an eye to appearances as the writer of that odious letter!

Cecilia felt a surge of protectiveness for the old dowager which disregarded any difference in age or station. She knew herself to be the more experienced of the two when it came to family relations; better than any, *she* knew how superfluous relatives were wont to be treated: They were pushed away and shoved into the first convenient corner.

But the dowager must not be permitted to suspect this, for it would only cause pain and shame to one who so obviously loved and took pride in her grandson. It was up to her to be clever enough to prevent the disaster, if such was planned, without unnecessarily raising the dowager's apprehensions.

She consciously smoothed the look of consternation from her face. "You are quite right, ma'am," she said with far more confidence than she presently felt. "I am persuaded that His Grace and I will deal together famously."

Her Grace had no choice but to accept Cecilia at her word. She laid aside the refolded letter and gathered up the abundance of invitations quietly awaiting their notice. They must decide which functions to attend.

They both enjoyed this part of their days. Together, the dowager and her companion confirmed their selections by sending notes of acceptance to some and regrets to others, working their way with practiced efficiency through the stack. Cecilia never thought of her employer as condescending in the slightest—nor, in fact, was she—for their tastes were in such accord that the issue of precedence never arose. And if Cecilia's mind churned with other thoughts, other fears, Her Grace was not to see it.

The social season was starting up in earnest. Masquerades, balls, routs, and soirées. They easily made their pick from the assortment offered, having long since agreed to preferring cards and conversation to evenings of musical entertainment. They took in the occasional dance party, however, to see and be seen like everyone else. And if Her Grace noticed that her companion's foot sometimes tapped along with the music, she was entirely too mannerly to comment.

Whenever they went out, Cecilia stayed close by her employer, discreetly signaling the dowager's attention to each speaker as required. Society might wonder why Miss Langley was so indulged as to be introduced, but, for the most part, all were sufficiently in awe of the intimidating old lady not to question it.

Since the precise hour of the duke's arrival was not known, the dowager and her companion resolved to make their rounds as usual. They were promised at a Venetian "breakfast" sponsored by Mrs. Drummond-Burrell, the party scheduled to commence at two that afternoon. Afterward, if His Grace still had not put in his appearance, Cecilia proposed that they take a walk through Hyde Park, a favorite exercise for them both.

It was while they were strolling leisurely along the dapple-shaded paths of this last-mentioned diversion that the second warning of change was given. At the sound of cantering hoofbeats, Cecilia casually looked behind her to see who it was that approached them.

She was so shocked, she nearly stumbled. But there was no doubting the identity of the oncoming rider, even dressed as he was *dernier cri*—for she could hardly mistake the face and figure of a man of such distinction. She at once faced herself forward.

What on earth could he *be doing here?* she wondered frantically. The reports in the newspapers indicated that the war was escalating daily, so it was inconceivable that he should be out on leave. No, it could not possibly be who she thought.

For a moment she was tempted to turn around again to confirm her observation, yet even in mufti, with sure and dreadful knowledge, she knew him. It was none other than her old staircase romancer, Colonel Trelwyn. He was here, mounted on a magnificent black stallion, riding through the park as if he owned it! Cecilia nudged her walking partner to the side of the footpath, hoping against hope to avoid notice. A meeting between them could only effect the most awful embarrassment.

But I am being absurd, she thought as she immediately called herself to order. She was sensibly reminded that he would hardly remember her, someone he'd seen but briefly in the dim light of a stairwell. And supposing he did recollect the occasion, he surely could not have identified her just from the few seconds she'd exposed her face at this distance, now, could he?

As if in earnest disagreement, Cecilia's heart began a rather desperate pounding as the rider came closer.

"Halloo!" he summoned as he neared.

Hopeful that her employer would not have heard, Cecilia forced herself to continue apace, ignoring the horseman drawing nigh. There was another group of strollers just a few yards ahead, so it must be to them that he called. He should pass by at any moment.

"Grandmother? Hold, I say."

Oh, please-God-have-mercy, no!

Cecilia's heart came to a complete stop before picking up its beat with uncomfortable, irregular thumps. With the greatest dismay, she heard the sound of hooves, slowing their forward progress . . . leaving the bridle track . . . pulling in alongside.

Her Grace caught the movement from the corner of her eye and glanced up. Cecilia was appalled when a look of welcome spread across the old lady's face.

"Why, Stephen my boy," the dowager trilled out in pleased accents. "So good to see you here. How did you manage to find us?"

A deep, masculine voice answered. "Iverson told me where you were, and since I'd not far to ride, I thought I would swing by to greet you. But didn't you hear me call?" He dismounted with an easy, flowing motion to join them on the path.

The old dowager darted accusing eyes to her companion, who shrugged back at her helplessly.

For the moment Cecilia was too stunned to feel anything of proper remorse, having several concerns of her own. Foremost was the astounding realization that when the man dismounted, he looked still bigger than ever. Being quite tall herself, Cecilia was unaccustomed to persons who necessitated her craning her neck like the veriest nestling.

During the scant space of an instant, he seemed to attend the dark red curls tumbling from beneath her gray gauze bonnet. Only a slight widening of black pupils indicated his interest, though, before he returned his attention to the dowager. All politeness, he said, "No matter, Grandmother, for I daresay your mind was elsewhere on this agreeable day. I take it you've been keeping well?" Neither he nor the dowager moved to embrace the other, such displays in public being considered bad *ton*.

"We go on quite fairly, Stephen, thank you for asking," Her Grace responded warmly. "Did you find your room to your liking? I had your letter only this morning, you know, and so there was not much time to make ready." She tossed Cecilia a significant look.

"My apologies, of course, ma'am. We've had a deal of rain in the north, which made my timing uncertain. I waited until the last stop before sending word—I hope it wasn't too inconvenient."

Pleased at these very proper sentiments, Her Grace gave Cecilia another pertinent look, then said, "There was not the least trouble about it, dear boy! However, it is time now for introductions." She nodded toward Cecilia. "Stephen, permit me to make known to you Miss Cecilia Langley, my new companion and friend."

The impact of the duke's slate-gray eyes left Cecilia bereft of speech. She had remembered that his eyes were dark, but now she saw that they had a strangely colorless, absorbing quality which seemed to soak up her very thoughts. With a slight shiver, she wrenched her eyes away and sank into a curtsy, ending the uncomfortable contact.

"Miss Langley." He acknowledged her with the briefest of bows.

Cecilia thought she discerned a hint of scorn in his voice.

The old dowager heard nothing of the kind, of course, but she did remark the unusual *pas*. Looking sharply from one to the other, she asked, "Stephen, do you already know Cecilia? It would not be surprising if you two had met, for she was on the Peninsula for several years with her father, Major James Langley."

Cecilia had initially chosen that name because it began with the truth and made it easier to cover any slip of the tongue. It was intended to confound anyone tracing her from Linscombe Hall yet was simple enough for her to remember. Now she had cause to regret her choice. The similarity in nomenclature might well give her away. Had he learned the name of the nurse at Santa Clara Infirmary? His next words reassured her.

"I do not think that I recall the name, ladies," he said slowly, searching first one face, then the other. "For I would never forget it if I had before been introduced to such 'Appropriate Company.'" He turned toward his grandmother with a bland smile. "I am indeed delighted if you have found yourself 'Suitable Female Companionship.'"

The sarcasm emphasizing these last three words was unmistakable and brought a crashing end to Cecilia's hopes that she might go unrecognized. And so, for the second time that day, she was glad that her employer could read lips and not actually hear. The reply to her note written on that late summer evening, so many months ago, still burned in her brain word for word. She could not fail to recollect her own phrasing as well, thus punctuated by his stinging tones.

Nonetheless, Cecilia thought she had the advantage. She knew she had done nothing to be ashamed of, or, at least, nothing really reprehensible. He, on the other hand, was guilty not only of propositioning a young woman whom he'd assumed to be unprotected, but all too possibly he stood guilty of nefarious designs on his grandmother's home.

Cecilia forgot how she had once thought his response to her trick of sending Marpessa to dine with him charming. She forgot the glorious sound of his laughter, and how she had chuckled right along with him. Instead, she was impelled to man her guns and fire for effect. Two could play at this game of trading words.

"How 'Perceptive' of you, sir," she flared out with some heat. "I 'Confess' that Her Grace has been an 'Angel' to me, taking me into *her* gracious home."

Ignoring this flanking maneuver, the duke chose to move into a weak area he perceived in Miss Langley's defenses. Recognizing the pert young nurse from Tôrres Vedras the instant she had turned around to look behind her, he resolved to withhold his own response until he could assess the situation more fully. She seemed willing to bandy words with him, but could she so easily justify her background? He attacked from a different quarter.

"Indeed, Miss Langley," he said in a leisurely manner. "Although, pray tell, if I inquire from friends in my old command for a Major Langley, what is it, I wonder, that they will find?" He lifted one finely arched, silky black eyebrow to a steep, almost jeering angle. Not for a moment did he believe that there was such person as she named.

For Her Grace's part, the old dowager could barely credit that her grandson was capable of the discourtesy she saw being demonstrated. When Stephen was in London just last fall, she had judged him a different sort of man altogether! This young giant with the implacable look was someone quite unknown to her. She could not hear the voices, true, but the exchanged looks of dislike on those two young faces were obvious. Before she could interrupt to defuse tempers, however, Cecilia showed herself able to hold her own.

"They—will—find—a—grave, sir." The young woman bit out each word separately, her chin held disdainfully aloft. "My father was one of those sent to report on the French at Burgos after Christmas, and his unit encountered an enemy patrol. Three men made it back, I believe, but Father was not one of them. And ... and I still miss him," she added with proud hurt. An involuntary spurt of tears glimmered beneath golden-flecked orbs.

It was this last admission which convinced Stephen that he had made a grievous error. A faint flush flew across his cheekbones, indicating awareness of the *faux pas* committed. Though he still had reservations about Miss Langley being what she claimed, he could not doubt the extent of her grief.

"My most sincere apologies, Miss Langley," he said with quiet promptitude. He bowed deeply before her. "We have had many, many losses, and I regret my unthinking words. Forgive me." Rising from his bow, he noted the dove-gray gown and black gloves, indicating half-mourning. The bereaved usually remained in full black for at least a six-month, but if Grandmother sanctioned this much return to wearing colors, he was not one to criticize.

But who is it, he couldn't stop himself from wondering, *that the red-haired miss really mourns?*

The dowager chose this moment to step between the two. "I see that our carriage has come for us, Cecilia." She nodded deliberately toward the landau they had used for their excursion to the park. "Stephen, we will expect to see you at supper." She ushered Cecilia to the awaiting vehicle without further ado.

Neither combatant being in any mood to argue, the party separated until evening.

CHAPTER TEN

"And just what was that all about, I'd like to know?"

As soon as she and Cecilia entered the open landau to return to Cavendish Square, Her Grace began demanding explanations. She was so overset, in fact, that she scarcely gave notice to the friends and acquaintances who waved to them from passing carriages. Even when the countess Lieven's distinctive equipage met them head-on, the dowager unknowingly gave that august Almack's patroness the cut. The dowager had something more important on her mind than being polite.

"Don't think to fob me off with any of your flummery, either, my young miss," she added crossly. "I'm not so green as to credit anything less than the truth! I want to know why Stephen was in such a pet, and why you pretended not to have heard him hailing us."

Uncomfortable in the falsehoods she had been living with, Cecilia debated over what she should answer and what she should keep to herself. More than the fact of her name or her being under age might cause trouble, not only to herself but to Miss Sheldon and the Dockerys as well, but of greater concern was the fear that if she confessed and was dismissed from service, who would protect the dowager duchess? *She* might quietly disappear again, needs be, but an old woman past seventy had far fewer options. Besides, leaving was one thing. Desertion in the face of the enemy was something entirely different.

Cecilia was more suspicious than ever that the duke, or colonel, or whatever else he was, would dislodge the dowager from Kelthorpe House. She might have been unable to get him to rise to the bait with her pointed remark about it being Her Grace's home, but Cecilia's apprehensions went unabated. She had more than enough reason to know that this man, duke though he be, was arrogant, presumptuous, and quick to impose his will. Oh, his apology for the rude way he'd questioned her about her father had been made quite prettily—he must be credited with having address—but the look on his face in the moments following his act of contrition could only be interpreted as *cold*.

She decided forthwith to continue as close to the truth as was possible without alerting the old dowager to His Grace's suspected perfidy. "I may have seen your grandson in Portugal," she finally answered. "But you must understand that there were so many men, so many faces, that I may not be perfectly sure it was he. There was some conflict with a visitor to the infirmary late last summer, although I thought I understood the name to be Trelwyn."

"Now, *that's* a fine taradiddle if ever there was," the dowager fumed. "Yes, Trelwyn is the family name. Stephen ascended to the duke's title at my son's death last year. But you cannot fool me into believing that if you had before seen my grandson, it was an occasion you cannot recall with any clarity. That boy," she said ominously, "is not one to be so easily overlooked." She screwed up her face into a expression of sheer ferocity.

Cecilia could see why Mrs. Dockery had called this woman a tartar. "Well," she replied on placating notes, "I did think there was something familiar about him, ma'am, but our meeting held nothing of import. Possibly, I was misled in my initial impression, and he may have been as well."

Cecilia was not about to let it be known how very distinctly she recollected the particulars. Her first experience of what could exist between a man and a woman, it was an occasion she was not likely to forget. The way her limbs had turned weak and how she had lost contact with everything, everything other than the velvety softness of his lips . . . The entire episode remained as clear in her mind as yesterday. While she doubted that the duke was so overset by the experience as she, from his insinuating speech today, she knew he recalled the events sufficiently to cause her discomfort. She decided, however, that she did herself no favor by dwelling on what was past.

"So, you would have me content with that?" the dowager grumbled, demanding a return of Cecilia's attention. "Very well, I won't press you any further. Apparently, you and my grandson have taken each other in aversion. You need not suffer one another's company, though. If you don't feel like joining us for supper tonight, I will make your excuses. Stephen doesn't yet know about my hearing problem—I deplore arousing anyone's pity—but he would have to learn of it one day, in any case. I suppose that it had just as well be now as later."

Keeping a disgruntled expression evident, Her Grace watched for Cecilia's reaction. *Ha!* the old lady thought to herself. The chit would have her think that a previous meeting with her grandson was so unexceptionable as to be forgotten? She was expected to believe that Stephen had formed that harsh, sneering look without cause? *The gel then brings up the family name, months later, yet would have it that the thing was of no importance?* "Well, what do you say, miss?" she prompted when Cecilia hesitated over her reply.

Cecilia wanted to say she would like nothing better than to retreat to her room for the evening. The thought of those chill and knowing eyes drinking up her thoughts was almost more than she could stand. But the man must not be allowed free rein to uncover the poor old lady's secret. Few people could withstand the killing effects of being the ben-

eficiary of another's pity, and certainly not someone as prideful as the dowager duchess.

Besides, Cecilia had to wonder if the self-
important duke would feel any such emotion. It
seemed more likely that he would view his grandmother's deafness as an embarrassment, proof of an
old woman's worthlessness. And if he then did decide to shuffle the old dear off to some dreary dower
house, away from the society she loved, it would be
far worse than what Uncle Andrew had planned for
a surplus niece. At least at Cousin Theresa's she
would have had the schoolroom to keep herself
busy. But the old dowager would have little to do
if she were sent away from London; Her Grace
would be giving up much more.

Unthinkable. Cecilia resolved that she must hold
her ground and be ready to spike his guns. "Well,
of course I wish to join you," she declared with all
the enthusiasm she could muster. "I'd not give up
an opportunity to get to know your grandson and
correct our little misunderstanding. There is no
need for you to rely upon yourself tonight, ma'am,
no need at all. Between us, you can go on as usual
without His Grace ever having to know of your affliction."

"Are you quite, quite certain?" the dowager could
not resist prodding. "I would not want you to be
uncomfortable solely on my account."

Actually, the dowager knew full well that she had
tossed the cat in among the pigeons, and she could
hardly wait to see what was caught! She intended
a front row seat to view the action, too. There was
something between Cecilia and Stephen. She just
knew it.

"I am entirely sure, ma'am," Cecilia insisted.
"We will spend a charming evening, enjoying one
another's company."

Under her stylishly modeled spring-green tur-
ban, the redoubtable old matriarch idly toyed with
the polished cabochons set into the head of her cane.
Amethyst, peridot, citrine, and pink topaz gleamed

softly beneath her fingertips. She remained quiet for the rest of the ride home, thinking that the evening ahead promised to provide more *divertissement* than she had uncovered in years.

Instead of going directly back to Cavendish Square, Stephen spent the next two hours covering most of the four hundred acres that comprised Hyde Park, trying to master his agitation. Like his grandmother, he was engrossed in his thoughts. He thus traversed the well-maintained grounds of the royal park in ignorance of the groups and couplets making their own afternoon promenades. Recognizing the newly invested duke, however, the *ton* merely judged such neglect as indicative of his natural, quite commendable exclusiveness.

As an officer and a gentleman, Stephen prided himself on his ability to maintain control over himself, presenting to the world a restrained aspect of unruffled composure. The exigencies of war notwithstanding, he knew he could be counted on to maintain a cool head in any situation. But there was something about Miss Langley's reappearance that unnerved him so that he felt the need for time to restore his temper.

He had been so *careful*, he considered, not to divulge his circumstances when he had invited that jade to his hotel last August. Too many people would seek to use a duke's favor. But he never had learned why she hadn't bothered to show up in person at their agreed-upon rendezvous. Nobleman or not, she had readily accepted his invitation.

With a principled man's dislike for mysteries, Stephen swore to get to the bottom of this one, no matter how deep Miss Langley's game.

Remembrance of whom—or, more precisely, *what*—had materialized at his dining table brought forth a fleeting grin. Had Stephen noticed, he would have realized that, brief though it was, it was his first real smile in months. But a fresh wave of frustration overtook him when he next remembered how he never had unearthed the purpose of the trick Miss Langley had played. He had never made it back to the infirmary to ask the sergeant-major—never found out anything more about her at all. A message that his ship would sail early had interrupted his plans, so with scarcely time to arrange for the sergeant's promised burgundy, he had made a scrambled, hasty departure for Lisbon. He had just barely made it, too.

It was evident that she had learned more about him, though. She had followed him to England; her appearance here went beyond mere coincidence. But since she must have known he was expected, why had she looked so stricken today when Grandmother gave him greeting? He felt positive that the young woman had seen him and heard his call, so why pretend to ignore him? There was no reason he could think of.

And she had found a way into his home. Stephen wondered how his grandmother, so remarkably astute in other matters, could have been so deceived by a nothing little camp follower.

As it had once before, honesty compelled Stephen to own that "little" was not the appropriate adjective. Miss Langley's height and form would cause any man to stand and take notice. He grudgingly admitted that she was a rare beauty besides; only nature could devise that particular shade of lush, dark auburn he'd noted beneath the brim of her bonnet. With that recollection, he had to eliminate the term "nothing" as well.

But "camp follower" was the one term of which he *was* certain. For the first time, the young duke—twenty-seven his last natal day—was glad he had come to London.

After his brief sojourn in the metropolis last August, following years of fighting while surrounded by dedicated men, he had been ill prepared for the superficial reaction of the *ton* to the war. Bored fops continuously sought diversion in their social engagements and sporting events, complaisantly ignoring the struggle against the Corsican menace in an endless round of pleasure-seeking. The latest wager booked at White's and the juciest *on-dit* seemed of far more interest than news from the front. Stephen had remained in the metropolis for less than a month before leaving its confines in total disgust.

But that was before receiving his grandmother's missive, reminding him to his duties. Gravely, he considered his heritage and her instructions.

Castle Kelthorpe dominated nearly thirty thousand acres of good Derby land situated at the base of the Pennines, those strong limestone hills called the backbone of England. The Trelwyn entail included another ten thousand acres and several great houses scattered about three counties, their combined production making the title one of England's wealthiest. Yet, as Grandmother had pointed out, he must have an heir. Unconsciously, Stephen leveled his broad shoulders, tucked his chin, and sat straighter in his saddle. He would not shirk any responsibility—not to his name and not to his family.

In this manner Stephen made his way back to Cavendish Square. He entered the mews behind the house and gave crisp, concise instructions for the care of his mount.

The old groom who took his reins merely nodded and tugged his cap. But when His Grace marched away from the area, the old man stared after him, amazed at his master's trenchant manner. "Gawd!" he finally exclaimed under his breath. "Not like he were the last time he were here, but more liken' to the old duke now. Jolly bedamned if he ain't."

The old groom shortened the reins and led the black off, cackling merrily to himself all the while.

"Stephen my boy, I am so glad you joined us early." Her Grace's eyes glowed with pleasure as her grandson strolled into the softly lit Rose Room sometime later that evening.

The duke looked more imposing than ever, *point de vice*, in fact. Over parchment-colored pantaloons of the finest leather he had elected to wear a coat of tobacco brown, cut and fitted to the waist in front and fashioned with elegant clawhammer tails. His athletic build made a fitting compliment to the inimitable art of that most famous of tailors, *the* Mr. Schweitzer of Cork Street. While the young duke had nothing of the dandy about him, no gracefully sloping shoulders or mountainous neckwear, the superb tailoring of his evening dress made a sight to garner accolades from even the most exacting of critics. To complete his ensemble, the duke eschewed sparkling jewelry, wearing only an engraved signet ring on his left hand and a single gold fob at his waist. Obviously no mere Tulip, he appeared every inch the highborn, most noble duke.

"I must always look forward to being in your company, Grandmother," he said, planting a kiss on her cheek.

He had entered the room ahead of time in hopes of finding her alone. He was eager to learn how the red-haired witch had insinuated herself into Kelthorpe House; instead, he was displeased to find that Miss Langley was already ahead of him and even now making him her curtsy. By the light of the candles, her hair shone an exotic cinnamon, the demure color of her dress accentuating its value.

How was it, he wondered, that anyone could look so enticing while wearing nothing but the dullest of grays? He was inexplicably made angry that it should be so, and he made no attempt to smother his annoyance. Dismissing Miss Langley's courtesy, he turned to address his grandmother. "I trust that tonight we dine *en famille*," he said pointedly.

"And so we do." Her Grace bristled. "Cecilia is by way of being family, and I would have it so. She is here at my express request and has no need to stand upon ceremony in this house. Do I make myself clear?" Her tone fairly crackled with authority.

Cecilia almost groaned aloud. She must appreciate the dowager's defense, but the last thing she wanted was for herself to be the cause of an overt breach between the old lady and the duke. His next words showed that she need not have worried.

"Indeed, madam," Stephen answered, his lids lowering to cover his expression. "You did say that Miss Langley had managed to become your companion, did you not?" He then turned a sardonic eye on the younger woman. "I regret the error," he drawled.

As he intended, Cecilia knew quite well what was meant. From being considered a drab of easy virtue, she understood that she had just been promoted to "designing woman"—as if she would so much as consider traveling an inch, and much less all the way to London, solely to pursue the grandiose Duke of Kelthorpe. What awesome conceit the man had!

The dowager made as if to speak, but Cecilia quickly waved her to silence. She was determined to draw the duke's fire away from her employer. "My dear duke," she challenged, golden glints shimmering in the depths of her eyes, "it appears that there is some, er . . . shall we perhaps say, *defect*? in your understanding. Is this a new problem for you, or have you always had conceptual difficulties?" She smiled sweetly to forestall any comment he might make. "Either way, if we cannot be admirers, one of the other, may we at least be civil? I do recall a brief incident with a colonel in Portugal, and Her Grace confirms that it was you." She paused for a moment to gather herself. "If you mistook my position there, or if something I did put you off, then I am truly sorry for it." She held his gaze steadily, hoping he would accept this at face value.

But such was not to be. Stephen bent his brow in seeming deliberation. "A problem with a name, was it, Miss Langley? I, too, remember a name, but I recall it as 'Marisa,' or something like that," he said smoothly.

"You are mistaken, Your Grace," she gritted out. "Her name is *Marpessa*, and she is—or, rather, was—my dog." She turned to her employer to explain. "Marpessa is a beautiful Briard that my father found for me when she was a puppy. I brought her with me from Portugal, but then had to leave her with a friend when I came here to London."

Completely at sea, the old lady merely nodded, waiting to see what else would transpire.

Her Grace was not to be disappointed. A persistent man, Stephen hadn't the slightest intention of giving up his pursuit so easily. Actually, he had remembered the dog's name well enough, but was bent on trying to ascertain the relationship between Miss Langley and the young man he'd spotted in the alley outside his hotel dining room, without disclosing a piece of intelligence that the enemy didn't know he possessed. The military had taught him such caution; he had hoped tonight to discover another much-needed piece to the puzzle.

With this thought in mind, he said, feigning innocence, "Marpessa. Yes, that was it. *Your* dog, do you say? My congratulations! A fine animal. But, pray, who is this fortunate 'friend' with whom you've entrusted such a precious possession?"

Seeing that Cecilia was not set to answer, his expression became even more benign. He said silkily, "Surely there is no need for you to be separated from your pet, though. I assure you that I would welcome such an addition. You must give me the direction and we will have her here in no time."

Cecilia was not fooled. She knew what sort of charm he could wield when the mood struck him, and yet, even as he spoke, she was aware of his eyes, glittering across at her like December ice. *Cold,* she thought. Cold and commanding. And she knew what he was really after—proof that she was less than she seemed. Indeed, it was happening just as Miss Sheldon had warned her: Without the protection of her family name, she was unlikely to be thought respectable. Perversely, Cecilia felt herself growing hot with anger.

Whether or not he was within his rights to seek clues to her background, the fact remained that he had only this day arrived. So how dared he offer to send for her dog without regard for the dowager's wishes? He should have asked permission before he set about rearranging the house, for no matter who held the title, this was Her Grace's residence. Still, if it was as she suspected, and he was capable of pushing his grandmother aside, just as well to know it once and for all. Cecilia decided to try to lure him into exposing his position.

Moving to an angle away from the dowager so as not to be "overheard," she concealed her fury and said in congenial tones, "You are entirely too kind, sir. Although I must, in all courtesy, refuse your generous proposal. I would never suggest to Her Grace that she should accept the inconvenience of a large dog underfoot. Besides which, a Briard should not be cooped up in a crowded city. Do permit me to ask you, though, just why did you fail to first consult your grandmother? She has lived here forever, after all."

The young duke stared. One elegantly skeptical, not to say derisive, eyebrow climbed to unprecedented heights; he tucked in his jaw and didn't speak for several moments. "I speak for Kelthorpe House," finally came his terse reply.

Cecilia froze at those abhorrently familiar words. She watched, horrified, as he stepped away from her to pour himself a glass of wine, looking as though he'd said nothing of importance. *I speak for Linscombe Hall*, her uncle had declared, compelling his niece to give up her name and all further claims on her family. *I speak for Kelthorpe House*, His Grace now said, disregarding any care for his grandmother.

And Cecilia knew what followed. How well she knew what happened to unwanted relatives.

When Iverson came to announce their dinner, Ce-

cilia was not even aware of it. The shock of hearing
His Grace's dreadful pronouncement left her dazed.
Unfortunately, her unmoving state prompted the
duke to move to her side and take up her arm,
which he proceeded to tuck beneath the soft brown
velvet encasing his own iron-hard forearm.

Brought out of her reverie by the contact, Cecilia
then made a mistake. She looked up at him with
wide, startled eyes, only to be overcome by the realization that she stood within inches of tightly
leashed strength—a strength much greater than her
own. Never had she been made so sensible of a
man's power. His commanding presence, combined
with his enormous height, made her feel so small!
Instead of pulling away as she should, she again
found herself mesmerized by fathomless dark eyes.
They seemed to hold some special fascination. They
challenged. They ensnared.

Cecilia could only be grateful when Her Grace
interceded, moving to take up her grandson's other
arm and requiring him to give her his attention.
"Shall we go in?" the elderly lady said brightly.
"And, Stephen, you must tell me if you remember
Caliban, that well-named hound of your father's. If
memory serves," she expanded while they took
their places at the table, "he once made off with an
entire side of beef which Cook had just removed
from the spit. Over a period of months, a series of
ill-assorted and disgusting bones kept finding their
way into the drawing room. It was forever before
we discovered where he had hidden the stolen trea-
sure; even then, Caliban hadn't the grace to appear
the least bit remorseful!" As the meal progressed,
the dowager continued to regale a mostly inattentive audience with stories of a succession of dogs
she had kept over the years.

Scarcely tasting his excellent supper, Stephen
studied Miss Langley from beneath half-lowered
lids. Her table manners were faultless, he noted,
reluctantly impressed. She even made an effort to
attend to his grandmother's monologue, when he

knew from the nervous glances she kept darting his way that she would much rather be elsewhere. Such consideration would never occur to someone not bred to the finer niceties, or at least he did not think so. So what, precisely, did that make her?

As for her refusal to send for her pet, the excuse she had given was just so much nonsense. It was common knowledge that Grandmother adored dogs—just listen to her now, going on and on about Caliban and the others. *Anyone* could speak for his grandmother on that head, so what gave Miss Langley to think that he, her own grandson, should not?

Stephen was also interested by the young woman's claim to owning the Briard. It set him to wondering anew about the mysterious young man in the alley. He broke off a scrap of bread, scarcely looking at it while he pondered the day's revelations.

At least his earliest fears that Grandmother had entered her dotage seemed unfounded. From the sharpness she demonstrated, Stephen concluded that her wits were in no wise deficient. He scowled at his bread crust suddenly, recollecting Miss Langley's deliberate insults regarding his own intelligence.

A twitch of a side-smile followed. He had to appreciate Miss Langley's wit, also her seemingly sincere offer to call a truce. Although he had no intention of assenting to a cessation of their warfare before discovering more about her, he would give her credit where due.

After the final wine was brought, Stephen excused himself from the company. He held membership in several gentlemen's clubs by courtesy of his title, and he announced his intention of locating some old friends who he thought might be in town. Since he could see that Grandmother and Miss Langley were set to spend the rest of the evening together, he decided that there was nothing to be gained by his remaining home tonight.

Before leaving, he stopped at the door to the rose-draped drawing room. "After you've breakfasted to-morrow, Miss Langley, I shall expect to see you in the library. I'll be there from ten o'clock on. Grandmother, Miss Langley, I bid you have a good night." Pausing to allow a footman to settle the folds of a dark gold silk-lined evening cape over his shoulders, he strode across the marble-floored hall and on out through the front door.

Icy tingles of trepidation trickled down Cecilia's spine. The feeling was immediately replaced by a very deep and *very* stubborn anger. Not content to deprive his grandmother of her home, shunting her off to who knew where, the duke seemed bound to dispossess her as well! Cecilia could only pray that he would understand about her special status at Santa Clara when she explained.

However, if Stephen Trelwyn could not approve of her helping the wounded—he, a soldier who had seen men die for the lack of proper medical attention—then she cared not a jot for his high-and-mighty opinion. Anyone too drenched in such conventional, insular appraisal to appreciate her endeavors was no one whose approbation she wanted. Even if she had no family connections she could admit to, even if her origins were truly as common as he supposed, he had no right to assume that she was in any way unworthy.

And from his very own mouth he delivered the proof that his were the only wishes that mattered. His words tonight condemned him. *I speak for Kelthorpe House*, he had proclaimed—words which might spell disaster for the dowager duchess.

Not that Cecilia feared he would do anything immediately; in fact, he may not yet have fully decided the matter. But the potential was there, only a fool could doubt it. Cecilia cudgeled her brain for a way to divert His Grace from his course.

The dowager, ensconced in a comfortable side chair, made no comment on her grandson's request. She sat quietly with a book of Molière's plays open on her lap while she watched Cecilia contend with what seemed to be a growing bout of the fidgets. Her young friend moved aimlessly about the room, apparently too restless to settle to either a book or her needle. It occurred to the dowager to suggest a game of cards, but with Cecilia's concentration in such an obviously uncertain state, the idea lacked appeal. She next debated about whether to intervene on the morrow and be present for the proposed meeting between the two young people. No, she thought it was better to let them thrash out their difficulties between themselves.

With a faint smile, Her Grace then reflected on the remarkable change in her grandson. From what she had seen of him before, she had judged him to be a mild-tempered, somewhat deferential sort who preferred to avoid open conflict. Yet today he was bent on relentlessly baiting a pretty girl without mercy—quite a radical change. She was secretly delighted that Cecilia was so quick to take him up, too, though Her Grace still did not know what lay behind their enmity.

Unlike her grandson, however, puzzles did not greatly trouble her. She was of an age to know that patience would, in time, be rewarded. Content to let events unfold as they would, she decided not to interfere unless needful to keep tempers in bound or events moving.

Finally, Cecilia picked up a small Argand lamp from a side table and moved it closer to one of the paintings. Something she saw there seemed to calm her, and she took a chair with the picture in view.

"Castle Kelthorpe," Her Grace commented after a while.

"What?" Cecilia jerked around as if startled awake from sleep. "I beg pardon, were you speaking to me, ma'am?"

"And who else do you see in this room?" the dowager asked with some asperity. "I said, 'Castle Kelthorpe.' The picture you seem so wrapped up in—it is a painting of the family seat. Do you like it?"

"Oh. Yes, I do," Cecilia breathed. "It is not like anything I've ever imagined before. Partly, I admire the prospect of looking down onto the battlements, just as if I were a falcon, flying away overhead. It does seem an odd notion, such a strange way of seeing things. There is also a kind of power in the view, a certain strength, when I compare the mountains nearby to the castle's walls. I seem to sense a sort of timelessness in each stone—nature's and man's." Cecilia shook her head, her curls set to bouncing, as she sought words to better express herself.

"I believe I know what you are trying to say," the dowager reassured her. "My husband used to tell me that Castle Kelthorpe was the pivot which held the family strong. I think you are seeing what he meant. Stephen's mother preferred town life to the duchy and so spent very little time there—not that I found fault with her for that, since I appreciate the comforts of London myself—but perhaps Stephen's bride will feel differently and make it a home again."

The duke's bride. The very answer Cecilia had been searching for!

If a wife could be found who preferred country life, there would be no reason for Her Grace to be removed from her house in Cavendish Square. She would be left undisturbed, all worries would vanish. Cecilia determined at once to make it her business to meet whatever young ladies might find favor with His Grace. She would find a way to encourage those most likely to appreciate living in the spectacular old castle.

Cecilia "Langley" would indeed be a "designing woman" . . . but she would weave her own designs.

CHAPTER ELEVEN

The prettily enameled pinchbeck timepiece depending from Cecilia's slim neck showed one minute past ten when she presented herself at the double doors to the library the next morning. Her Grace was not yet stirring; for a fleeting moment Cecilia wished she might have pleaded her ameliorating presence. A footman liveried in Kelthorpe gray and silver awaited her nod before opening the doors to announce her.

Nothing in Cecilia's face gave away the fact that she'd spent a fitful night, sorting through a turmoil of impossible facts, improbable plans, and undefined emotions. What puckish fate had seen fit to reintroduce her to Stephen Trelwyn? On a glorious black stallion he came charging back into her life, and, quite suddenly, her future no longer held the promise of the quiet, rewarding days she had once envisioned.

Surely, though, with the war in the Peninsula raging, the duke could learn little in eight weeks, the time he had allotted himself for finding a wife. Indeed, he might never learn the whole, Cecilia thought with expanding optimism. Either way, though, she vowed to complete her self-assigned task of protecting the old lady who had been so very kind to her.

Her mission today was clear. She must relieve the duke's mind about her previous occupation; accordingly, she had dressed this morning with care. She had chosen to wear the lovely lavender lawn Mrs. Dockery had provided, then had brushed her hair until it gleamed with healthy brilliance. In deference to a military man's penchant for order, she had arranged each curling tendril, each fold of her gown, into meticulous order. Even the tiny bows fastening her sandals had been tied with exactitude. Her appearance must be faultless.

The larger difficulty lay in knowing that she had *somehow* to maintain control of her temper. Even the façade of an equable disposition proved difficult with Stephen Trelwyn around. She'd made an awful cake of herself at the Hôtel Quieroz—well she knew it—but something about the man did aggravate her so! He goaded and mocked her with such offhanded ease that she feared for her tongue every time they met.

Still, necessity dictated that she allay his fears. Only by incurring his respect could she further her plot to influence his choice of a bride, and, she thought wryly, it should all be quite simple, should it not?

"Miss Langley, you are very punctual this morning." His Grace looked up from his seat behind an enormous, yet exquisitely inlaid desk.

As the footman closed the library door behind her, Cecilia sank into the requisite curtsy.

"Oh, no need for the formalities," he said, observing her movement. "Do sit down, please. I'll be finished with this in but a moment." He returned his attention to the stack of papers in front of him.

Not greatly reassured, despite this auspicious beginning, Cecilia made her way over to a button-tufted wing chair of tanbark leather. She arranged her skirts with an air of casualness. She was glad of the chance to examine her adversary at close quarters, for every time she had looked down the table the night before, she had discovered dark eyes already upon her own. She had been unable then to take his measure. Now, while his gaze was lowered to the papers on the desktop, she found herself at leisure to make a closer inspection.

She noted that the sides of his midnight-dark hair

109

were neatly trimmed and feathered back, rather longer now than it had been in Tôrres Vedras. A heavy black wave dipped near the center of his forehead to give him a devilish, nearly rakish look. His lightly tanned jaw was freshly shaved, its clean, severe contours decidedly masculine, while the white folds of his neckcloth emphasized the width of his shoulders, outlined as they were in Bath coating.

Her eyes strayed to his lips. They were fuller and softer now in his relaxed state than they had seemed yesterday. Perhaps convivial company the night before had influenced his mood and would make him more amenable to herself—or so she could only hope. Set straight, his lower lip was just slightly thicker than the upper, she saw, and she could not prevent herself from remembering how pleasant it had felt when . . .

"If you will be good enough to give me your attention please, Miss Langley? We have a matter to discuss, you and I."

Slate-dark eyes, all too knowing, were set squarely upon her own. With a sinking sensation Cecilia worried about whether His Grace had seen her as she so blatantly considered his mouth. And how, she wondered, ashamed, could she have become sidetracked when her objective was so important? This was no time to be floating in dreams like a spooney.

In a rare occurrence, Cecilia felt a rush of color flood her face. *Oh, twice bedamned and blast the man!* she thought heatedly.

She struggled to keep her voice neutral and her features expressionless, or, at least, as much as her flushed cheeks would allow. "Yes, Your Grace?" she asked with caution.

"Yes, Miss Langley," His Grace allowed in the most repressive of tones. "As the head of my family, you will agree that it is my duty to investigate your acquirements and your antecedents. In view of our previous meeting, I think there is good reason for me to question your fitness to reside in this house and, ah . . . shall we perhaps say, *associate*? with its residents. I will tolerate no impropriety. You do understand?" A silky brow rose over one eye to accent his meaning.

Cecilia understood very well. The man was the posterior portion of a donkey, that's what! He believed she had followed him all the way from Portugal, and was telling her that she was unwelcome as company for his grandmother—and for himself. And he was mocking her again! He had deliberately copied her style of wording from the night before to throw back into her face. For so many years she could rightly take pride in a dependable humor, yet this man had only to come within yards of her to set all to naught. But it was imperative that she curb her inclinations. She must somehow charm him, disregarding any cost to her dignity.

Using her best imitation of Cousin Theresa, Cecilia simpered, "Most certainly, Your Grace. It would not do for the reputation of this house, nor for my own good name, to have any irregularity occur. As I think Her Grace has told you, I am of gentle birth, though you once mistook that fact, I believe." She dropped her eyes to her lap as she sought to convince the duke of her right to his proper regard.

Although determined to look modestly downcast, inexplicably, she found herself drawn to face her opponent. She took a deep breath and her voice leveled without her realizing it. "My father was an infantry major," she said with collected quiet, only a faint golden glow in her eyes giving evidence that she struggled to hold herself in check. "He was a career officer stationed at Tôrres Vedras until the first of this year. It was entirely with his permission that I volunteered to help in the infirmary there on a regular basis, and, while I will not say that he was greatly enthusiastic when I began, Father didn't believe in anyone remaining idle during wartime. Quite frankly, Your Grace, neither do I.

111

So I took responsibility for seeing to the men's comfort, dispensing the medications Dr. Fosgate ordered and applying changes of bandages as needed. I wrote letters for those who needed a scribe, sharing duties with the Sisters of a nursing order of nuns. And, contrary to what you might have presumed, at Santa Clara Infirmary, we employed orderlies for such personal assistance as a female could not render."

To Cecilia's dismay, she felt her cheeks staining bright red again. Damn. *And damn again.* How entirely stupid! She had never once been put to the blush by the men at Santa Clara.

Oddly, whether from some delicacy of feeling or for some other reason, His Grace sat quietly, allowing her time to compose herself. If she didn't know better, she might suppose he was being intentionally kind when he consciously averted his eyes from her flaming cheeks. But whatever his intent, he appeared to find the details of a nearby paperweight of immense interest.

After a few moments, she managed to go on. "When Father was killed"—her fingers twitched, trying to cross themselves against telling lies—"I had no one left to care for me. My mother's family are all long since gone—they were the Mayfields of Alnstone in Sussex, and a highly respected old family, should you be interested. At any rate, having no other means of support, I came to London, seeking a situation of employment."

"And how came you to this house, Miss Langley? For you may well understand my surprise at finding you here—and my concern at such an unlikelihood as your presence represents." No expression could be read on his wonderfully handsome face.

Cecilia's conscience-stricken fingers again twitched in her lap. "Mr. Lawrence Dockery, your grandmother's legal adviser, also ministers to my affairs," she said stiffly. "It was he, or, rather, his wife, who recommended me to this position. And you must know that I had no idea that you were

112

related to Her Grace, since I knew the only name you had given me: Trelwyn. There was no reason for me to mention our previous meeting to anyone, so there was none to warn me, you see." She did not add that had she known of the kinship, no power on earth could have induced her to come.

Would he turn her out? Nothing she had said was really a lie: Her relatives certainly did not care for her, her mother's family had been Mayfields, and she had given the rounded little solicitor the management of her stashed resources. Mrs. Dockery had arranged for her employment here, and Cecilia truly had not suspected His Grace's connection to the House of Kelthorpe. It was not a *total* departure from the truth. Or so Cecilia consoled herself before going on with her story.

"After returning to England," she continued as calmly as she could, "I went to Mr. Dockery for advice. I had to find some way to supplement my income, for there was not enough money for me to do else. And," she confided, "while my being here may be somewhat uncomfortable for you, I must say that it is intensely embarrassing to me." She sat up a fraction straighter. "Is there anything else you wish to know?"

Stephen leaned back in his chair and surveyed the young woman seated before him. Glossy, clipped curls framed the classic oval of her face, even as the delicate tint of her lips and cheeks were flatteringly highlighted by the lilac coloring of her gown. The weight of the timepiece hanging between her breasts pressed the thin fabric into a deep hollow, effectively displaying the rich depth of a woman's figure.

But what kind of woman? That was what he was here to find out.

Her story *could* be true, he supposed; her bearing was certainly that of a woman of refinement, and her manners bespoke the well-bred young lady. He'd begun to have second thoughts about her status even before this interview. However, he was

113

not mistaken that she had openly flirted with him in Tôrres Vedras. He determined to cover this point with his next question.

"Tell me, then, Miss Langley, about our first meeting—"

"Oh, I know what you are going to say," she interrupted, leaning forward with her hands gripping the tufted leather chair arms. "You tried to make an assignation with me that day on the staircase, and you are wondering what happened to your fine plans. But you will please recall exactly what was said! You made an assumption"—she narrowed her eyes in accusation—"and told me where we should meet. I admit that I allowed it to appear as if I agreed, but you may recall that I did not speak the words, for I was not at all flattered to be thought of as a . . . as what you thought." An irrepressible gleam lit her eye. She sat back, grinned, and said, "Do not say you weren't pleased with my substitute."

Stephen found himself tempted to match her open smile. "And so I was!" he agreed, chuckling. But he quickly brought himself back into control, his voice a shade harsh as he struggled against an urge to feel a great liking for the young woman. "Ah, but then, Miss Langley, you cannot expect me to take all of the blame. You did allow me certain liberties, I think?"

"I did *not*. Well, I mean, I did," she recanted, reluctantly. "But I didn't know you were going to, well, to do *that*, and I suppose I was rather off guard. And maybe a bit curious, too," she admitted in a spurt of honesty. "However, that is all it was, sir! And if you think, as you have already implied, that I came to your grandmother's home to seek you out, let me assure you again that nothing could be farther from the truth. I have no doubt that you are considered vastly eligible by any number of people, but if that is what I had wanted, why, I had only to tell Father what had occurred on the stairs. And

114

wouldn't that have been just too bad of me?" She tossed him an impudent smile.

"Such *sauce*," he stated, eliciting no more response from her than a light, gurgling laugh. Yet there was no mistaking that she had spoken truly. The spirited and forthright way she had proclaimed her innocence finally convinced him.

So be it. With no more ado, Stephen moved from behind his desk and drew Cecilia up from her chair. "Then I am to be grateful to you?" he said low-voiced. "Another one of your angelic displays?"

His expression was alight with new friendliness—and possibly something more—while his voice took on an indulgent, even playful tone. "You turned down the opportunity to fix me in parson's mousetrap, Miss Langley . . . Cecilia. Are you not now at all sorry for it?" His big hands seemed to pulse with life as they held her long, slim fingers firmly within his grasp.

"Your Grace. . . ?"

"Stephen," he corrected her almost tenderly.

"But—"

"My name is Stephen and I would hear you call me so. Don't let us deny ourselves the privilege at this late date, Cecilia." Her name was a gentle whisper parting his lips.

"S-Stephen, then," she said, staring up into teasing, smoke-colored eyes, eyes that made her forgetful of her real interest in the outcome of this exchange. His hands felt so warm and alive against hers, clasping each of her fingers securely with gentle strength. She could not help but wonder what it might be like to have such a man for a husband, to have any husband at all, for that matter. What would it be like, she rhapsodized, to travel life's road with such a man? What would it be like to have her own home?

Home.

Just as quickly as this thought formed, Cecilia stiffened and snatched her hands away. Once more her traitorous emotions had betrayed her. How

115

could she so quickly, so easily, be lulled by soft gray eyes and a mellifluous voice? Since when, she thought in disgust, was a handsome demeanor and warm hands all it took to make her lower her shield? The man was really too entirely dangerous.

In a voice turned husky with distress at her lapse, she said, "Marriage is not a thing to undertake because of a single kiss, and, to be fair, I must shoulder at least half the blame for what happened." She gripped her recently freed hands together in front of her, as if eager to keep them to herself.

Not understanding the reason for the rift, Stephen resented the abrupt cessation of intimacy. Rejected, he took masculine refuge in renewed antagonism. "But surely your father had the right to know of my offense," he derided. "A gentleman must protect what is his to care for; you cannot but agree. What was it that made you keep our little secret? Hmmm?"

Cecilia was nearly undone by the intrusiveness of his question. A tilted black eyebrow served to disconcert her further, but she steeled herself to answer him back as truthfully as she dared. "Until that day, Father had reason to be proud of me. Why should I have exposed my own folly when no real harm was done?"

Her sense of humor seemed to return when she added another thought, one which took Stephen by surprise. "Besides that," she assured him, "Father would not have considered the addition of 'one of those demmed spoiled colonels' sufficient compensation for the loss of his daughter—the daughter who so agreeably managed his house and comforts. No, I think he would not have cared for the connection, not even if he'd known that the particular colonel involved was the heir to a dukedom. Oh, you did not know it"—she smiled impishly—"but you were in far more danger from Marpessa. She was waiting downstairs for me and would have charged to my rescue if I had so much as squeaked!"

At first irritated by the ease with which she had

116

thrown off his question, Stephen found that he could not hold out against Cecilia's bright riposte and winsome smile. As for whether she had intentionally set him up for a fall on the steps of Santa Clara Infirmary, he realized that it was just the sort of thing she *would* do!

Not about to let the minx get the better of him again, though, he quickly framed his reply. He was immensely startled to be interrupted from an unexpected quarter.

"Stephen? What goes forward here!"

Unnoticed, the dowager duchess had opened the library door and now stood smacking her cane against the floor. Condemnation writ wide, Her Grace's snow-white brows rose in eloquent disapproval. "You have been in here, closeted with Cecilia, for what in some houses would be deemed an unseemly length of time," she snapped. "I'll have an explanation, if you please."

Mouths agape, the couple turned in unison toward their interrogator. The dowager glided into the room, the soft swish of her favorite pongee silk sounding about her ankles.

When she had come downstairs earlier, Her Grace had gone to the tradesmen's receiving room directly across from the library. Leaving the door open a crack, with a keen eye, she had watched Cecilia pause, then square her shoulders and motion to the footman when she was ready for entry. But as the minutes had dragged by without anyone coming back out, the old lady had decided it was time for her to go in and see what was amiss.

The sight of her grandson and her companion standing but a few feet from each other—instead of remaining in chairs like civilized persons—had led the old dowager to the conclusion that she had interrupted a potentially emotional scene. Yet their amicable, hectoring expressions quickly put paid to any serious fears. Stephen wore an I'll-get-you-for-that look, and Cecilia looked like someone who had already gotten in a few good swings.

117

That notwithstanding, the dowager could not resist deviling the pair. Without changing pace, she went to the bell-pull and summoned a servant to bring them refreshments. "I daresay I'm pleased to see that you two have come to terms," she said, deliberately perverse, as she took up a seat on a leather sofa. "So much more agreeable, don't you think?"

Neither Cecilia nor Stephen knew what to make of this change in tack. Rebuked one minute, applauded the next?

"Grandmother, we were just reminiscing about the war—"

"Ma'am, I was going over my background—"

Never did a woman smile more enigmatically than the dowager Duchess of Kelthorpe. The two young people's words, tumbling one over the other, confirmed her opinion that she had done right to barge in. When she had summoned Stephen to town the month before, she'd been afraid that a diffident nature, combined with vestiges of grief for his father, would make him unappealing in the marriage mart. But now? Now he was as animated as a fond grandmother could wish.

Silently, the dowager gave heartfelt thanks to Miss Cecilia Langley, paid companion. Handsome young dukes would always attract the matchmaking mamas and their ambitious daughters. *Lively* handsome young dukes could have their pick.

"Tut-tut," she said directly, settling herself more comfortably on the sofa. "I merely remind you of the appearances. I don't wish to chide either of you, especially since you seem to have resolved things yourselves."

Changing the subject as the underbutler returned with the requested tray, Her Grace then said, "Cecilia, I believe we are committed to Lady Jersey for her rout party tonight. Perhaps, Stephen, you would care to give us your escort? You are in town for a purpose, so you may be interested in attending in order to renew your acquaintance among the *ton*. All the world and his wife is sure to be there, including Prinny, I'm told. What say you, my boy?"

Cecilia held her breath while waiting for the duke's answer. It was as though fortune were falling her way. If His Grace would consent to go out with them to the countess Jersey's, she would be well on her way to implementing her plan, despite this disastrous interview. And surely he would take advantage of the opportunity. At a rout party, or "drum" as they were sometimes called, a hostess invited at least three times as many guests as could comfortably fit under her roof at one time. Stand-up refreshments and background music would be the only diversion offered, since the guests were expected to circulate and amuse themselves amid the company. He couldn't pass up an evening which would provide him with such an effective means of reconnaissance; at Lady Jersey's, he would meet nearly every marriageable young lady on the town.

"I should like that above all things, Grandmother," he answered with scant hesitation. "I have no other commitments tonight and would be more than happy to accompany you."

Cecilia choked down an urge to crow in triumph. Apart from the fact that she had been granted the chance to begin guiding His Grace in making his nuptial selection, she was thrilled at the promise of catching her first glimpse of England's "first gentleman." Since coming to London, she had been intrigued by the gossip that constantly followed the notorious Prince Regent, known as Prinny to his intimates, so this would be her grandest outing yet.

Cecilia, too, pushed all other thoughts aside to savor the dual opportunity presented. Not even an afternoon of her favorite needlework helped to calm her as she eagerly anticipated the evening's pleasure.

Directly after an early supper, Iverson held out Her Grace's swansdown-trimmed wrap, while the first and third footman assisted the duke and Cecilia with their shorter evening capes. Cecilia could scarcely breathe, she was so excited.

As their little party started out the door, however, Her Grace's dresser came scurrying down the stairs with the dowager's fan, an elegant conceit with countless tiny diamonds pavéd into the frame. Apparently, it had been left behind. In the maid's rush to catch them up before leaving, inadvertently, she brushed against a table with a large flower arrangement set upon its center. The vase and its contents crashed to the marble-tiled floor.

Cecilia jumped as if shot. His Grace whirled around, all senses alert, and the poor abigail began loud wailing in distress at her clumsiness. Iverson attempted to calm the stricken maidservant, at the same time, giving orders to the two footmen on duty to fetch broom and dustpan for cleaning up the mess.

While Cecilia went to take charge of the fan and reassure the distraught servant that her conscientiousness was appreciated, and that surely no great harm was done, Stephen's eyes followed after his grandmother, who had gone on ahead to the waiting carriage. She had not been a step ahead of them when the accident occurred, yet Her Grace had not noticed the commotion.

A thoughtful look marked his features. Presently, he offered Cecilia his arm to their coach.

CHAPTER TWELVE

A trio of creamy beeswax candles burned low on the bedside table. According to Cecilia's little watch pendant, laid to rest beside the candelabrum, it was half after two in the morning. Propped up against fat, downy pillows in white lace-edged casings, Cecilia sat back, balancing a squat jar of ink with her knee, busily penning a letter to dear Miss Sheldon. There was so much she wanted to say to her old friend and a question she needed to ask.

Of foremost importance to her letter was the news of the duke's arrival at Kelthorpe House. Momentous revelation. Yet Cecilia did not fully confide in her friend, for she had never told anyone about her misadventure with a certain insinuating colonel. She had no inclination to do so at this late date; not even her dearest friend needed to know *everything*.

Neither did she publish her fears about the duke's plans for his grandmother. Disregarding the odd kindness she had seen from him, Cecilia was sure that he meant to take his place in the world and might thus turn his grandmother out. The mortification she felt over her own relatives' poor treatment now caused her to shy from relating the fact of another innocent person caught in a similar trap. So she didn't mention her intention to sway His Grace's choice of a marriage partner, either.

But so much had happened in the short time since she had last written, and the question which had arisen tonight needed an answer without delay. Returning from Lady Jersey's party not an hour ago,

Cecilia thought it a good time to write for advice undisturbed.

When the Duke of Kelthorpe—she refused to think of him as *Stephen*—had first consented to go out with them that evening, she had rejoiced in his decision. He was making it easy for her to mark his interests so that she could begin steering his attention toward appropriate young ladies. With the barrier of his poor opinion of herself fairly overcome, the next phase of her plan should have been veriest child's play. Unwittingly, however, she had left out one important factor: She did not know any young ladies. Her calls with the dowager had given her the introduction to a goodly number of prominent society matrons, and such gentlemen as enjoyed a shuffle of the pasteboards, but Cecilia had gone to the Jerseys' rout without the acquaintance of a single marriageable girl. Not one.

Nibbling the tip of her plume, Cecilia contemplated her predicament.

What she was most in need of was her old mentor's counsel on how to make friends with other girls of her own age. Cecilia thought of them as the white gown and ribbons brigade—such costume being *de rigueur* for debutantes. Without giving away her real reason for asking, she returned her pen to paper and simply wrote that with the Season getting under way, she would very much like to develop a few friendships, assuming that someone in her position could do so without seeming too forward. In closing, she implored her old governess to recommend how she should go on, and begged Miss Sheldon to make an immediate reply. Carefully inking the bottom of her paper, Cecilia drew the likeness of a fiercely snarling dog.

As she snuffed out the candles, a tear spun from the corner of her eye. Her throat constricted painfully and she gave a watery sniff. Tightly hugging a pillow to herself, she tried pretending that she could hear Marpessa's sleepy breathing on the rug beside her bed, a familiar, comforting sound for so many years. Oh, she missed her pet quite horridly, it was true! For a moment the tear threatened to spill out onto the linens.

After nuncheon the next day, Cecilia pocketed her completed letter and prepared for her weekly visit to the Dockerys. Her Grace had insisted from the beginning that she make use of the Kelthorpe landau on her half-days, since the dowager thought it demeaning to her consequence for her companion to use a hired conveyance. Mrs. Dockery had also begged Cecilia to make free of their carriage, so Cecilia allowed the Kelthorpe coachman to take her to round Kennington Oval, thence returning to Cavendish Square via the Dockerys' vehicle.

Sally greeted Cecilia upon her arrival. The little blond housemaid bade her welcome and took her into a tidy, sunlit back parlor, where Cecilia soon was joined by her chatty hostess. When pleasantries had been exchanged and the tea tray brought in, Cecilia pulled out her letter to Miss Sheldon, along with the coins to pay the post. Mrs. Dockery refused the offer with admonitory clicks of her tongue, just as she did each time.

"Why, certainly we will see your letter off, dear Cecilia! Mr. Dockery will be happy to take it to the posting office, the same as he always does. If I had a niece, which I don't, of course, I would wish her to be just such a young lady as yourself and would not allow any talk of payment. Come to think of it, Mr. Dockery *does* have a niece, but she lives in America with her husband, so that hardly counts, does it? How you would stare, Cecilia, if I told you how much it costs to send her a letter—the *moon*, at least. Not that I regard it, for I enjoy maintaining a wide correspondence, oh, I do indeed. And Mr. Dockery says that another letter is just the thing to keep the country informed. I'm sure that dear Jane is always pleased to hear from you, and I am delighted to be of service in the matter. Don't give it another thought!" Mrs. Dockery buttered another scone and popped it into her mouth.

"So, what is the latest at Kelthorpe House?" the round little woman next asked, her face alive with interest. "It must be positively edifying to go out and about in such elevated company as the dowager duchess keeps; mixing with the *haut ton* can only be called exciting. I think we must also soon go shopping for you for a new gown or two, because you cannot have sufficient changes of dress for all the gadding about you are doing. Not that you don't look lovely today in that delightful pearl gray, and the lace I had you use on the collar was just the right touch, even if I *do* say so myself, but—"

Cecilia assured her hostess that she had no need to add to her wardrobe just yet, but that she would accept her kind offer, and gladly, at a later date. She then undertook a description of her past week's activities. She knew how much Mrs. Dockery loved hearing about all the fashions and foibles of the Polite World; she had quickly understood that the little solicitor's wife thrived on learning what was lately considered important in the highest circles. And frequently, Mrs. Dockery made the oddest, most amusing connections between a particular fad and the reason for it. Cecilia thought some of her comments either very astute or else remarkably naive, but she never was quite sure which.

She had expected Mrs. Dockery to pounce on her description of the Regent, whom she had caught a glimpse of through the crowd the night before, but instead, Mrs. Dockery evinced far more interest in domestic concerns.

"A grandson, you say?" Mrs. Dockery seemed overwhelmed by the news of their increasing numbers at Cavendish Square. Her questions thereafter came rapid-fire. "How long will he be staying, and what is he like? Why has he come? Describe him, dear girl!"

"Well," Cecilia answered at a pause in the spate of inquiries, a slight pucker forming betwixt her brows, "His Grace stands a full head taller than I, and must weigh a solid sixteen stone. He has quite the widest shoulders I have ever seen, but he moves well, nonetheless. Black hair, smoke-gray eyes, and he won't drink claret after supper. Prefers his hock, he says. He's come for the purpose of seeking a wife—he's three years under thirty—and I suppose he will return to his home acres at the end of the season. Or, at least, I hope so," she added in fervent tones.

"Well, of course you do," Mrs. Dockery sympathized. "Having someone interfere with your peace, giving out directives and making a nuisance of himself with all manner of special requirements— it must be absolutely awful. Why, he probably gives you orders up and down and then expects you to *toady*, no doubt. It is no wonder to me that you should wish him at Jericho, and quite right, too!"

"Oh, no, it's nothing like that." Cecilia laughed rather ruefully. "While I wouldn't say that the duke is a comfortable addition, he is really very polite and doesn't stand upon his dignity overmuch. That is, no more than is acceptable from one in his position." Cecilia was surprised to realize that she spoke no more than the truth, for His Grace had been remarkably considerate, even obliging at times. He had allowed her time to recover from her embarrassment yesterday when she was trying to describe her duties at Santa Clara, and then, just last night, she had heard him assure the dowager's much-stricken abigail that the broken vase was of no account, when it had been a Sèvres! Such thoughtfulness was indeed kind, however unexpected.

"No," she went on with her answer to Mrs. Dockery, "the duke is not a demanding sort. Rather, he is a self-possessed man with a something you might call 'completeness' about him that doesn't seem to require much by way of others' attentions. It's just that—well, it's just that he has such a cool, commanding aspect that is always *there*, if you know what I mean."

She wasn't altogether sure that she knew herself what she meant, but Mrs. Dockery seemed satisfied, apparently understanding that the subject was discomfiting, if nothing else. The plump little matron returned to the topic of the Jerseys' rout party, prattling cheerfully on about what-was-what and who-was-who, effectively taking Cecilia's mind from her own concerns.

"I am *so* glad you came today," Mrs. Dockery finally said as Cecilia prepared to return to Cavendish Square. "Your visits are always quite a treat. And you may be assured that I will send your letter off to Jane straight away."

In spite of her fears that she would be unable to meet young ladies of good background, Cecilia soon learned that nothing was more easily done. Overnight, she found herself highly sought after by countless young misses, even before her plea for guidance reached the county of Sussex.

The reason for this phenomenon was simple. Cecilia shared an address with the most eligible *parti* to come on the town in years.

Miss Langley, does His Grace like to ride in the park? At what hour does he go there? Dear Miss Langley, will the duke be at Almack's on Wednesday next, do you know, and is he engaged yet for the cotillion . . . for the waltz . . . for the first country dance? Hardly flattering to herself, Cecilia concluded, but certainly convenient.

In fact, if her task was not so serious, Cecilia would have greatly relished the spectacle of seeing every female in London throwing herself at the Duke of Kelthorpe's head. From girls barely out of bib and tucker to overripe widows on the catch for a fortune, women flocked to any event that might attract his presence. Hostesses scored the success of their parties based upon whether or not they could boast the young duke's attendance. For if he

126

came, the ladies would follow, and then *their* hopeful swains would swarm through the doors.

From the letter to his grandmother announcing his intentions, Cecilia and the dowager had both assumed that His Grace would go about his own pursuits without their company. And he did spend his days out riding, driving, visiting at the clubs, and so forth, while she and the dowager met for their usual round of afternoon card parties and teas. But their evenings took a different course almost from the first. His Grace seemed intent on conforming his schedule to their own, attending most of the events they had selected to entertain themselves.

Additionally, he had insisted upon being their escort each week to the exclusive assembly at Almack's. Cecilia had soon found herself a regular guest in those famed rooms on King Street behind Pall Mall, where the *bon ton* met during the Season. It had been no trouble for the dowager duchess to procure her a voucher, although, of course, Cecilia did not dance or otherwise partake of the festivities. Her Grace's rank was sufficient to allow Miss Langley the entrée, but black gloves prohibited revelry.

Aware of these strictures, Cecilia was nonetheless excited beyond measure on her first evening within those hallowed rooms. Her Grace had warned her beforehand that Mr. Colnet's orchestra was no more than passable, the cardroom sadly flat, and the refreshments not even worth their mention. But Cecilia was by no means disappointed. In Almack's, she discovered that the company was everything marvelous to behold.

Beau Brummell languidly quizzed all the guests; the countess Lieven relentlessly snubbed any she did not consider up to the mark; even as white-ruffled dresses, trimmed in every shade of the rainbow, twirled around the dance floor in time to the music. Matrons vied with one another in the cut of their gowns and the brilliance of their jewels, while unattached gentlemen, wearing the regulation white waistcoats with knee breeches, circled the rooms like so many hungry sharks, making themselves agreeable to the daughters of prosperous houses. All in all, it was a gorgeous display.

And while she was there, the major's daughter used her time well. By the end of the second week of His Grace's residency, Cecilia could tally her prospects for the nuptial honors at four: Miss Janet Whitte, a buxom blond beauty who proudly traced her ancestors back to the Norman conquest; Anne, Lady Carruthers of Berkshire, the already-wealthy heiress of three bachelor great-uncles, and a baroness in her own right; Lady Arabella Dumont, tall, darkly lovely, with impeccable credentials; and Mrs. Catherine Peasely, a war widow with the sweetest nature Cecilia had ever encountered. These were her candidates.

They were chosen because the duke had shown each one at least a modicum of favor, and because at some time in the last two weeks, they had professed a preference for country life—well, not all of them, Cecilia mentally corrected. Three had made such claims, but Lady Arabella was entered into the lists because of an overheard statement regarding antiquities. It seems that the lady *adored* anything Gothic, and especially old castles. Thus, each was judged suitable to become the next Duchess of Kelthorpe.

Now it was time for Cecilia to bring attention to her selections. Giving the matter some thought, she decided that the best way to go about the thing was to have the young ladies do the deed themselves. If she could inspire her candidates' confidence, such that they would believe that His Grace had already singled them out for his notice, they would set their caps and catch him fair. Pleased with her stratagem, Cecilia resolved to commence the action this very night at Almack's Wednesday subscription ball.

"You don't say so, Miss Langley!" Miss Whitte's eyes showed avid interest when Cecilia approached her in the ladies' retiring room. The beauteous Miss Whitte had no difficulty believing that she had found preeminence in the Duke of Kelthorpe's esteem; without a sign of reluctance, she snapped at the bait. "Blondes *are* all the rage this year"—she preened before her reflection in the large looking-glass—"so I cannot pretend I'm surprised. And you say that the dear duke is *shy?* With a little nudge I can overcome that!" Guinea-gold curls were turned this way and that, admired by their possessor as Miss Whitte prepared to reenter the ballroom to impress her latest conquest with her unparalleled charms.

Lady Carruthers proved equally interested. Twenty-four years old and proud of her position in the world, she had rejected every suitor to her hand—callously, some said—hoping for just such an opportunity to come her way. "He is the sixth duke of the line," she whispered with barely suppressed excitement. "You do realize, Miss Langley, what that means? I shall have precedence over very nearly every lady in the realm. And only *bashfulness* keeps him from speaking? That should cause no problem, no problem at all!" Eager to convince the duke that he had no need to dissemble with *her*, the baroness hurried away from the refreshment room where Cecilia had cornered her.

After making a check to see that her employer had no immediate need of assistance, Cecilia next gave her attention to the ballroom, where couples twirled and turned in graceful movement. She had seen Catherine Peasely on the dance floor earlier—a lissome figure in Olympian blue silk, cunningly draped to enhance an impossibly tiny waistline. Cecilia's favorite in the running, the petite widow had lost her husband at Corunna four years before. She was still young, definitely comely, and apparently in no rush to remarry, and Cecilia feared she would also be the most difficult to enlist in the cause. She was soon to be proved disappointingly correct in her apprehensions.

"Miss Langley!" A sunny smile from Mrs. Peasely greeted her approach. "I am glad to see you here tonight. And Her Grace is certainly in looks, is she not?" She nodded toward the dowager, beautifully gowned in dotted gauze over emerald-green satin. Her Grace was sitting in conversation with old Lord Rutheven, her favorite cicisbeo, and Cecilia readily agreed that the dowager's extended years were scarcely noticeable.

The young widow then bestowed a sweet smile on the escort at her side. "You must please allow me to present Sir Malcolm Wrotherby to you, Miss Langley. He's an old friend of my family in Shropshire, and he and my brother went to the same schools together. We have known each other forever and ages."

Cecilia evidenced her pleasure at having the acquaintance, while the gentleman referred to bowed shyly, before turning back to his companion. He accorded Mrs. Peasely the most worshipful, besotted look Cecilia thought she had ever been privileged to see.

"Though the formal announcement is not yet made," Mrs. Peasely spoke confidingly, "Malcolm has done me the honor of asking me to be his wedded wife." A blush suffused her cheeks, and Cecilia saw a gentle tightening of Sir Malcolm's hand on her arm.

"Then I am delighted to be among the first to wish you both happy," Cecilia replied with all sincerity, thinking that if Mrs. Peasely had found such devotion to replace her loss, very well and good. She liked the young widow and rejoiced in her obvious happiness. And yet, strangely, it was relief that she felt most of all. *Relief that Catherine Peasely would not be the one to endure the misery of marriage to Stephen Trelwyn.* What else?

Her search of the assembly rooms was less successful thereafter. Lady Arabella was nowhere to be found; a few subtle questions brought to light the information that her ladyship had accepted an invitation out of town and was not expected back for several days. With her list shortened to only three names, Cecilia prayed that the raven-haired beauty would return to London soon. Lady Arabella might be just the one to succeed, and frankly, Cecilia had serious doubts that His Grace could be snared by either one of the self-consequential two she'd earlier set on his trail. His Grace had a keen awareness of his own worth, certainly, but he was not so horridly obvious about it as those two ladies appeared to be.

A few days later, she thought the matter even more urgent when she was party to a conversation between Stephen and his grandmother. She and the dowager were sitting quietly in the morning room, reading the latest periodicals, when the duke sauntered in, a cogent look in his eye. Cecilia had a premonition of danger as she watched him position himself in front of the dowager's seat.

"You ladies appear content this morning, as if the world suited you well," he began in an innocuous vein. "How I do envy you! My own life has lately grown rather unpleasantly complicated." He brushed a speck of lint from an otherwise immaculate sleeve of Brunswick green superfine before rounding zinc-gray eyes on his grandmother. "It seems," he said in measured tones, "that there is a rumor about that I have developed a fondness for two, let us say, *well-endowed* young ladies. Albeit more precise to say that only one boasts monetary enrichment. I won't embarrass you with their names, Grandmother, but they have each of them assured me that their only reason for pressing me for my *proposal*"—his voice strengthened appreciably—"was their certain knowledge that I would welcome their attentions."

With no sign of discomposure Her Grace laid her reading aside to ask with detached politeness, "What can you mean, dear boy? Just what rumor have you heard?"

Cecilia held her copy of the *Courier* in stiff fingers as she fought to still the trembling which threatened to expose her.

"You know quite well, Grandmother." The growling menace in his voice was unmistakable to Cecilia's ears. "May I remind you that I expressly forbade you to interfere in my affairs?"

"Certainly you did so. Quite right, too!" the dowager added. "I have always believed that a man should choose his own wife—that is what we are talking about, I gather? In no way would I seek to rule your decision on such a matter. But why so reluctant? No reputation will suffer from what is said in this room. Just who has been plaguing you, and how?"

The duke considered the upright figure seated before him. He did not appear to notice Cecilia, sinking ever deeper into the cushions of her chair some feet away. "Doing it too brown," he said with a sardonic lift of his brow. "Miss Janet Whitte and the baroness Carruthers, as I'm persuaded you well know. They've both of them taken the bizarre notion that I suffer from such an excess of sensibility that I'm unable to come out and declare myself. I think it was the baroness who put it best only this morning when she cadged onto me in the park. She said I 'must not be reticent with the lady so soon to bear the name.'" His eyes glittered an opaque gray and he unconsciously flexed powerful shoulders. "Well, madam, what have you to say?"

Without taking her eyes from her grandson's outraged face, the dowager replied in the mildest of tones. "Say? There is not much *to* say, dear boy. If the ladies you name have the idea that you bear a *tendre* for them, I have had nothing to do with it. It seems to me more likely that, being coming sorts, they have built up their own fantasies as they chose. Young girls today have such deplorable manners, altogether hiddy-giddy, you'll agree. But *I* certainly would not wish their like on you."

Cecilia sat quietly, pleading in silence that she be permitted to drop into oblivion unnoticed. Her heart thumped so loudly that she could hardly hear what was said; the din in her ears beat time with her blood, pumping upward with shocking force.

Those jingle-brained ninnies! she thought in angry dismay. Two more clumsy, clunch-headed conspirators could hardly be imagined. She had known Janet Whitte had flower-fluff for brains, but she'd expected rather more diplomacy from the baroness. No help for it now. Cecilia could only keep her head down and pray the shots missed her.

Stephen stood frowning over his grandmother's words. Before he could speak further, however, Her Grace voiced another thought.

"I believe I may know what it is, dear boy. Someone has played a trick on you. Perhaps among your acquaintance, some of the younger men thought it a very good joke, and they expected to have a fine laugh at your expense. Yes! That must be it," she insisted.

"Well," he owned, albeit grudgingly, "you could be in the right of it there. The Bucks were ever ripe for a lark, and I suppose it would hardly be the first time such a May game has been played. I'll do some investigating," he said with dark promise, "and when I catch them out—"

But Her Grace took exception to this. "Come, come, Stephen," she protested. "Surely you can manage a prank better than that? You must go on as if nothing at all is amiss. That's the best way to confound them. You've enough town bronze to avoid the clutches of those bold-faced gels, too, I'll make my wager, and they'll soon tire from your lack of attention. Neither Miss Whitte nor the baroness has ever had a shortage of gentlemanly suitors, from what I hear, so there's no need to fret yourself that they'll suffer from the experience. As for the perpetrators, seek them out if you will, but the Bloods are likely to hear of your inquiries and laugh all the more."

Stephen sighed in something like frustration. "Right, then," he said finally. "But I hope I may depend upon you to assist me in scotching any gossip that comes your way."

"Consider it done!" Her Grace agreed. "Now, off you go about your day. Gentleman Jackson's Saloon, is it?"

Catching the shrewdness in her look, he laughed. "So, you've forgiven me already for riding roughshod over you, ma'am? And now you're hoping that someone will draw my cork, just in case your little lesson hasn't completely soaked in? Too, too clever!" Unexpectedly, he scooped the old lady up from her chair and enveloped her in a fierce hug. He pressed his lips to her softly wrinkled cheek in a hearty kiss—completely flustering his grandmother . . . and his audience as well.

Doubting her eyes, Cecilia sat stunned. She felt a grin slowly spreading its way across her face, tribute to the spontaneous affection just demonstrated. It was the first real sign of attachment she had seen His Grace exhibit toward the dowager.

"I should have known better than to think you had a hand in this, Grandmother," he continued with all sincerity. "I am very sorry to have suspected you of such goings-on." He set her down gently and then sent Cecilia a dazzling smile. "I beg pardon, too, for having made you a witness to my bad temper, Cecilia," he added brightly. "However, no matter how slowly it may seem, I am learning that you ladies know just the right tactics for bringing a misguided fellow back into line." He sent her a cogent look, marking her recognition of his meaning. After executing a perfect military salute, he jauntily marched out the door.

Cecilia didn't know what to make of it. Could she have been wrong about his intentions? Did he actually care for the old lady? The mere thought that she had herself committed a profound injustice called up all the roses into her creamy-skinned cheeks, making her glad that no one else could have reason to suspect her foolish, misguided interpretations.

Was it really foolishness, though?

Perhaps. Then again, perhaps not. Like His Grace, she suspected coincidence, and he *had* asserted that he was master of this house in words she could not like. Reluctantly, she accepted that the duke was not nearly so arrogant as she had at first thought him, though; he was simply more assertive than most men. Having been a regimental commander, and of the famous Ninth at that, she really should have made allowances. Then, too, for all of his being a nobleman of the highest rank short of royalty, he was also, truth to tell, surprisingly disinclined to the usual displays of bigwiggery she'd witnessed in his fellows of the peerage. Hadn't he teased her just now, and as good as admitted that he'd appreciated her trick on him last August?

She might have seen it sooner. The man who could laugh at himself was not a man who would forever condemn others for faults out of hand. More, it was clear that her plans to protect the dowager were all quite unnecessary. With a softer blush, Cecilia remembered the warm kiss he had bestowed on his grandmother and the generous, devastatingly handsome smile he had had for herself. Her heart seemed to expand at the memory.

Uncertainly, she reconsidered her own plans. Her first two candidates had been entirely too *coming*, that was sure—but even in the light of her new discovery, she wondered if she shouldn't hedge her bets and continue with her campaign. Even did he love his grandmother, as she now believed he did, it was still possible that the wrong wife could influence him away from the dowager duchess.

Yes, she might be needed here still. Cecilia resolved to continue her efforts to find His Grace an amenable wife—just in case.

With a softly drawn sigh, she returned her attention to her reading. Thirty minutes passed without a line from the *Courier* soaking through to her consciousness, although page after page was turned.

She was relieved when the dowager duchess put her a question.

"Cecilia," the elderly lady said, her voice gentle, "did I not see you in conversation with Lady Carruthers at Almack's the other night? I cannot quite imagine what anyone sees in her, or in Miss Whitte, either. You must be more circumspect in your friends, I think."

No reply seemed to be expected as the dowager returned her attention to her magazine. Cecilia, fighting to preserve her countenance, was left to wonder what, if anything, the canny old lady suspected.

CHAPTER THIRTEEN

"Stephen! Damn your eyes, I never thought to see you here in London, rubbing shoulders with us ne'er-do-well fribbles! The way I heard it, when you sold out last autumn, you stayed in London for less than a month before you left again, swearing you'd never be back. Well, what about it, old man?" A huge hand belonging to a proportionally sized young Colossus, slapped the duke hard across the shoulders.

"Viv," Stephen acknowledged laconically, unshaken by the pounding blow. "Irrepressible as ever, I see."

The two large young men stood in the vestibule of their club, the duke just arriving, and his acquaintance appearing from within one of the club's inner rooms. Stephen was modishly attired, all masculine elegance in dark-green Bath coating, long trousers, and Hessian-style boots, while Lord Emberley wore a handsome Guards uniform with a major's insignia haphazardly pinned to each side of his collar.

"Ahhhh," exhaled the red-coated major with a singularly wounded look. He placed one large paw over his barrel-shaped chest near his heart. "You come not to praise us but to bury us?" he paraphrased waggishly. "We're not so bad as all that, I'll have you to know. But, tell me, when did you get in, anyway?"

"The last week of April," the duke replied. "I looked for you, but Whitehall said you were on leave for a fortnight."

Lord Emberley grinned broadly. "I must have left London just about the time you got here, then. But come on, man! Let's tilt a glass to Wellington and the Battling Ninth Light. May they do us proud in our absence!" His Lordship signaled to one of the discreet servants for which White's proprietary club was rightly admired, ushering the duke over to a vacant settle to await their order.

When they were seated, Stephen asked, "So you've been back for what—six months now?—and still on commission? That scrawl you sent to tell me your news was damned hard to decipher, I don't mind admitting, and there were one or two words I never did unscramble. I had no reply from you to any of my letters, either, Viv, which meant I had to depend on Grandmother for reports on your progress."

"Never claimed to be a penman," Lord Emberley answered, impenitent. "Now, let me see. It was Hallowe'en night when I was hit, and I made a ship home almost immediately. Spent the next two months in bed—took a fever don't y' know—but I don't scruple to tell you that I got bloody tired of lying about while m' mother carried on and made a great to-do over me. I'd intended to sell out at first, but with the shortage of officers here at home, I ended up letting the War Office talk me around to staying on. Must have been my distinguished record that convinced 'em," he added innocently.

Lord Vivian Emberley, earl of the same name, had been one of Wellington's subalterns until he stood too close to a British field cannon. It had exploded unexpectedly, taking his left hand with it. Stephen was glad to hear that his friend had survived the ordeal in good spirits and had been reassigned to a staff position with the prestigious Horse Guards, his disfigurement notwithstanding. And as Stephen well knew, Major Lord Emberley, a bluff, hearty fellow, was a fine officer who had more than once been cited for conspicuous bravery. He and Stephen had been firm friends all their years on the

Peninsula, and, any appearance to the contrary, they were equally glad to see each other.

"You are serving it up too rare and thick, Viv," Stephen could not resist teasing. "More likely, they wanted to keep a closer eye on your antics." His expression next turned serious. "It doesn't bother you too badly, then?" He gestured toward the missing member.

Laughter dispelled his concern. "Not a bit of it!" the earl asserted. "Learned to ride one-fisted with Wellington, and a good surgeon fixed me up right and tight." His expression quickly altered to one of woebegone disappointment. He said, sounding deeply grieved, "Hated all the condolences, though. Wrote replies to the worst of 'em—rotten way for them to treat a fellow, wouldn't you say?"

Stephen had to pause a moment to adjust to this revelation. "So, you didn't answer my letters because you thought them *good* letters?" he finally asked, amazed.

"That's the barber. Just so! No need to tell a friend in so many words. Friends know how it is. And you can call on 'em if you need 'em, too."

Amused by such logic, Stephen went on to another subject. "By the bye, Viv, while I was at Whitehall I checked for a name on the casualty lists—a major stationed with the infantry at Tôrres Vedras. I'd heard he was killed on a scouting mission sometime early on in the year. Whitehall's records don't list the man, but I would like to confirm the report. Any ideas on how to go about it?" His look held only casual interest.

"Tôrres Vedras? Must have been with the Third Foot, then. The devil's in it, they took a heavy beating at Badajoz, worse luck. Lost every single one of their officers, so I heard. I didn't know anyone from the Third myself, but then, I sailed out of Lisbon directly. It never does to rely on those lists, though, that much I can tell you. Nincompoopery things! Two friends of mine—who are both very much alive, as it happens—were reported dead betimes. And one of 'em *twice!*" Major Lord Emberley snorted at his beloved military's well-known inefficiency.

Stephen was reluctant to drop the subject, but a soft-footed waiter approached, forestalling further questions. Just as well, he concluded, for it was unlikely that his friend held more in the way of information. Also, he preferred not to exhibit more overt interest, lest Viv become too curious about the reasons for his inquiry.

"Well, man, have you found yourself missing the bugler's call to reveille?" the earl asked after their drinks were poured and the agreeable toasts made. "Don't say you've succumbed to the lure of soft living. Can't say as I'd blame you if you had, though. I confess, I appreciate my beef twice a day; may even catch up on the meals I missed on the Peninsula—oh, say in another month or two." Vivian Emberley chuckled delightedly to himself at this witticism.

Stephen languidly raised an eyebrow. "Why, Viv, haven't you heard?" he drawled in tones much unlike his usual, more precise speech. "I've become a farmer. Up with the roosters every morning, don't you know."

The earl's deep guffaws drew disapproving stares from more dignified patrons come to enjoy the quiet White's usually offered. Ignoring these more staid members, his lordship roared out happily, "What a crammer! Can't picture you taking the easy life. Oh, no, I'll not credit that you've gone from commanding colonel of the best disciplined unit in the Peninsula to ordering field hands about their business."

Shaggy, sun-bleached brows wiggled under a shock of hair of the same wheat color. Not an unhandsome man, the earl nonetheless looked hugely unkempt next to the duke. They were of a size, yet Stephen Trelwyn seemed darkly dangerous, sleek, and self-controlled. The earl looked like nothing so much as a big, friendly blond bear in a scarlet uniform.

140

"I do assure you, it's no more than the truth," Stephen replied serenely, taking a sip of his wine. "Nothing catches my interest so much these days as a discussion of the rotation of turnips and clover. I am quite in alt whenever sheep are mentioned within my hearing, while as for the Acts of Enclosure—"

"Pitchin' it too deep!" Major Lord Emberley grinned good-naturedly. "You'll never convince me you're not interested in a demmed sight more of the world than that. Something brought you to town, and I'll bet it wasn't the thought of any land-grasping Enclosure Act, either."

Stephen barely accorded a smile to this sally, replying in the blandest manner. "No, Viv, I haven't been reduced to seeking to increase my fortune by taking title to the commons of my home villages; although, God knows, it's done often enough. Actually, I'm here on personal business for a few weeks . . . Hoby does make the best footgear, you know." He eyed with lazy approval the flawlessly finished boot encasing his foot, resting casually on a stool in front of him.

Not believing for a moment that this was all the reason for his friend's sojourn in London, the earl refused to pry. Vivian Emberley might ever present a good-humored, jovial face to the world, but he was not an unintelligent man. He knew to a nicety when to leave well enough alone. "Have you seen Beecham yet, Stephen?" he asked merely. "No end of a good fellow, Beecham. He and I are working on a project together that you might be interested in. Fact is, that's why I wasn't here when you arrived back in town. Been out drumming up support for the venture and, seriously, we could use another good man on it."

"You mean Pen House?" Stephen asked, his eyes sparking with interest. "Yes, Sir John told me how he was backing a plan for a hospice to provide interim care for invalided soldiers returning from the Peninsula. I ran into him while I was out looking

141

for you, and we supped together—right here, in fact. I've already instructed my solicitors to put me down for a subscription, but John didn't tell me that you were one of the patrons. I agree that it seems a good way to assist those men who are willing to make the effort to overcome their wounds and lost limbs. Moreover, the scheme set me to thinking on an idea for a project of my own."

Stephen's voice gained enthusiasm as he elaborated. "I've written my steward to see how many more cottages my estates can support. Once the men who come through Pen House are healed sufficiently, they'll need to find permanent employment. I don't doubt that some will be agreeable to relocating if they should find they can't return to their previous homes, and my man Cawley is canvassing the neighborhood squires to see if they can provide still more places. There were many in my regiment who could have benefited from such a program; I've already sent a message to my old sergeant-major to pass the word out to those he thinks good candidates for us."

Vivian smacked his knee gleefully. "Glad you signed on, man! A few more backers like you and I'll be well satisfied. 'Pon my oath, if more'd ever had to spend time in one of those butcher's shops they call surgeries, they'd have my fine appreciation of what we're trying to accomplish here. Those places are absolute horrors, I can tell you, and, once the men are mustered out, here at home they get no help at all. I was never so glad as when I got back to London and had my own physician take a look. But too few of the enlisted men can afford the kind of subsequent care I got, and a demmed shame it is, too!" he concluded ardently.

Stephen called to memory the little whitewashed building at Tôrres Vedras. It was his good luck never to have been injured himself, but he'd had plenty of occasions to visit his men in field hospitals and had marked the distinctions between them and Santa Clara Infirmary. Those men fortunate enough to receive care at Santa Clara had much to be grateful for. The doctor in charge must be the one responsible for the improving innovations; he made a mental note to correspond with Dr. Fosgate to ask if he would be willing to pass on some of his ideas for their use at Pen House.

Strange that he should remember the physician's name when he'd heard it only once. Even more strange how he recalled, and with such sharp accuracy, every word Miss Langley had ever spoken—or written. Not eager to pursue *that* thought at the moment, Stephen unconsciously smoothed the pleats at his cuff and resolutely changed the subject.

"So enlighten me, Viv, how else have you been spending your time? I know the War Department values your services"—he eyed askance his friend's rumpled red tunic—"although it is rather alarming to think of dear old England in the charge of such hey-go-mad devils."

Vivian only laughed at him.

"Not shackled yet, are you?"

"Devil a bit!" Vivian Emberley's deep laughter was heard yet again. "You always were up to every rig and row. How did you know? I am honored to be affianced to the sweetest little lady in Wessex, Miss Emmeline Moorehead. She's to have a Season before the engagement's officially announced, and since you're here, you'll have the privilege of meeting her before much longer. Lady Smithers is her godmother—deuced good sort of woman, Lady Smithers—and she'll be sponsoring Emmeline's come-out ball. Emmy's all in a pother because she's late in coming to town due to a slight mishap at home. She'd planned to be here by now."

"Nothing serious, I hope?"

"No, not at all. Seems Em and her rapscallion young brother had a wager about a regular rasper of a fence she cleared quite handily—a good seat there!—but which he came to grief over. It was naught but a sprained ankle, but the sawbones put

143

him to bed for two weeks. Lady Smithers agreed to set back the date after Emmy said she didn't feel right about leaving her brother so soon," he added approvingly. "Should be here in a few days, though. Be sure to answer the invitation, won't you?"

"With pleasure." Stephen's eyes smiled warmly. "I wouldn't miss it for the world. I'm eager to meet the young lady who can bring down such a mighty oak as yourself."

The earl looked to be not at all abashed. He was as proud as any peacock, and it showed. "But what about yourself, man," he asked in return, "anything doing in that direction?"

"Not just at the moment. I'm too busy avoiding traps for the nonce," came Stephen's dry reply. "Although, and I tell you this privately, I am on the look-out for a bride this spring. The estates go to some ramshackle grandson of a great-uncle if I don't get myself an heir before I cash in my chips. There's been a Trelwyn at Castle Kelthorpe since the walls were raised, and Grandmother would never forgive me if I were so blind to my duty as to let everything pass to a virtual outsider. Unfortunately," he continued in flat, disgusted tones, "this year's crop of marriageables seems to offer only gibble-gabbling prattleboxes and avid social climbers. Too coming by half, I'd say." Stephen's eyes grew hard at the thought of Miss Whitte and Lady Carruthers.

Nodding wisely, Vivian Emberley was gratified to have discovered the reason for the duke's visit to London. Stephen smoothed his expression and rose to take his leave.

"I've an appointment to keep, Viv, if you'll excuse me. I'll look to see you at the Smithers' party, if not before."

As he stepped out onto St. James's Street, Stephen pondered the idea of his friend as a married man. Viv was the last fellow he'd expected to give up his freedom, yet it was easily seen that the earl was top over heels. But, as a duke, he did himself have much more to consider than a sweet face or venturesome style. If that was all marriage required, he might as well pay his addresses to Miss Langley.

The very deuce. Had his wits gone begging? What brought such a nonsensical thought into his head? Even were he not of high estate, he would never align himself with such an improper young miss. Why, that one had no more idea of how to go on than the greenest halfling. He'd spent a good many hours in her company these past three weeks, and he was constantly amazed by the thin line she walked between charming audacity and outright disrespect.

Correctly behaved most of the time, considered unexceptionable by persons of *ton*, she managed nonetheless to present a character of distinction which Stephen wasn't sure he approved. When she'd been informed by Lord Rutheven that "our Shakespeare epitomizes the height of language usage," Cecilia had not hesitated to refer the marquis to a perusal of Roman orations and rhetoric, specifically the additions of Cicero. Apparently, Cecilia's father had kept a very odd assortment of books. And Stephen had to admit that she'd made her point in a manner that gave no offence. Rather, he was astounded to hear Lord Rutheven back down and beg her forgiveness for having spoken so rashly. Remarkable. Especially considering what a stickler the marquis was known to be.

Stephen quirked a smile as he took up his reins and pointed up his leaders. Skillfully, he traversed the busy streets of old London, eventually bringing his curricle to a halt in front of a venerable address in Fleet Street. He instructed his groom to come forward and walk the horses, though not too far, as he didn't expect to be long. The interior of the building was a misaligned warren of offices and shadowy, twisting corridors branching off in so and so many directions, but an obliging clerk, presumably set to await his coming, promptly directed him to the tenant he sought.

145

One Lawrence T. Dockery was the man he came to see, and once led into his office, Stephen beheld a spry, stout little fellow, sporting an impressive cravat tied in the complicated Maharetta. However, his look of sagacity was reassuring.

Mr. Dockery declared himself most honored to be of service. "But you need not have put yourself to the trouble of coming to me, Your Grace," he said. "I was very happy to make the appointment here, of course, but would have been pleased to attend you at your convenience." The rotund little lawyer's bright eyes looked a question.

"Thank you very much," Stephen responded, "but I expected to be in the area, in any case. The matter which brings me is somewhat delicate, you understand, and I didn't want to call attention to your involvement."

All congeniality, however curious he must be after this intelligence was imparted, Mr. Dockery stood waiting for further enlightenment. The answer was not long in coming.

"I wish to verify the credentials of a Miss Cecilia Langley, whom I think you recommended to my grandmother's notice. I am not satisfied that she is quite suitable for the position, so I was hoping you could tell me more about her."

"How now? What's this?" Mr. Dockery exclaimed, drawing himself up to his full five feet and four. His previously affable expression dissolved in a trice. "Do you say that Miss Langley has exhibited some particular vulgarity? Her conduct is found wanting in some way, perhaps?"

"No, certainly not. Her manner is everything correct." Stephen fell on the defensive himself, for he found he couldn't tolerate that his own earlier doubts about Cecilia's sense of propriety be thus voiced by another. *He* might criticize her, but he would not permit someone else to do the same. It was ridiculously perverse, he knew, but he couldn't seem to help himself.

"Then, Your Grace," said the little solicitor in

confusion, "I confess myself at a loss to understand you. What is it that is wrong? A finer young lady I've yet to meet, for she's a gentlewoman in all respects; you cannot seriously doubt it. Why, she lived under my own roof and has graced Mrs. Dockery's table, I'll have you to know, and we find her all that she should be. Further, you must be aware that Her Grace has relied upon me any time these last thirty years," he sniffed, "and I believe my judgment is to be depended upon."

"Yes, yes! That's agreed," Stephen said with some asperity. "I do not fault Miss Langley's manners or your competence. I hope only to learn something more about her background—her family and upbringing. I want to know if you have certain knowledge of her father and of her mother's people," he persisted.

"But of course I do," Mr. Dockery declared. "Is that all that's disturbing you? Sit down, Your Grace, sit down and be comfortable," he begged, motioning to a neat table and side chairs. Once they were seated opposite each other, Mr. Dockery bent his elbows on the tabletop and steepled his stubby fingers with a thoughtful air. He said, "I can assure you, sir, that the Langley affairs, though modest, of course, are totally in my hands. As for the distaff side—"

"You mean the Mayfields?" Stephen clarified.

"Yes, the Mayfields," said Mr. Dockery, seemingly pleased to be on firm ground. "There's none left of that connection since the line died out some years ago, leaving poor Miss Langley without further support. Oh, a sad day it was when we learned of the major's death, I can tell you. Such a gentleman! A fine officer!"

"And do you also happen to know about any young men in her life?" Stephen next asked, a shuttered expression on his face. "Naturally, any attachment must be of interest to me—ah, to us." The image of a slender, shadowed figure with a postillion-style hat still nagged at him. He was, in fact, in danger of becoming obsessed by the thought of Cecilia having a secret involvement.

Apparently, however, his timing with this question was not of the most propitious. The pudgy little solicitor, relaxed and leaning back in his chair, suddenly slipped bonelessly forward to slide right under the table! His rounded middle was all that saved him, catching on the inset table skirting before Mr. Dockery quite reached the floor.

"Goodness me!" he squealed in stricken tones after righting himself from the foolish position, straightening his ruched-up attire with quick little tugs and pats. Then, in only slightly less aggrieved tones, "*What* an idea, Your Grace! Oh, dearie, dearie me! I am absolutely certain that Miss Langley has never . . . I mean, she just isn't the type to . . . ? Well, I am absolutely sure that there is no previous attachment. It's completely out of the question, Your Grace!"

Stephen was beginning to feel not a little foolish himself. Everything was exactly as Miss Langley had proclaimed, and the niggling doubts which had brought him here now seemed preposterous. Necessarily, he apologized for whatever remarks seemed out of order, but the dapper man of law would have none of it.

"Tut-tut, don't give it another thought," Mr. Dockery cried, well appeased by the expressions of repentance. "No offense meant and none taken. It is certainly your right to look into your grandmother's affairs, but in this instance there is absolutely no reason for your further concern. None at all!"

With long experience in judging men, gained on the battlefields of Spain and Portugal, Stephen acknowledged the able opinion offered. Taking his leave just a short time later, he did not see Mr. Dockery sink back into his chair and remove a large square of cambric from the pocket of his waistcoat. Mr. Dockery then vigorously applied said cloth to his face, blotting up the scattered beads of moisture which had sprung from his pores. Nor did His Grace see when that gentleman, so widely renowned for his integrity, rolled his eyes and blew his lips outward in a universal gesture of heartfelt relief.

The lady Arabella Dumont finally returned from the country house party which had kept her away from town. Cecilia spotted her at Holland House during an afternoon entertainment, gorgeously attired in crisp white muslin trimmed in light blue velvet ribbon. She wore a matching turquoise parure of great price. With her jet-black hair and alabaster skin—not to mention her respectable fortune and antecedents—she was undoubtedly a well-qualified candidate for His Grace's hand.

As soon as the dowager was settled in with her particular cronies, Whigs every one, Cecilia begged to be excused for a few moments. She then eased her way through the crowd of literary brilliants and political lions to reach the dark beauty's side. She checked over her shoulder to see that the crush prevented her employer from being witness to her contact, for she had a vague suspicion that the shrewd old dowager sometimes saw more than she should.

"We have missed you, my lady," Cecilia ventured upon her advance. Barely acquainted, Cecilia was not at all certain of her welcome acceptance by the proud young peeress.

As if in agreement that the approach was unseemly, Lady Arabella deigned the briefest of nods. "Miss Langley, it is kind of you to have noticed my absence, I'm sure," she said in a lofty accents.

Then, apparently remembering Miss Langley's connections, she asked with rather more friendliness, "Do you go to the Rowling reception tonight? There is to be dancing afterward, I'm told, and Lady Rowling's ballroom can only be admired, don't you think?" She took in Cecilia's dull gray mourning dress with no hint of compassion before adding, "I think the flooring there is quite the best I've ever had the pleasure to dance across."

Ignoring the slight, Cecilia answered, "I have not

149

yet had the privilege of visiting their home, but I'm convinced you may be right, my lady. Yes, we are committed to Countess Rowling this evening, though I don't know how long we'll stay. Her Grace sometimes enjoys watching the dancers, but the duke rarely takes a turn on the floor. Soldiers have injuries, you understand. . . ." Cecilia allowed her voice to trail off dramatically and in a manner that would certainly tantalize one as romantically inclined as she believed the lady Arabella to be.

"An injury, Miss Langley?" Lady Arabella's deep-set, chocolate-brown eyes filled with sympathy. "But I don't quite understand. Is something the matter with His Grace? I don't recall ever hearing that he was wounded; why, I'm almost positive that he was not."

"Oh! Of course, nothing's wrong." Cecilia cupped her hand over her mouth in pretended dismay. "I only meant that, um . . . a slight hurt. Please do forgive me, my lady, I should not have mentioned it at all. Pain can be endured quietly—most days, that is." She maintained a guileless look throughout this disjointed speech, then drew a deep breath as if gathering her scattered wits. She offered Lady Arabella a look so soulful that it would have done credit to Marpessa. "Lady Arabella, pray do forgive my wayward tongue. I just wanted you to know that if His Grace doesn't ask you to dance, it can only be because something is, er, bothering him, if you take my meaning. He speaks so highly of you that there can be no other reason if he doesn't solicit *your* hand for the waltz tonight. And I do so hope that I may rely upon your discretion. For if His Grace learned that I had spoken of this after he's been so very brave, well, you must see that it wouldn't *do*."

"Certainly, I shan't refer to what must cause discomfort." Lady Arabella's dark eyes welled up with unspent emotion as she passionately clasped her hands to her bosom. "I take it that His Grace doesn't want his wound talked about, and you are

150

so right not to mention it directly. Oh, such courage our valorous war heroes have. I would do nothing to slight His Grace's gallant sacrifice!"

Cecilia wondered whether the lady would be so sympathetic if an injured man were not of such high estate as the duke, but that concern was irrelevant for the moment. She was just glad that Lady Arabella's nature was so incurious as to omit further questions about the nature of His Grace's supposed injury. However, confident that her maneuver had succeeded—and congratulating herself that only the tiniest untruthfulness had been employed—she then excused herself and returned to the dowager's side. She didn't notice the keen look the dowager duchess gave her; she was unaware that a break in the crowd had exposed her tête-à-tête with Lady Arabella, or that her conversation had been closely monitored.

Much later, after everyone had exchanged their afternoon dress for evening wear, the party from Kelthorpe House was announced to those already arrived at the Rowlings' ballroom. Cecilia and the dowager retired to the cardroom, while His Grace chatted with various acquaintances and perused the occupants of the dance floor.

He was soon startled out of his complacency when a young lady with whom he'd only once before spoken—and that in the most casual way nearly two weeks before—came up to have speech with him. It was surely not at all usual for a gentleman to be so boldly approached. "Thank you, no," Stephen answered the young lady's query. "I don't believe I'd care for any of the punch at this moment." Nonplussed, his right eyebrow rose to astonished heights.

Stephen was mystified. Why, he wondered, should an attractive young debutante, and an Incomparable at that, come up to him, proposing to bring him refreshment? At least a dozen footmen were in Lady Rowling's employ, half of whom were in the ballroom, offering selections of drinks from their trays.

151

He couldn't at first imagine what had made the young lady ask such a thing, but he was not behindhand in returning the compliment. "It would be my pleasure to fetch you something, though. What might I bring you?"

"Oh, no, nothing for me!" Lady Arabella looked flustered at his suggestion. "I shouldn't dream of putting you to the trouble, Your Grace. I just thought *you* might care for something." With a determined look on her beautiful face, Lady Arabella then glanced about and gracefully waved toward a pair of gilt-trimmed chairs. "But if it pleases, could we not sit down for a moment, perhaps over there?" she asked him.

"As you wish," he replied courteously. He offered his arm and escorted her to the preferred seating.

Dressed in white lace over pink étoile satin, Lady Arabella was unquestionably alluring, and Stephen was not unaware of her several attractions. Tiny clusters of lustrous, white-rosé seed pearls adorned her shell-like ears, and her glossy black hair was curled and pinned in the most appealing style imaginable. But as entrancing a picture as she presented, the duke refused to be distracted by the feminine arts. The old military adage came to his mind: *Where there are two, there well might be three!*

When they were seated, he spoke in lulling, silky tones. "You mustn't hesitate to confide in me, Lady Arabella, for I cannot help wondering what it is that brings such a Brilliant to my side. I am surely the envy of every man here and most conscious of the honor you do me, but, by any chance, you don't happen to find me shy, do you?"

"You are shy? I did not know it!" Lady Arabella turned a quizzical, heart-shaped face around to him.

"No, of course not. I only wondered if you judged me so."

"Surely, Your Grace, as one of our highest peers, any show of reticence must be thought most unbecoming in you. Do you not think so?" Never very powerful in her understanding, her ladyship's look of pretty confusion was so obviously genuine that Stephen felt at once free to discard his suspicions.

"Yes, it would, rather, now that you mention it," he said in dry tones. "I don't believe we need concern ourselves, in that case. So, with that settled, would you not care to dance with me instead of remaining here on the sidelines?" He rose to his feet in expectation.

"Oh, no!" she disclaimed, her dismay apparent. "I much prefer to sit and talk, please believe me. I have this age been wishful of becoming better acquainted with one of our nation's heroes, for I do so admire a man who is willing to fight, even to *die*, for his country." A soft blush lightly stole across her flawless cheeks at the bold admission, followed by a look of satisfaction as His Grace regained his seat. With every sincerity, she said, "You must know I feel so very helpless when I hear the news of the war, Duke. Why, anyone of refined sensibilities must be *unspeakably* saddened by the terrible suffering our men must endure. For me to be in the presence of such bravery quite takes my breath away."

Not for a moment did her ladyship regret her presumption in speaking out. The duke had mentioned shyness to put her at her ease, she knew, and it was incumbent upon her to show him that she appreciated his thoughtfulness. Most men, she was aware, were of so much rougher a nature—so basely coarse and crude! Yet here was a man who entered into the finer feelings. Enraptured, she studied his noble brow, oblivious of the faint sarcasm in his tilted smile.

"Ah. You follow the actions of our troops, then? In that case, what think you of our current effort to take Burgos? Wellington seems to believe we should give it another go after that stony fortress resisted his endeavors October last."

Lady Arabella shivered unaffectedly at this. "Your Grace!" she cried, much shocked. "Surely I may esteem our gallant soldiers, particularly our *wounded* soldiers, without going into detailed interest. That would be conduct unbefitting a lady, you must agree. No more such talk, I beg you!"

Stephen, in fact, did not agree. Still, he knew it was the way of their world to protect the Fair Ones from anything even remotely unpleasant. Consciously covering his thoughts, he politely changed subjects. "A waltz is just beginning, my lady. I insist you grant me the pleasure of taking the floor with you. Come." He stood and extended his hand.

The handsome smile that accompanied his request was not one for any female worthy of her sex to ignore. Upon seeing the ease with which His Grace had arisen, Lady Arabella agreed to his proposal. She supposed that either his dreadful injury was not paining him tonight, or else he was making a special sacrifice in her honor. Either way, it behooved her to accept his offer. She could appreciate what a striking pair they two would make, and she was not about to forego the opportunity of showing off her new champion before the *haut ton*.

Certainly, the beautiful couple with their shining black locks were noticed. From the cardroom where she and Her Grace had been practicing their skills, Cecilia looked out toward the ballroom in time to see the results of her machinations. Twirling to the violins' music, Lady Arabella and the duke gracefully circled the room, their matching jet-black hair drawing the attention of one and all. Cecilia had to ruthlessly smother her own feelings at the sight, squelching the tingle of envy which threatened to make itself known.

Her plan was well in motion. That was what counted.

CHAPTER FOURTEEN

One week later, disconsolately, Miss Cecilia Langley picked at a wilted flower in the middle tray of a heavy crystal and silver epergne centering the long, mahogany dining table. *I wonder when I shall ever have back the use of my own name?* she mused sadly.

She knew that it could be years before she would be free to use "Linscombe" again; indeed, she might never be able return to the name of her birth. But where normally a pragmatic nature precluded useless speculation, for some reason Cecilia now was wont to rail against her chosen fate. The loss of her name seemed to epitomize what had become an unhappy predicament.

Forty guests were expected to dine at Kelthorpe House this Thursday night, including Lady Arabella Dumont and her esteemed parents. Cecilia had necessarily cut short her visit to the Dockerys that afternoon in order to assist with the evening's plans and make herself ready. She would much rather have declined to attend. Why this should be, when she should have been eager to observe His Grace's progress with the dark damsel, she could not have told exactly. But so it was.

Cecilia was aware that Stephen Trelwyn was seeing Lady Arabella regularly during this past sennight, either for rides in the park, an evening at the opera, or some other outing to which they had been invited. More and more he left his grandmother, and herself by extension, to their own devices while he pursued the next duchess. Lately, instead of showing interest in his grandmother's preferred activities, he chose to attend the balls and musical evenings Lady Arabella favored.

Cecilia considered that she rather resented the loss of His Grace's near-constant company. She missed his dry comments and the skilled wordplay which so often could surprise a laugh out of her. Quickly, before these maunderings traveled further, Cecilia pulled her thoughts away.

No regrets, she scolded herself; the whole was exactly according to plan. "Then why do I feel so glum tonight?" she inquired of the blameless tabletop.

She and the dowager had a most satisfactory relationship. Her Grace saw to it that her companion was everywhere received, and Cecilia enjoyed each new acquaintance. The young crowd found Miss Langley's calm good sense comfortable, and the older ones seemed to hold particular respect for her card-playing abilities. She and the dowager had been exceedingly gay these past weeks, delighting in every sort of splendid entertainment, even since her grandson's defection.

So why this vast depression?

The duke had not an inkling that anyone had meddled this time, Cecilia was sure. In fact, he seemed in a fair way to making Lady Arabella a proposal. Gossip had it that the dark beauty was not immune to his charms, either, and in an overheard conversation, Cecilia learned that the betting at White's favored an early wedding. The *beau monde* agreed that they made a handsome couple, and Cecilia knew she should be congratulating herself on her achievement.

Why, then, should she feel so gloomed?

The dowager duchess had sent her down to the supper room to see that everything was in order before the guests arrived, but there was really nothing left to do. The chandelier of cut Venetian crystal was polished beyond fault, and beneath its happy influence, the tableware rested in glory. Linens were immaculately displayed with nary a fold

156

out of place. The tea rose she toyed with between slender fingers was not even truly wilted; it was limp only because the stem had not been set deeply enough to reach the water.

The neglected cutting seemed to sum up Cecilia's mood.

"Is there anything the matter, Miss Langley?" The head butler had noiselessly entered the room, and his question broke into her thoughts. His glance encompassed the room's appointments with approval, though he seemed concerned lest she had found something wrong with the arrangements.

"Oh, Iverson, I didn't hear you come in. No, nothing's amiss. It's lovely, quite perfect." She was privately relieved at his interruption to her otherwise morbid thoughts.

"Are you certain, miss? 'Tisn't too late to make a change if you think it needful."

"Oh, I'm certain Their Graces will be more than pleased," she answered. "While as for how you managed to do so much, and on such short notice, I'm sure I'll never know. It was only late yesterday that the final numbers were made; you are quite a marvel, really!" She dipped a curtsy to the astonished butler.

The tips of Iverson's ears took on color as he pulled smartly at the hem of his properly striped waistcoat. "No more than I should be expected to do, miss," he said gruffly. "Nothing out of the ordinary, I assure you."

Tucking her arm under the august butler's black-clad sleeve, Cecilia made haste to correct him. "Not so, I say. When we attended a gathering last week at the Reedwilders', I noticed that their man didn't manage nearly half so well. Things there were all ajumble when more guests came than were expected. Oh, it led to quite a to-do. *You* would have managed it much better, I'm sure."

Cecilia, in her heelless satin slippers, was still an inch or so taller than the worthy Kelthorpe butler as she held his arm and smiled into his face.

"Iverson," she continued with conviction, "I've seen the most ridiculously clumsy butlers that you can imagine: butlers with rumpled stocks and creased jackets, rude and stupid butlers, and houses so disordered that you'd swear they had no butler. But you, sir, are a prince among your peers! Unobtrusive, considerate, thorough—and from the *uncanny* way you seem to know what's wanted before it's even asked for—well! I'd accuse you of being a mind-reading Gypsy, did I not know better." She twinkled down at him, her usual good humor reestablished.

Flushing to the roots of his silver-sprinkled hair, Iverson couldn't prevent an answering smile. "Now, miss, 'tis good of you to say so, and don't think I don't mean it! But I consider it an honor to serve fine people like Her Grace and the duke—and you, too, Miss Langley. I'll admit to a bit of uneasiness when you first came to us," he said truthfully, "but the way you've brightened up this old house has not gone unnoticed below stairs. It's we who thank you, miss, 'deed it is." He patted Cecilia's hand fondly.

"Ah, a mutual admiration league, is it?" came a languid, drawling voice from the doorway.

Leaning against the light-painted wood, the duke's silvery eyes examined them with a derisive lift to one eyebrow. Dressed in darkest gray, white, and a gorgeously embroidered waistcoat, his insouciant posture silently magnified his criticism.

Poor Iverson's earlier rosy flush turned an even darker red. The normally unflappable butler looked miserable at being caught in what could rightly be called a compromising position; it was not at all proper for him to be consorting in such manner with young Miss Langley, and everyone there knew it. But in vain did he try to release her hand from around his arm.

Cecilia did not blush. If anything, her creamy complexion paled at what she considered an unwarranted attempt at humiliation. She was, fact be, angered past all bearing.

"Admiration, indeed, Your Grace," she flashed out. "And when was the last time you thanked someone for their help, especially those who do the many little things that are all too easily taken for granted? Or do you prefer to glide through life without gratitude for the people who must cater to your whims day after day? And when, may I ask, will you learn to appreciate that every single person in this house works hard, hours upon hours, just so that you can have an easier time of it!" Outraged gold flecks glittered from within wide brown eyes.

She was just working up to what she thought she wanted to say, unconsciously invoking the principle that the best defense was a good offense, when her words were cut off midstream.

"You will halt this damn nonsense."

The duke swiftly moved forward to stand just inches in front of her, his fury radiating to the very corners of the room. She was so startled by his shout that she dropped her hold on Iverson's arm.

That blameless servant jumped back at least a foot, but his presence seemed forgotten while His Grace focused on Miss Langley. "Do you *dare* to criticize me?" Stephen roared. "Just who do you think you are?" Metallic glints sparked from his eyes as he loomed before her, dwarfing her by his height and sheer mass.

He dominated Cecilia's view. She struggled to bring glittering gold to meet shimmering silver without flinching. Deliberately, she lowered her voice. "This is not an army barracks, Your Grace," she observed, grimly defiant. "I am not one of your troopers, you are *not* my commanding officer, and there's no need for your shouting for all the world to hear. But if you must ring a peal over my head, then, please, feel free to do so—*after* we are alone."

Uncharacteristically abashed, Stephen permitted no change of expression to give him away. He snapped an order to Iverson to please excuse them forthwith, doing so with less belligerency than might have been expected. As soon as the hapless butler managed a shaky bow and exited with whatever dignity he could manage, the duke returned his attention to the real object of his ire.

His jaw made rigid by the effort, he, too, lowered his voice. Deadly deep tones issued from his thick chest with controlled menace. "So," he growled, "you would accuse me of vile heartlessness toward my hirelings? Allow me to inform you that you know nothing whatsoever about it. I have *never* failed in my duty to any of my servants and I'll not let such defamation be spoken unchallenged. Each person in my employment is appreciated, *and* well paid for his work—more than in most houses, if you'd care to know."

Cecilia was immediately put in mind of her own generous salary. If she was so well paid, albeit by the dowager, it stood to reason that it was indeed the custom of the house. That Stephen could be in the right of it, and she in the wrong, did not sit too well. Moreover, she had never found it easy to back down from a chosen stance. But an innate sense of fairness refused to permit that she ignore her error. Pale gray silk skirts whispering, she sank down to the floor in an exquisitely graceful curtsy. "Your pardon, sir," she said softly, "I did not have the right to make such a charge, and I beg for your forgiveness."

All but unmanned by this show of contrition, Stephen's discomfort increased a thousandfold. She made him feel like the veriest tyrant! *Damn* the wench for her provoking ways, he inwardly raged . . . then he damned himself again for acting such an oaf. He didn't know what had upset him so about seeing Miss Langley standing close to Iverson; he thought it perhaps due to a certain estrangement he'd noticed of late between himself and his grandmother's companion. They had been on comfortable terms for some weeks, until just lately, when she

160

had seemed to become more remote. The change had irked him, leading to tonight's explosion.

The cut-crystal prisms cascading overhead scattered their light across Cecilia's bowed head. Her uniquely colored curls, darkest red, yet bright, glowed up at their viewer. Stephen felt his anger dissipate as quickly as it had come. He leaned down to take up her hands. He drew her to her feet, regretful of his temper and his foul display, wanting to recapture their earlier friendship.

With one tapered finger he gently but inexorably raised her chin. "My beautiful angel," he whispered, "look at me."

For long moments Cecilia's thick lashes hid her expression. Then she raised her eyes to meet his.

Strangely, Cecilia felt as if she might willingly drown in the mist-gray depths before her; no longer did anger cause the opaque, metallic glitter that had earlier marred the surface of his eyes. Now their expression was smoke-soft, absorbing, ready to drink up her thoughts. Held immobile by the moment, Cecilia let herself be captured by something she did not understand. She felt only the force of his eyes, the warm touch of his hands—unwilling or unable to release herself from this man's compelling look.

She, too, had missed His Grace's companionship but had deliberately avoided him since her plans for him were well in train. Also, any reminder of his interest in the lady Arabella seemed to fill her with an odd sense of loss. Yet now, the firm curves of his lips seemed to invite her touch, and a vivid memory of the feel of his mouth tempted her to partake of its resilient softness once again. Her hand seemed to rise of its own accord, wanting to reach up and brush the texture of his lips, the enticing fullness beguiling her.

None knew what might have occurred next, for the faint sound of the street knocker broke the spell. Cecilia jerked back and snatched her hand away before it achieved its objective. She grabbed up her skirts in something awfully like panic, casting her eyes about in search of a speedy exit.

Hurriedly, and without uttering a single word of excuse, she ducked her head and made for the back staircase, which—thankfully!—led away out of sight of the front hall. The kitchen servants were all fully occupied with the dinner preparations, so none was spectator to her undignified charge up the steps. Verily, Cecilia felt pursued by the legendary ten thousand devils.

At the top of the staircase, she turned to slip away down the corridor leading to her employer's door. She was prodigiously alarmed at the way she had forgotten herself! Breathless, feeling unsure and almost frightened by what she'd nearly done, she quickly tapped for permission to enter.

The dowager, every pure white hair in place, was perched on a stool before a gauze-skirted table. As soon became apparent, she was in quite a state of her own. "What kept you, gel?" she snapped. "My dresser told me I was complete to a shade a good half hour ago! I've been waiting up here all alone, when I should already be downstairs. I was beginning to think everyone 'loped off and forgot me!" She picked at the surface of a swanskin powdering puff, her vexation apparent.

"No, of course not, ma'am!" Cecilia croaked. Clearing her throat, she forced herself to regain command of her voice. "I was in the dining room and lost track of the time"—this, with more truth than she knew—"but I believe I heard someone arriving at the door as I was coming up, so we'd best go on down if you're ready."

"Well? That's what I just said, isn't it? I think your wits have gone begging tonight, Cecilia!"

Cecilia thought so, too, but this was no time to brood over her own galaxy of stupidities. The dowager had worked herself into a rare state and needed her companion's particular support. Best to get Her Grace downstairs so that the old lady could stop fretting and begin to enjoy the evening.

"Where's my fan, gel? The ivory-painted one."

"It's right here, ma'am. And I have your wrap as well." Helping the dowager adjust the generous length of a costly Malines lace shawl, Cecilia handed the old lady her favorite jewel-encrusted cane. The dowager had no need of its assistance for walking, but Cecilia had learned that Her Grace thought the accessory lent extra authority to her years.

Together they stepped out into the second floor hallway. Seeing that no footman stood by to overhear, Cecilia paused for a moment and turned to face her employer. "I want you to know that I'm sorry for the delay, ma'am," she said contritely. "Truly. I realize that I've been horribly remiss."

"Hush, now!" the dowager barked while patting Cecilia's hand in a consoling manner. "No need for apologies, and well you know it. If it comes to the point where I can't get into a taking around my own friends without them misunderstanding ... hrumph! I'm just nervous with so many people coming tonight; it's hard to conceal the appearance of inattention when I'm required to act as hostess. It has been *years* since I've dared do my own entertaining. But tonight I shall feel confident with you at my side."

This statement made it necessary for Cecilia to ask pardon yet again, but Her Grace would have none of it. "Such stuff, Cecilia," she grouched. "You and I may say just what we like to each other, I trust. No need to be putting yourself low. No need at all. We'll come through this, all flags flying." Her Grace reached the head of the grand staircase and began her descent with a firm tread.

By the time they reached the main drawing room, Cecilia felt herself so much restored by the dowager's bracing words that she even managed to deliver Iverson an encouraging wink as he held open the doors. His posture at first seemed tense, but he appeared to unbend slightly at her cheerful gesture. She hoped the duke did nothing further to up-

163

end the sorely tried butler but was herself most careful to avoid His Grace's eye as she followed the dowager into the stately apartment. Inside, two liveried footmen wearing traditional white-powdered wigs were at work, serving drinks from chased-silver trays.

Cecilia had met most of the just-arrived guests on previous occasions, and she bobbed her curtsies and murmured her pleasure at seeing them again. She paid especial attention to the dowager's position, determined that the old lady should suffer no further lack of support this night. She made certain to give her the proper cues, using the private signals they had long since worked out. Usually, a skillful repetition of a particular remark clued Her Grace to the expected reply; she would read Cecilia's lips and could thus quickly catch the gist of what was said.

The spacious Blue Drawing Room had been thrown open for the occasion. So named for the rare blue-veined marble used to construct its several high, arched window embrasures, the room now swirled with luscious fabrics and colors, attesting to the notion that London was indeed the center of Fashion. Lady Arabella was a vision in translucent gossamer silk, gathered over a satin underdress of bright citron yellow; her parents were attired in equal good taste, very much what one would expect from a family with their prestige.

Cecilia suddenly felt altogether tired of her dull mourning colors, and no matter that the material was finer than any she had ever owned before. She found herself wishful that she might wear something more attractive, more eyecatching, herself.

She would have been surprised to know that her wish was echoed by another person in the room. Stephen was in the process of concluding that Cecilia's particular shade of hair, vibrant in the light from dozens of lamps, might be better displayed against the brighter color of Lady Arabella's gown. Perhaps an old gold would be even better, and deep forest green would be splendid against Cecilia's dark red curls. So lost was he in this speculation that he had to give himself quite a mental shake when interrupted by one of his guests.

"I say there, Stephen," said Vivian Emberley brightly, "who's the Fair One who just came in with your grandmother? Damme, what a dazzler she is! Need you to introduce us, old man."

Stephen's eyes narrowed with displeasure at these encomiums. Without reference to his friend's request, however, he raised his quizzing glass as if the better to examine Viv's choice of evening wear. Forsaking a uniform, the young giant's coat was doubtlessly shaped by the hand of a master, yet the extremity of its lines came nowhere near approaching the Duke of Kelthorpe's level of understated excellence. Stephen allowed his glass to fall. With a sigh he said, "My dear Viv, the young *lady* you refer to is Grandmother's companion, so I'll thank you to be more respectful. And aren't you forgetting something? The estimable Miss Moorehead would hardly be gratified at your comments, I think."

Major Lord Emberley looked a funny cross between insulted and chiding. "Dash it, Stephen, nothing of the sort! Just appreciating bounteous terrain, don't you know."

"Yes, I do know," His Grace said dampingly. "I suppose I must make the introduction you desire, but I'll tolerate no barracks manners here, and so I warn you." Stephen suffered a painful twinge at his use of the word "barracks." Cecilia's earlier wielding of that word returned in a flash; his jaw tightened at the memory.

The earl was speedily taken aback by what seemed an unfounded attack. Before he could voice his protest against the Turkish treatment, however, the dowager duchess joined them.

"Stephen," she broke in, "you must excuse your friend for a moment. I don't believe he's yet met Cecilia."

Put to rout, Stephen abandoned his peevishness. Truth to tell, he was horrified by the way he'd let Viv's bantering remarks disturb him—remarks similar to his own thoughts, at that. It was churlish to have chastised his friend; he clapped the earl on the back by way of asking his forgiveness. "I'll permit Grandmother to do the honors, then," he said. "Miss Langley will be enchanted, I'm sure."

"Lead on!" the earl cried, happy to do as he was bid. He gave Stephen a triumphant smirk, or, at least, something as close to a smirk as his typically good humor allowed.

Cecilia looked up as the dowager duchess approached her. Her Grace had an unknown, very large but pleasant-looking gentleman in tow. By his size and age, Cecilia assumed him to be a friend of the duke's. Whatever else he was, though, she thought him an impressive addition to the company. From his puce-colored velvet lapels to the paste buckles on his evening pumps, all was correct at first glance. Still, she thought the gentleman's neckcloth was just slightly off center . . . yes, it was definitely askew . . . giving him an endearingly mussed appearance. In Cecilia's opinion, he looked like nothing so much as a mischievous, if overlarge schoolboy.

"Cecilia, I make you known to Vivian, Earl Emberley," the dowager said as they reached her. "My lord, I give you Miss Langley, my delightful companion and friend."

"Oh, delightful, indeed," the earl said as Cecilia curtsied. "I must ever bow before such entrancing loveliness!" He made a sweeping gesture before her.

"Bah! *Flatterer*," the dowager cried, turning to Cecilia. "Be careful he doesn't turn your pretty head, gel. He and Stephen have been friends this age, and the young scamps are together in some project to change the established way of things. They dare attempt to prevail upon me for support. Ha! I may even give it!"

Lord Emberley executed an especially deep bow

before the dowager duchess. "My most heartfelt thanks, dear lady, for your all-too-kind consideration. I know we may depend upon you in the end, so please accept my small expressions of gratitude. We shall be proud to count you among our esteemed supporters." Comical, fluffy-blond brows jiggled in good spirits.

Her Grace did not seem affronted by this piece of forwardness. She gave every evidence of being rather pleased at the presumption, graciously nodding her acceptance. "It seems a sound enough plan," she said.

"But what is this project, ma'am?" Cecilia asked, curious. "If you don't mind my asking, that is."

"I'll leave the earl to tell you," the dowager replied. "He's quite at the center of it, and will know best how to describe the idea. But watch your purse; this one will have your shillings before you know it!" So saying, she went off to have a word with one of the footman quietly circulating with the refreshments.

Vivian Emberley turned back to Cecilia with a winning smile. "I've not before had the pleasure of meeting you, Miss Langley," he said sociably. "You must tell me all about yourself. How long have you been at Kelthorpe House?"

Cecilia, while liking the earl's open manner, was yet careful to guard her reply. "It is kind of you to inquire, my lord, though there is not a great deal to tell. I am engaged as companion to Her Grace and have been here just over two months. But don't think to put me off, please, I'm eager to know what Her Grace meant about the plan you have undertaken to effect."

Not at all slow to conform to her bidding, the earl was happy to speak. "We call it Pen House," he began, "an idea originated by Sir John Beecham. It's a shame he's out of town tonight, or he would be here and could tell you about it himself. You see, Miss Langley, it's our intention to set up a recovery area for men returning from the Peninsula, since so many of the wounded don't get all the care they should. Some of us thought we might like to help out. Do something about it, don't y' know."

"You mean to create a hospital?"

"Well, yes and no. Oh, we'll have our own sawbones, of course—er, excuse me, miss, I meant to say surgeon—but anyway, the idea's sort of grown to include our finding work for the men who come through. After they're well, that is."

"What a marvelous idea," Cecilia said excitedly. "So you intend to do more than just sew them up and send them on? Oh, outstanding, my lord. I approve!"

Stephen drifted over in time to hear this last. As their host, he felt it his duty to steer the party on to lighter subjects. "You'll forgive my intrusion, but this is hardly the place for such serious converse," he reasoned mildly. "Not that the topic is unimportant, merely inappropriate to a social evening, I think."

In this, however, Stephen underrated his opposition.

Cecilia half lowered her lids in a play of disinterest. "Oh, good gracious, me," she said, first dipping each word in dainty droplets of sarcasm—only later wondering where she found the temerity after her earlier, forced volte-face. "How could I have been so insensible, Duke? Of course, we must confine ourselves to discussing the agreeable weather. Or, perhaps, we should remark the furnishings, or be seen sharing the latest *on-dit*? Why, Lord Emberley and I must be *ever* so indebted to you for sending us to the rightabout. I should be cast right down into the dismals, did you not remind us of the proprieties."

The subtlety of her words was not lost on either of the gentleman. "Give it over, do!" Vivian Emberley exclaimed, laughing heartily. "And you, Stephen, coming it much too strong. Wasn't two days past that I heard you say that the ladies held no opinions on matters of any real import! I'm think-

168

ing Miss Langley has showed you up good and proper!"

"And I think Cecilia's more the exception than the rule, Viv," Stephen responded sardonically.

"Oh, yes, certainly," Cecilia quickly put in. "Why, Her Grace would never interest herself in something like, say, Pen House, now, would she?"

The earl's eyes danced back and forth between the erstwhile opponents. "What-ho! Another hit!" he announced, full of glee.

Caught in a trap he suspected he'd built, Stephen manfully made shift to acknowledge his defeat. "And that puts me firmly in my place, doesn't it?" he said whimsically. He had to laugh. "Indeed, I should have known not to count on either of you to behave in the expected manner. Do continue your discussion, with my blessing."

He strolled off, leaving Cecilia elated with her victory. She turned back to the earl, wanting to return to their earlier topic. At that moment, however, she recognized something that had been teasing at the back of her mind. "But, you are a military man, sir!" she impulsively blurted out.

Thinking it was his empty cuff which had finally caught her attention, the earl ruefully eyed the offending sleeve-end. "Indeed I am, miss. Obvious, what?"

Following the movement of his eyes, Cecilia promptly corrected his inaccuracy in judging the reason for her question. "Wrong conclusion, my lord!" she crowed, her eyes sparkling as she grinned irresistibly. "It was the rod down your spine which gave away your secret. Only a soldier stands that particular way, and, as the daughter of a major, I could not fail to recognize one of His Majesty's defenders. I've followed the drum myself, if you must know—and had you three good hands, you still could not fool me!"

"Oh, famous!" the big man shouted. Vivian Emberley's ready laughter quickly brought attention from others in the room. He admitted that he, too, bore the rank of major and was currently commissioned by the Guards. For those who missed the exchange, the earl retold the tale, laughing anew with each telling. Soon the joke was shared round, the good-natured chuckles lasting until Iverson announced that dinner awaited their pleasure.

Not everyone enjoyed the merriment, however. At the end of the hours-long meal, when the ladies withdrew and left the men to relax with their wine and tobacco, Lady Arabella Dumont drew Cecilia apart in the grand marble-tiled foyer. "It was most uncalled for, Miss Langley, to draw vulgar attention to Lord Emberley's sad plight. Levity is to be deplored in such instance, you must agree."

Unprepared for this attack, Cecilia faced her antagonist and said slowly, "Nooo, I don't believe that I *can* agree with that. It was Major Lord Emberley who shared the jest with everyone, not I; and if he's comfortable, then why should we not be?"

"But where are your sensibilities, Miss Langley? For I would be excessively shocked to learn that you could be so horridly unfeeling—so insensitive to another's pain!—especially since I know you to be a gentlewoman. You must share my sentiments. And, now that you are made aware of the inappropriate quality of your remarks, I am persuaded you will understand better how to go on. I needn't remind you that as ladies both, however unequal our stations, it is our part to sympathize with the shame Lord Emberley must feel at his loss."

"Shame?" Cecilia asked. "Shame, did you say? But what can you mean, my lady? I shan't pretend to be aware of the circumstances under which Major Lord Emberley was injured, but I doubt he did anything for which he should be ashamed!"

"Well." Lady Arabella sniffed. "I didn't mean to imply that his service to his country was somehow lacking in honor. I referred, rather, to the sense of humiliation one must feel when one is less than whole."

"Less than—? No such thing, I assure you!" Cecilia said with strong good sense. "Why, the gentleman has a right to take the greatest pride in having surmounted the worst effects of his injury. I have nothing but respect for any man who overcomes such adversity."

Not wholly grasping the significance of this, and unaccustomed to having her superiority questioned, Lady Arabella nodded with satisfaction. "Quite, Miss Langley. I am so glad that you now understand."

But if Lady Arabella missed the meaning of Cecilia's imputation, there was another who did not. Preparing to rejoin the party across the hall, Stephen came upon the two in time to overhear the interchange. Giving Cecilia a look she couldn't interpret, he submitted, "And I also understand, having been set aright once myself this evening. But come, ladies, shall we rejoin the others?"

Lady Arabella at once laid a proprietary hand upon His Grace's arm. Turning her back on the dowager's companion, and without so much as giving it a thought, she swept into the Blue Room with all the perquisites of her position.

Cecilia, thus deprived of escort, sought a much-needed refuge with her employer. She felt confused by Stephen's words, and she reflected upon how the evening seemed one for cutting up her peace. There seemed to be no end to its discord! Never before one to develop headaches, Cecilia feared that she was in imminent danger of just such a malady.

Led by Lord Rutheven, the other gentlemen filed in momentarily. Lady Dumont spoke up when all were returned. "Your Grace," she addressed their host, "you must prevail upon my Arabella to entertain our little assembly. She sings and plays with exceptional, even superior talent, if you will credit that a fond parent does not boast overmuch. I'm sure she would be agreeable to playing for us if *you* made the request. My daughter must ever wish to please, and I think you have only to say the word!" She tittered meaningfully.

Seeing no recourse but to accede to this suggestion, Stephen appealed to Lady Arabella to honor them with a recital.

Accordingly, and as convention required, the young lady dithered prettily for some minutes before acquiescing to the flattering entreaties. While she went to seat herself before the rosewood pianoforte, the others comfortably situated themselves in the chairs dispersed around the room. Lady Dumont conjured up her daughter's favorite sheets of music to deposit on the music rack, while Lady Arabella requisitioned the duke's assistance in adjusting the stool. She then gracefully positioned her fingers over the polished ivory keys.

Cecilia and the dowager almost collided as they quietly rushed to a backless bench farthest away in one corner.

"Knew I should have hauled that oversize hunk of terror out and burned it!" the old lady muttered darkly. The Broadwood-built pianoforte stood innocently on its handsomely carved legs, quite unconscious of its censure. "Why ever is it," Her Grace continued on a raspy whisper, "that the gels insist on thinking everyone must be enthralled by their musical efforts?" Her Grace was particularly disgruntled because she had been about to suggest that the card tables be set up, when Lady Dumont had usurped her in the matter.

Unaware of any disaffection in the ranks, with her skirts circling about her in the most becoming way, Lady Arabella favored her listeners with a smile before launching into a sentimentally sweet ballad of love unrequited. Stephen had taken up a place alongside the keyboard to turn the pages of her music, and, as Lady Arabella's practiced notes rolled out, he stood tall and sinfully handsome by her side.

Free to observe him as he was thus occupied, Cecilia couldn't help but to admire his unruffled poise. There was something altogether too seductive about the man for her to resist as she knew she ought.

172

She felt a desire, a pulling sensation, whenever he was near. It made her want to step inside the space of his arms, where he might hold her safe from the world. She wanted him to hold her with all his great strength, to hold her forever close, so that never again would she feel unwanted or unloved, someone of no value to be discarded at will.

Oh, she had tried to keep away from him. She had reminded herself constantly that she mustn't encourage him like she had on a darkened staircase so long ago. That was a happenstance not to be repeated. But was he aware of the feelings he aroused in her? And just what did it signify—to him—to her? Cecilia had no ready answer. She knew only that she suffered a strong attraction whenever he was near, one which must be avoided.

She was distracted by a different thought. She recalled the duke's response when he had come upon her and the Dumont in the hallway not so many minutes ago. She gathered that he'd heard some part of the dispute, but she couldn't be sure whether he had meant to take her part or Lady Arabella's. Surely, no one of sense would think Major Lord Emberley to blame for his unfortunate injury. His Grace would be the first to agree. Perhaps not, though, if the raven-haired beauty was all but promised to him. Loyalty might make him take her ladyship's part.

And what matter if he did? "Miss Langley" had enjoyed his good opinion when she had thought she needed it to stay at Kelthorpe House; why should she care whether he thought well of her now, when she knew Her Grace was in no danger from him?

Yet it did matter. Terribly.

Squaring her shoulders above the backless seat, Cecilia tried to suppress her foolish yearnings and concentrate on the music. However, when Lady Arabella thrust her high, dulcet voice into yet another song, Cecilia became aware that her seatmate was contending with certain problems of her own. The dowager duchess seemed to be having trouble controlling an uneasy twitching. Certainly Her Grace was far too well bred to permit any obvious show of distress, but her slight, annoyed movements alerted Cecilia, sitting so close beside her.

The old dear must be bored silly. With her acute deafness, she could scarcely hear the music, could see little more than the backs of her guests, and, doubtlessly, she was fatigued by the whole thing. Even before age brought a decline in her hearing, the dowager would be the first to admit that she could not enjoy young girls' recitals.

Cecilia set herself to devising a solution to Her Grace's predicament.

Surreptitiously, she tapped her employer upon the wrist. Looking down, the dowager made her a slow, regal nod. To the rest of the company the pair seemed relaxed thereinafter, sitting quietly with their eyes on their laps. Song followed song as the peeress's repertoire was gradually reduced, while the hostess and her companion gave every evidence of pleasure at the entertainment provided.

Only Stephen discerned the true reason for their nearly motionless state. His eye made out the tiny movements of the two ladies hands; an old children's game was in progress.

Paper . . . scissors . . . rock!

CHAPTER FIFTEEN

"More coffee, Your Grace?"

"Just leave the pot where I can reach it, please" came the inattentive answer.

"Very good, Your Grace. Will there be anything else?"

Assured that nothing more was required, the underbutler arranged the silver urn within reach as instructed. He then left by way of a discreet side door, leaving the young duke alone in the pastel-carpeted breakfast room.

Stephen absently sipped from his cup. The delicately made china gleamed whitely through his strong, sun-browned fingers. With his back to the open windows overlooking the gardens beyond, he relaxed to the feel of warm sunshine streaming across the width of his shoulders. It was time to rethink his relationship with his grandmother's *séduisante* companion, he decided.

At first he had been merely intrigued by the episode with the young miss in Tôrres Vedras, then was angered and made suspicious by their unexpected reunion in Hyde Park. The subsequent meeting with Cecilia in his library had served to totally disarm him, however, and in the last few weeks—well, in the last few weeks he had discovered that he enjoyed her bright if sometimes perilously outspoken company. He realized that with each new incident he had become further and yet further involved with the audacious red-haired beauty. *But had he really been about to kiss her beneath the chandelier's soft light?*

Oh, yes. He knew he had.

She tempted him, taunted him, and completely entranced him. Those huge warm brown eyes lured him to plumb their depths and dared him to excite her passion. And he knew that passion rode just beneath the surface of their relationship. He felt the strength of desire every time they met, and the signs were unmistakable that she felt it, too. He yearned to have her in his arms and in his bed, to see her eyes become softly drugged by his kisses and to hear her cry out for him. Why this should be he did not question. He simply accepted it as real.

Even at the first of the evening, in the dining room, when she had gone on the attack over what she had regarded as his mistreatment of his servants, he had wanted her. She had stood there so gallantly, so bravely, that for a moment he had found himself eager to add his own shield to her cause. It didn't seem to matter whether he had been the reason for her raised sword. For Cecilia was a woman who had faced the worst sort of reverses in life with precious little help from anyone. Yet, without hesitation she had leapt to the defense of one whom she thought needful. He admired her for it. He wished there was some way to assure she could hold to that gloriously *undaunted* outlook forever.

But the dilemma he faced this morning was not so much about the particulars of his attraction to the tall young miss, or her attraction to him. It was more a problem of ethics. Lingering over the remains of his early meal, Stephen considered the delicate circumstances.

It was not only unseemly for him to give in to his desires and form a private liaison with one of his household, it was patently dishonorable. Affairs of that sort were not conducted right under one's own roof, after all. Unfortunately, honor also prevented him from initiating a proposal to Cecilia that she should change her current position and become his

176

mistress, not even did he set her up at a separate address. That would impinge on his grandmother's prerogatives.

Of course, Cecilia might come to such a decision on her own—although he scrupled to insinuate that she *should*—since, by her own admission, she was of no more than mediocre background and without any great family name to uphold. But supposing the beguiling young miss did indicate a preference in accordance with his own. Could he then in good conscience take her into his possession . . . were she willing . . . and did she make the suggestion herself?

Stephen straightened in his seat as pride gave him the answer. Disregarding the fact that his world would find nothing amiss if he took Miss Langley to live in a separate establishment; as a gently bred young woman, she deserved better from him. "And she *is* under my protection," he admitted aloud.

If only he could trust himself . . .

Another thing bothered him, too, something about the young woman that didn't sit square. A touch of mystery lingered about her origins, even after he'd quizzed that Dockery fellow and all seemed in order. But no. He really had no reason to harbor doubts about Cecilia's right to his regard.

Stephen scowled in self-disgust. No help for it. If he couldn't conquer his desire for Miss Langley, then he must avoid her, and that was that. Grandmother seemed satisfied with her companion's service, so he could not interfere despite his own desires. He must not let his personal wants get in the way, either, of another matter begging his attendance. He was in London for a purpose.

Lady Arabella Dumont was a bit of a moonling, true, but she was a great beauty with all the customary attainments. Of impeccable family, she would make an admirable duchess, and, if she wasn't able to understand the front page of the *Review*, what did it matter? It was the way of their

177

world for a wife to attend to domestic and social concerns, leaving politics and statecraft to the husband.

This last thought left him feeling weary. There were fully four weeks left before the Season ended, though—plenty of time to make up his mind before coming to any marital decisions.

While Stephen remained at his morning meal, Cecilia had gone out into the spacious back gardens behind Kelthorpe House to engage in her own reflections. After an irksome night, she had risen early, taking her embroidery threads to check them against a bed of periwinkles. She proposed to use the color to adorn a reticule and slippers for the dowager, decorating those items with stitchery designs of her employer's favorite flower.

Ascertaining the appropriate shade, Cecilia claimed a sun-warmed bench in the rose arbor, well out of sight of both the house and the mews. A double-dished fountain made a pretty tinkling sound close by, while birds scolded and chirped in the shrubbery.

Since the duke often strode out the back way rather than wait for his horse or his sporty new curricle to be brought around to the front, she had chosen her spot of concealment so as to avoid further encounters between them. At least, not until she had got her thoughts together. After last night's events, she felt the need for privacy to consider her proper response. Hours spent the night before, wadding up bedpillows, first one way and then the other, had left her feeling hagged.

The man is causing me to loose my sleep! she silently cried to the cloudless skies.

No. She must face the truth. She had caused her own problems.

His Grace—Stephen—never had been the blackguard she had so foolishly tried to paint him. She had known it for some time now. Her original misjudgment might have stemmed from his ofttimes

178

high-handed ways, but her sordid suspicions went beyond anything he had brought upon himself. Instead, Stephen had proved to be an upright man who would never mistreat his kin, a man whom her father would have approved. Clearly, too, her plot to influence his bride-choice had been unnecessary, so why had she persisted, more especially in the terrible expectation that her identity might any day be discovered?

When she'd seen the great hug Stephen had given his grandmother after he had wrongly accused her of meddling—accusations caused by her own attempts to fix his interest with Miss Whitte or the baroness—that's when *it* had happened. That's when she had, without any real awareness, decided to stay as long as she could and bedamned to the consequences. She had persisted in her plot to find him a wife, clinging to the excuse that she was assuring Her Grace's future. What had made her do such a thing?

Possibly, she had acted from stubbornness. She hadn't wanted to leave her comfortable place here, so she'd forged ahead with her plans to arrange Stephen's life for him. She had, willfully, it seemed, convinced herself that she needed to ensure against His Grace settling on a wife who might later threaten his grandmother's position. But if, indeed, that was the reason she'd stayed, it would make her guilty of a fault that Miss Sheldon had often warned her she was prone to: self-blinding opinionations. Was that why she had kept to her place at Kelthorpe House?

There was no sense in denying the risk she ran, either, for it was a guinea to a groat that the duke had sent queries to the Continent long since. While another might have convinced herself that the library interview had satisfied the duke about her history, Cecilia was not such a hoddypoll. She knew that only the irregularities of wartime had prevented his learning the truth. Oh, she had brought herself to a pretty pass and no mistake.

"So what's to do now?" she questioned in a whisper borne aloft by the May morning breeze.

She squared her slim shoulders, pulling her spine upright. A decision had to be made whether to leave now—something that in prudence she should have done weeks before—or whether to chance discovery by remaining a bit longer. Forcing herself to search out the truth, though, she had to admit that there was more to *it* than that. There was something else that compelled her to stay, and she must ruthlessly seek out the reason. Gingerly, she probed a sensitive area in her memory.

Was it because of some absurd idea about the first, indeed, the only man to have kissed her? Perhaps that was why she had remained here. Last night when she'd looked into Stephen's eyes and stared at the petal-soft curves of his mouth, she'd caught herself contemplating a future filled with his kisses. As if a duke would ever consider a union with a virtually nameless Miss Nobody! Yet she had, for a moment, leaned into his arms and felt herself suffused with a desire to give her every thought into his care, to touch him more intimately. . . .

So. There it was, then. No more roundaboutations. Cecilia suddenly knew the name for *it*, the name for what she was feeling. She recognized what had caused her absurd and, indeed, quite dangerous behavior.

It was *love*. Oh, yes, she had been stubborn all right, stubborn in misreading her heart!

Certainly, she had known that love was something that often grew with time, but somehow she'd never expected it to come creeping up like a sly and clever cutpurse. With a sinking sensation, she wondered if this newly recognized emotion wasn't why she had stayed on so long.

"Oh, damn and blast. The whole thing is impossible," she muttered to the sky. If His Grace for an instant suspected her feelings, he would laugh himself into a fit. Sought after by the most glamorous exclusives in the kingdom, he would never give her a second look. She was too tall, too outspoken, and far beneath him in fortune and name. Or, rather, the name was good. Her father had served the crown with distinction, and Uncle *was* a "1661 man." Could she but tell of it.

A sparrow in a nearby bush was considerably startled by an unusual word Cecilia once learned from a trooper whose rifle misfired.

Even if her story was never uncovered, though, she couldn't remain and watch Stephen wed another. It would be agonizing, devastating, to watch him march down the aisle with the lady Arabella. But would it not be even more unbearable to leave now and lose all contact? Not with the man who had so boldly teased her, sternly corrected her, and then called her his "beautiful angel." That would be asking too much.

She was decided, then. She would stay for as long as she could. She would continue to assist her employer—she'd become adroit in that charade, at least—and she would remain until and unless her fraud was discovered. Of course, she would have to leave then, and hastily.

"A ha'penny?"

Cecilia gave a little jump and turned toward the speaker.

"I'm offering for your thoughts."

The duke, wearing highly polished top boots and dressed for riding, stood but a few feet away. Although she'd troubled to take shelter from casual discovery, he had glimpsed her bright hair through the leafy arbor, its color contrasting against the softer pinks of the roses.

She practically stuttered in stupefaction at his sudden appearance. "N-no thoughts. T-truly. And you shouldn't sneak up on me so!" *How mortifying to be caught woolgathering, and now of all times.* She ducked her head and clutched the silks she'd carried out to the garden.

Unaccountably ignoring his earlier promise to

avoid temptation, Stephen was nearly as much surprised as she when his footsteps had brought him to her side. Still, he couldn't resist teasing, "Evasive moves, Cecilia? I had thought better of you. This cannot be the same virago who made me such a blistering denunciation last night. Come, come. Tell me what you were thinking of."

"Um—er—?" She frantically searched for an answer. "Oh! Colors. Yes! I was just wondering if I'd chosen the right shades for my embroidery." She hastened to hold up the bundle of silks she'd brought out for comparison.

Pretending to accord the matter his attention, Stephen studied the blue and green threads she held up for his inspection. "Periwinkle, is it?" He touched the skein she'd already chosen. "Ah, this one, I think." The lines at the corners of his eyes spread fanlike into a warm smile. Cecilia caught a fascinating glimpse of strong white teeth.

He sat down on the bench beside her to confide, "You cannot misdirect an experienced campaigner with such false maneuvers, you know. It was another matter entirely that put that pensive look on your face. Perhaps you think I criticized you too severely last night. . . . No? That's not it?" He seemed to read her answer, though she said not a word. "Possibly, you were thinking of how much you enjoyed the music after dinner. Have I got it right yet? Hmmm. No, I can see that's not it." His lips parted in a slight, knowing smile. "Or, perhaps"—he leaned closer, reading the truth in her eyes—"you were remembering . . . this."

If she'd not already been seated, Cecilia would have fallen down in shock. Gently at first, he touched her lips with his, before pulling her closer and yet still closer. As his kiss deepened, she welcomed his lips, eager to discard her confused and muddled thoughts. Liquid warmth welled up within her, suffusing her limbs with marvelous heat. Somewhere in the hazy reaches of her mind, she decided that his first kiss was as nothing compared to this! She felt impossibly drowsy and yet remarkably alert, all at one and the same time. Each breath he drew became hers. The strong hand at her nape was her guide. Spinning beyond time, she responded to each movement he made with heightened perception. *Oh, my love!* her heart sang out, willing the kiss to go on forever.

With a show of reluctance he completed the contact as gently as it had begun. "Have I guessed right?" he asked softly, exploring the sweet curve of her cheek with his forefinger.

She couldn't seem to open her mouth. She tried clearing her throat, but still the words wouldn't come. Anyway, what on earth could she say?

More than anything, Cecilia found herself wanting to confess the truth to him—all of it—everything. She wanted to tell him who she really was and why she'd run away from Linscombe Hall; most of all, she wanted to tell him that she loved him with all her being. Her brain, once more in control, begged her to reconsider. She should make objection, strong objection, against his remaining so near.

Without waiting for an answer, Stephen reached for a curl that lay close to hand, twiddling the soft, shining strand against his thumb. Coaxingly, he asked, "Were you remembering last night, Cecilia? Or were you remembering another date: one afternoon last August, on the stairway of a little Portuguese infirmary?"

His questions killed any protest she might have made. She could only nod, her eyes overlarge, waiting to see what might happen next.

But Stephen didn't know *what* should happen next.

Here he was, in the broad light of day, disregarding that very code of honor he'd so lately invoked. Not that he cared for any breach of social precepts—a peer of his distinction had no need to consider the gossip's tongues—but to have broken faith with his own principles of conduct was, for him, a real scandal. No help for it now, duty bade him rectify the wrong he had done.

"Miss Langley," he clipped out smartly, springing to attention and staring at a point just above her head. "I cannot ask your forgiveness; my actions are inexcusable. I will speak to Mr. Dockery and obtain his permission to pay my addresses." He consciously concealed the violent turmoil seething within his breast.

At this, Cecilia blinked roundly and seemed to locate her voice. She bounded to her feet, her bright eyes discharging angry gold sparks. "Confound you, sir, you'll do no such thing! Oh, how dared you to think I would allow it?"

Reluctantly, he faced her. He took in her brave stance and almost gave in to an urge to gather her close and hold her fast. He fought to counter his foolish desire with words to resolve this crisis. Taking refuge in the brisk military style of speech which had served him so well on the battlefield, he said, "I regret your feelings, but emotions cannot be of any concern to us under these circumstances."

Actually, being in the midst of an unprecedented turmoil of mind, he was less aware of the content of his words than of the need for recompense for his beastly actions. Holding himself under stringent control, he continued. "And I take full responsibility as is my right and proper duty, Miss Langley. You must know that an offer of marriage can be the only solution to my trespass."

He should not have been astonished when Cecilia responded with the unexpected, instead of the gratitude which should have marked her reply. "Oh?" Her voice rang with challenge. "So it was perfectly all right for you to kiss a nameless nurse in Tôrres Vedras, was it, but not so well to kiss a Miss Langley of Kelthorpe House? What chivalrous conceit, sir! Well, I think that I should have something to say on the topic, and I say you will not speak of this occurrence to anyone. I forbid it, do you hear? Furthermore," she raged, "if you don't care to apologize—and indeed, I agree that there's no reason you should be sorry for what, after all, I allowed—then you must accept *my* apology and have done with this farce!" She directed him a scathing look and then turned on her heel, quitting his company without so much as a backward glance.

Left thus in a state of bewildered bemusement, Stephen watched her graceful, if hurried, exit. He'd offered his hand for the first time in his life and been flatly rejected. He felt a strong sense of the greatest ill usage.

Farce? She *forbids?* Did she really think he would accept her answer? There was a world of difference between a hospital drudge and a duchess's companion, and nothing she could say would change that. He set off in speedy pursuit to tell her again, and in terms she could not fail to understand, that he would have her to wife—whether she willed it or no!

With long, ground-covering strides he followed his quarry straightly into the house. Through the lush conservatory stretching across the back of the building; past the unoccupied, sunny breakfast room; and on into the pink-floored front hall. His progress was rapid. Ignoring the various servants halted mid-act as he traversed the several rooms, he was intent only on overtaking Cecilia's lead. Before he could obtain his objective, however, Iverson interrupted his progress at the base of the main staircase.

The butler held out a travel-stained packet. "A special post for you, Your Grace. From the Continent, I believe." If Iverson associated the duke's errand with Miss Langley's rush through the hall not one minute before, nothing of it showed in the servant's demeanor.

Stephen nearly groaned in frustration. By now Cecilia would have made it to her own bedchamber, where he certainly could not follow. He resigned himself to delay. "Very well. Thank you," he said brusquely, accepting the proffered letter. "And,

Iverson, send word up to Miss Langley—and Grandmother—that I desire their presence in the library in an hour. In precisely one hour."

Experienced troopers had snapped to in sprightly form in the face of such clipped, authoritative tones, and the head butler to Kelthorpe House was no exception. He all but ran to effect his errand.

CHAPTER SIXTEEN

Destiny decreed still further complications to a situation moving swiftly from bad to worse. Whatever the contents of the letter Stephen held, it would soon be discovered that other correspondence, all of a domestic nature, was also having its effect.

Miss Jane Sheldon had discerned something actionable in the last parcel of mail she had received from the metropolis. For weeks she'd been content to let matters unfold as they would, but upon receipt of her latest intelligence, the loyal old governess had forwarded a reply and had at once packed up her traps. And as she had gone about arranging for transport, more news was passed on by an old acquaintance which urged her to her purpose.

Thus, while Her Grace's guests were making their way to Cavendish Square early on Thursday evening, Miss Sheldon was at the point of stepping down from a hackney carriage in the Kennington area, just a few miles away.

"Quite thrilled to have you here at last, dear Jane!" Mrs. Dockery cried in welcome. "It was *such* a relief when I had your note to say you were coming, for I certainly don't know what's to do." Mrs. Dockery then went on dramatically, "Oh, I just couldn't think how to manage. Poor Cecilia was here not two hours ago, and you wouldn't have recognized her, such a long face she had. I didn't tell her that you might come for a visit because she was looking so sadly *pulled*, don't you know."

Neatly attired in a lightweight, three-quarter-length spencer and a matching toque in a practical dark blue color, Miss Sheldon entered the well-lit foyer of the Dockerys' home. Pausing to give her old friend a hug, she turned to instruct the jarvey where to set down her bags.

A shadow was seen moving up the walkway in the gloam of early evening.

"Great heavens, what *is* it?" Mrs. Dockery shrieked in awful tones. "Quickly, Jane! Shut the door!"

Miss Sheldon glanced over her shoulder. "Amelia, calm yourself. I have brought with me Cecilia's pet, Marpessa." The big Briard had hopped down from the coach and was bent on following Miss Sheldon inside.

"Oh, I see. A pet," Mrs. Dockery conceded doubtfully. "But, Jane, when Cecilia referred to the dog she'd left in your keeping, I thought she meant, well, a dog. This looks more like a—a nightmare! Does she . . . does she bite, do you know?"

Miss Sheldon's soft chuckles made their own answer. "Marpessa, say hello to my friend, please," she directed.

A deep "woof" came in response.

The plump little solicitor's wife made a droll face, though she was far from being reassured. "Well, if you think it's safe, then I suppose it must be. And there's plenty of room in the back garden," she added hopefully. The Briard stood nearly waist-high to the two little ladies, so Mrs. Dockery might be forgiven if she felt herself overwhelmed.

"No need, Amelia," Miss Sheldon answered. "Marpessa is entirely civilized and much used to being indoors. We've quite enjoyed each other's company for several weeks now, you see, and have come to know each other very well. You may depend upon it, she will do nothing to cause us discomfort."

But a horrendous great howl at once belied these words!

From somewhere within the house, there came a

lamentable noise that had the waiting jarvey boggle-eyed in terror. Miss Sheldon had taken his fare from her reticule and he saw it waiting, still held in the palm of her hand. He snatched up the sum, turned, and plunged down the steps, not pausing even to count out his tip! At the posting house he'd debated with himself about carrying such an unlikely pair; now he was sure his worst fears were about to be realized.

Barely aware of the driver's precipitous retreat, Miss Sheldon hastened toward the continuing sound. She was closely followed by her hostess. The door to a small sitting room stood wide open; apparently, this led to the source of the commotion. Crouched in front of a chintz-covered sofa, with her muzzle aimed at the ceiling, Marpessa loosed another great, agonizing note just as Miss Sheldon and her hostess made it through the doorway. The deep, baying outcry brought servants up from every corner of the house.

"Dear me," Miss Sheldon exclaimed in dismay. "Whatever could be wrong? Oh, you did say that Cecilia was here earlier? Did she perchance sit over there?" By now Jane Sheldon was shouting her words, pointing toward the offending sofa. She could hardly be heard over the din caused by the unhappy canine, not to mention the excited squeals and screams emitted by various menials rushing to the scene.

"Yes, yes! To be sure, she did!" Mrs. Dockery raised her voice in answer. "But what does it mean? Oh, Jane! What do we do?"

Miss Sheldon hurried over to her grieving charge and snatched up a front paw. Magically, the wailing notes came to an end.

While Miss Sheldon soothed the Briard, Mrs. Dockery looked on in amazement. Seeing that things were under control, Mrs. Dockery thanked her servants for their response before shooing them out. When these last were returned to their business, the goodwife's questions flew thick and fast.

"Do dogs always go on like that? Doesn't she like it here after all? I must be agreeable to keeping it . . . her . . . here if you think it needful, but will she *sing* for us again, do you think? I do hope not. I cannot imagine how we should manage—and did the neighbors hear it? How embarrassing if they should complain! Can we somehow keep her a little less *vocal?*"

With Marpessa safely quieted, Miss Sheldon pledged the dog's cooperation. "Please do forgive the outburst," she said with a chagrined look toward her hostess. "I think it must have been the smell."

"Smell? Do you say *smell!*" Amelia Dockery looked properly outraged. "Why, my dearest Jane, whatever can you mean? Mr. Dockery assures me that I keep house perfectly well. I know it to be true—I've always taken such pride! There cannot be a single reason why Cecilia's pet should take exception to my housekeeping, for I'm sure Sally cleaned in here, just like I asked her to, right after this afternoon's visit. And anyway," she then wailed, "we had only tea and buns!"

"Amelia, you miscomprehend my meaning." Miss Sheldon barely stifled her laughter at her old friend's concerns. "I meant only that Marpessa must have located Cecilia's scent, telling her that her mistress had recently been here. Briards are very perceptive and loyal dogs, and she's most eager to be returned to her proper owner."

The solicitor's spouse allowed herself to be mollified by this answer. "But, Jane," she next asked, "how on earth did you manage to get her to stop like you did? One minute it sounded as if we were sure to raise the dead, and then you came in, and—just like that—it all ceased. It was the most amazing thing! I *know* that I should never have managed it so—"

"Easiest trick there is," Miss Sheldon interrupted. Like Cecilia, she knew not to hesitate to break into her dear friend's chatter. She calmly went on with her explanation. "You see, Amelia, a dog, by its nature, will not bark or howl if someone gently holds its paw. I cannot say that I understand it exactly, but it's a method my father once taught me. There," Miss Sheldon said with a final scratching of black silky ears. "I think we need concern ourselves no further about Marpessa. And I'm afraid we've worse things yet to consider. Just as I was setting out from Hazelmere, the Linscombes' housekeeper saw me and gave out a piece of news that I expect will substantially affect matters here. We're in the suds, Amelia. Dished, in fact."

"No, don't tell me," Mrs. Dockery moaned, clapping plump hands over her ears. "Not another word until I've seen you to your room and made you comfortable. I don't know whether to be glad or sorry that Mr. Dockery is away from town just now, but whatever horrid thing has happened, can we not leave it until after supper? So very bad for the digestion, my dear, unless it simply cannot wait?"

Miss Sheldon nodded her head at this. "No reason why we can't eat first," she replied. "I'm feeling half starved, and there's nothing to be done until the morrow, in any case. By all means, let us have our meal in peace." She followed her hostess up to the bedchamber prepared for her, the Briard trotting obediently, if reluctantly, at their heels.

Only after a very nice dinner of stewed hare, lamb cutlets, and a wealth of spring vegetables, removed by a blackberry tart, did they return to the topic of Miss Sheldon's reason for visiting. Requesting that a tea tray be brought to the sitting room, Mrs. Dockery signaled her readiness to listen.

But Marpessa had something to add. She had been shut out of both the dining room and the back parlor while the meal was served, and so, at the reopened door to this last-named room, she went immediately to the preferred sofa and once again threatened to "sing." Grabbing a forepaw, Miss Sheldon barely averted a second disaster.

"*Dear* Jane," Mrs. Dockery advanced, observing

191

the occurrence, "we really must reunite Cecilia with her pet at the earliest possible moment. Do, please, say you will consider it."

Eyeing the heavy black paw resting in her hand, the old governess was not behindhand in making her agreement. "But first," Miss Sheldon said ominously, "I must pass on Mrs. Tucker's latest account."

From that moment forward, she was assured of Mrs. Dockery's attention. It took all of an hour to explain the matter, mainly because Mrs. Dockery had not before heard the story of Cecilia's chaperone on shipboard, Mrs. Perkins, nor about certain other details of relevance.

"And so," Miss Sheldon finished her report, "Mrs. Perkins lately saw Cecilia here in town, asked a few questions, and then sent word to Sir Andrew of her findings. According to the Linscombes' housekeeper, we may expect him in London in two days or less."

Her words had every effect she could have wished for.

"Great heavens, what's to be done?" Mrs. Dockery gasped. "Though I suppose I should have expected it, what with Cecilia out and about so much, but, I confess, this has caught me quite by surprise! I gathered from the first that Cecilia's actual name needed to be kept our secret—even Mr. Dockery doesn't know the whole—but if what you say is true, and the poor girl is also underage, the baronet can drag her back quicker than a cat can lick her ear. All our plans, Jane!" she cried out in dismay. "If we hadn't enough problems already. What with Kelthorpe too blind to see what a rare *prize* our girl is, and now this nasty, odious Mrs. Perkins—I'd like to just pinch her, I would!"

"Pleasant thought," Miss Sheldon agreed. "However, I must hold myself to blame that Cecilia is now in such sad case. In my conceit, I wanted to grant her the opportunity of coming to London to become acquainted with a nice young man who

192

would see what a darling she is. I never meant for her to fix upon a duke, yet from your letters, we must believe that she has."

But Mrs. Dockery would not allow it. "Indeed, Jane, it is not your fault," she instantly declared. "You see, I *knew* the dowager duchess had a handsome young grandson just out of the military, and I also knew that he and Cecilia were likely to meet. Why, I even hoped that they would. To be sure, I was overjoyed when he came seeking a wife, and, rather than counsel Cecilia to guard her heart, as I should have done, I actually encouraged her interest by asking about him each week. I thought she *deserved* to aim as high as she pleased!" Her plump little chin quivered as she then snuffled out her next words. "Yet from all I could tell, he sounded so ideal. He has been a military man and most sensible throughout his command. But now? Now the poor girl is made most unhappy, and it is all my doing. That's the reason I wrote and asked if you could come, Jane. I've made such a mess of things!" The lawyer's goodwife blindly pulled a napkin from the tea tray to catch up the tears trickling down her round cheeks.

Marpessa, sensitive to the emotions surrounding her, came to lay her fine black muzzle on Mrs. Dockery's knees. Much appeased by this show of support, Mrs. Dockery dried her eyes and timidly rubbed a finger in the hollow between the dog's sympathetic eyes.

"Well," Jane Sheldon said firmly, "we will just have to risk stirring the waters, it seems. Our appearance at Kelthorpe House cannot make matters any worse, and the sooner we put it to the touch, the quicker the matter can mend. Who knows? Something may yet develop."

"And we must not delay!" Mrs. Dockery added. "There's word about town that the Duke of Kelthorpe is any day expected to pop the question—and to someone *quite* unsuitable."

* * *

Shortly after the hour of ten the next morning, the Dockerys' smart carriage drew to a halt before Kelthorpe House. Iverson recognized the equipage and promptly gave entry to its occupants, though he did wonder why no one had informed him that visitors were expected. When the Briard wove her way in through the open front door, he next questioned his eyesight—as did two footmen and a startled housemaid—particularly when the huge dog passed them all by and started a beeline trot right up the grand staircase. They stood frozen, immobile, as Marpessa reached the top and, without a sound, disappeared down the corridor leading to the ladies' wing.

Such effrontery.

Just as the butler sought to make his objections known, Miss Sheldon demanded his attention. "That is Miss Cecilia's pet, so I trust you won't mind," she said with authority. "Also, if you would be so kind, please inform Miss Lin—Miss *Langley*, and Her Grace, as well, that Miss Jane Sheldon and Mrs. Lawrence Dockery have come to call. You might mention that we are here on a matter of some urgency."

Iverson rose to the occasion. At a gesture, the gaping servants were called to order and he himself did the honors in showing the visitors into the Rose Room. Normally, they would have been taken to a lesser waiting area, but something about the situation made him decide that his choice was the more suitable. He was familiar with Mrs. Dockery's association with the house, and whoever this Miss Sheldon might be, she certainly seemed respectable enough.

On his way first to the dowager's apartments, Iverson met Cecilia in the above-stairs corridor. Her expression was one of such shining happiness that he knew he'd done right not to impede the monstrous canine's progress. Not fifteen minutes ago, after he'd delivered notice of His Grace's summons, Miss Langley had looked so woeful that it had near wrung Iverson's heart. But Miss Langley had nonetheless thanked him for the communication, just as she ought.

"Iverson, look," she now exulted, making an effort to hold her voice to a reasonable pitch. "It's Marpessa. My 'Pessa is here, do you see?" She bent to dig slim fingers into the Briard's thick ruff while the dog gazed up at her adoringly.

"Yes, miss. So I understand," the butler returned, pleased that she showed such ladylike restraint. Not that he'd have blamed her did she shout her good news, for it was obvious that the dog held a special place in her affections. "And you will find a Miss Sheldon and a Mrs. Dockery in the Rose Room, awaiting your presence as well, miss. I'm on my way now with word to Her Grace to come and join you." He was further approving when Miss Langley remembered to say most politely that she was obliged, before she sped on her way.

The dowager, with years of experience to add polish to her decorum, showed herself equally capable in meeting the unprecedented events. When she had her communiqué about visitors, the butler received no more than a cultured "Thank you, I'll be down directly."

Scarce able to modulate her steps, Cecilia descended the staircase with Marpessa following right behind. She kept dashing anxious looks over her shoulder every so often, as if to be sure that her pet was really with her and not a mere figment of her longings. When she greeted her friends and embraced them both, still, her eyes kept returning to her minion.

"Oh, Miss Sheldon, I cannot say how much this means to me. I was never so surprised as when I heard that precious scratching at my door." Cecilia dropped to the floor to chuck Marpessa under the chin. "You cannot know how much I've missed her! But I must say she is looking very fine from your care, and I thank you from the bottom of my heart."

Cecilia then hopped back up and squeezed tiny Miss Sheldon once again.

"And you have been missed as well, dear girl!" Mrs. Dockery spoke up. "Such a commotion last night in the parlor when your beastie got wind of your presence. I daresay there's not been so much excitement in my house in who knows how long! Not that I minded *too* much—not since it's over— but Jane knows a trick that she must teach you. Now that I know the way of it, I may even consider a sweet little pug for myself. Now, I wonder why we don't have a dog already? I had no idea that they were so very interesting, or so remarkably *devoted*. Yes, I must speak to Mr. Dockery about a pug. You understand that we will prefer something a bit smaller than—"

Her voice faded to a halt as Iverson opened the wide paneled door to announce the dowager duchess. Both Mrs. Dockery and Jane Sheldon rose immediately and sank into curtsies, while Cecilia ran to give Her Grace a great hug.

"Isn't it wonderful, ma'am?" Cecilia cried. "This is my very good friend, Miss Jane Sheldon, come with Mrs. Dockery to bring my Marpessa to visit me. I am so excited, please forgive me, but it's been so very hard—!" Her eyes brimming with tears, Cecilia bent to hide her face in the Briard's heavy coat.

While Cecilia took a few moments to recover herself, the dowager requested the butler to set out refreshments. "Coffee," she declared. "Very strong coffee, and perhaps some sherry as well."

Iverson made no sign that he found the order for this last beverage in any way unusual, though it was not yet eleven of the clock. He, too, had collected that the occasion might call for something more substantial than tea; the expressions on Mrs. Dockery's and Miss Sheldon's faces indicated that there was more afoot than had yet been disclosed.

When the butler shut the door behind him to effect his errand, the dowager duchess bid everyone to be seated. "Cecilia," she remarked, "I don't think your pet is the only reason for our receipt of this visit." She turned a sharp eye on the visitors. "Am I correct, ladies?"

Mrs. Dockery drew a long breath and said simply, "Yes, Your Grace. We are here because Miss Linscombe needs us. Miss *Cecilia* Linscombe."

At this, Cecilia sucked in her breath and bolted upright from the green-and-white striped fabric of the sofa she was just sharing with Mrs. Dockery. She turned to Miss Sheldon, reading the necessity for the revelation in her old mentor's decisive look. "Uncle?" she faltered.

"Ah," the dowager supplied in smug tones. "You must mean Sir Andrew. So, he's finally caught on to his niece's whereabouts, has he? Well, well. I had wondered how long it would be before he found us out."

Now it was Her Grace's turn to be met by three sets of eyes, each pair centered upon her own. These did not include Marpessa's, who had settled herself at Cecilia's feet for a nap, such respite being long overdue after her many canine excitements.

"Ma'am? You mean to say that you knew? But that's impossible!" Cecilia gasped in dismay. It was just one shock too many, and Cecilia dropped back to the sofa cushions in total disarray. The Briard shifted slightly to lay her head atop her mistress's feet, merely giving an unconcerned moan of sleepy content.

The dowager did not keep her audience long in suspense. She condescended to explain. "When I first received Mrs. Dockery's inquiry, Cecilia, I instructed her husband to seek out certain information for me. He was at first reluctant to do so for reasons I think you know. But I persisted in asking until the answers were supplied, and he was sure that I meant no one harm. It seems that neither of us was entrusted with the entire story"—the dowager paused to give Mrs. Dockery and her friend an admonishing look—"and he was therefore only too willing to delve further into the matter. More especially, once additional facts came to light."

A bumblebroth of confusion followed this. Mrs. Dockery went pink at the thought of her spouse holding her to blame for not telling him the whole story. "Indeed, I never would have guessed myself that dear Cecilia was so young," she lamented, babbling in her distress; while Miss Sheldon set about assuring Cecilia that she'd no idea Mr. Dockery's perspicacity would have uncovered so much information, and, as the original conspirator, Miss Sheldon then begged Amelia's pardon for having been the instrument of such marital discord as might result. Cecilia, meanwhile, was exclaiming to the dowager that she never meant to cause trouble, and was it possible to forgive her? She was truly sorry for it, but hadn't known what else she should have done.

"Oh, give over," Her Grace finally entered. She rapped her cane in exasperation. "Ladies, ladies! There's nothing to get in such a tizzy about, I assure you. We'll come about in no time."

Iverson opened the door at this juncture, his entry putting paid to further divulgences while the restoratives were laid out on a table. The old dowager serenely poured coffee for those with that preference, while her butler served sherry to herself and to Cecilia.

"And when may I expect a call from the bar-on*et*?" the dowager asked, emphasizing the last, diminutive syllable. "I presume that it will be sometime soon?"

Told that he could arrive at nearly any time, Her Grace caught the butler's eye and instructed, "You will show Sir Andrew Linscombe in when he arrives, Iverson. The Blue Drawing Room, I think. Oh, and, Iverson," she added, "he may ask for our Miss Linscombe here, but instead, you are to send for me."

"Very good, mum," the butler replied without inflection. Bowing to the correct degree, he quietly left the room, just as though this latest request were in no way remarkable. Why Her Grace wanted the Blue Room opened for a mere baronet might have caused him to privately wonder—it being the grandest room in the house—but more, if he understood correctly, Miss Langley was somehow become a "Miss Linscombe." But Iverson kept his expression noncommittal, as only the most superior of servants can do.

"That's that, then," the old lady said with high satisfaction. "Never fear that I cannot manage it, for Mr. Dockery agrees with me in thinking that this Sir Andrew Linscombe is not the man to destroy his precious reputation by annoying a duchess. No, nor even a dowager duchess! Now, ladies, I think the only one we have to feel apprehensive about is . . ."

But before she could finish her speech, the doors burst open to allow in His Grace. A singularly forbidding expression evidenced his displeasure. Apparently, he'd not slowed enough in his trek from the library to be informed that there were guests in the house, since he stormed halfway across the room to the occupied seating area before the presence of visitors registered.

Cecilia looked up and, understandably, resorted to a deep drink of her sherry. Imbibing without the needed degree of concentration, however, this resulted in the liquid passing down the wrong way, causing her to choke and cough loudly as she tried to regain her breath. Marpessa, too, was stirred from her dozing, and, at seeing another old friend come upon them, she charged toward the newcomer with a glad whine.

"Good gad!" His Grace quite rudely expostulated. "Grandmother, who are these people and what are they doing here? I explicitly requested you and Cecilia to attend me in the library at this hour!" His arrogant demand was somewhat diluted by his going down on one knee to fondle the Briard's waiting ears. "Oh, for God's sake," he added unsympathetically as Cecilia continued unsuccessful in her attempts to smother her strangling sounds. "Take some water, Cecilia, do!" An excoriating look accompanied this instruction.

Iverson had included the mentioned liquid on the tray, and Cecilia grabbed a napkin square, pouring herself a glass of water to soothe her mistreated throat. As soon as she regained control, she voiced her exception to the duke's treatment of their guests. "Well, of all the insolence!" she said recklessly, sent to the very limits of her endurance. "You've gone beyond the line this time, Stephen, and I tell you, I will not have it!"

"You—? *You* will not have it?" he answered in angry surprise, raking her down with a look of cold fury. "Just who in blazes set you up to judge my deportment, I'd really like to know? I am in *my* house and I'll act as I please whenever—"

"Oh, yes. Yes, indeed!" Cecilia broke right in. "You are the one who, only last night, was telling me what a considerate fellow you are. Yet here you stand, dismissing my friends and in a manner I can call only disgraceful! Explain yourself, do you dare." Cecilia drew herself to her full five feet and nine, looking the epitome of righteous outrage.

"An excellent point, dear boy," Her Grace cackled, swiveling her head back and forth to catch every word. She seemed enormously enlivened, but upon remembering the niceties, she amended, "Though I shall insist, Stephen, that before we continue, you first permit me to bring Mrs. Dockery and Miss Sheldon to your notice. They must be tired of having to stand for so long while awaiting your attention." She nodded to where the two little ladies stood ready to make their curtsies. "They've brought us a piece of news, along with Cecilia's— what was it again?—oh, yes, her Marpessa."

Recalled to his surroundings, Stephen offered apologies for his uncivil behavior. He exchanged courtesies, though an air of abstraction accompanied his attendance to the necessary obsequies.

Mrs. Dockery and Miss Sheldon traded meaningful looks unobserved. Both seemed to read some special significance into these happenings. Their particular satisfaction may have arisen from the time when they heard the two young people exchange the use of their given names.

After the amenities had thus been seen to, the duke bethought himself of his purpose in searching the household for his errant grandparent and her companion. He withdrew a letter from his pocket and inserted it into Cecilia's reluctant hands. "Yours is the next explanation, I believe," he said with dangerous calm.

Even with Marpessa so close by, Cecilia felt the force of the threat, especially since her vaunted protectress had returned from her greeting to the duke and had promptly lain down again to snooze atop her feet. Cecilia silently cursed Marpessa's unawareness as she struggled to concentrate on the paper given to her hand.

She read the lines therein contained. At the last, she sighed and said softly, "Yes, it's all true." Then, with a feeling of unaccustomed cowardice in the face of so many events gone out of her control, Cecilia passed the sheet on to the dowager duchess.

"Paulites?" Her Grace asked after scanning the lines. "Cecilia, you never told me that the Sisters at Santa Clara were of that order—Roman, of course, but so very exclusive," she said as an aside to her solicitor's goodwife. "Well and well! I knew you'd had good training, gel, but I had no idea you were so fortunate as to serve with the Order of Paulites. And such accolades for you from Dr. Fosgate. I don't know exactly what 'oil of camphor' is, but he says here that you implemented the practice of using it to painlessly remove bandages, making his job very much easier. He also writes that we may credit your skills for actually saving more than one man's life. I had no idea, dear girl!"

Stephen looked more baffled than ever. He interrupted to say, "But, Grandmother, do you mean you knew about this? You knew all along that Cecilia was an impostor? And if you did"—his voice rose aggressively—"why did you not see fit to inform me?"

"Because it wasn't my secret, Stephen. Anyway, why should I have done so? Cecilia is in my charge, after all, and there's been good reason for what's been done. A girl of nineteen cannot easily refuse her uncle's dictates."

"Nine*teen!*" Stephen exploded, whirling round to look at Cecilia. "Do you dare to tell me that for all of this time I've been set on my ear by a child of only nineteen years? I can scarcely credit any of this! And what 'uncle'?"

"Well, of course she's nineteen," his grandmother replied. "How old did you think she was? She certainly never told me otherwise, and I hardly suppose she would mention her age to you at all. As for your last question, Stephen, we are sometime in the next day or so expecting Sir Andrew Linscombe, a Sussex baronet. He is Cecilia's uncle and he intends taking Cecilia away from us." She sniffed in obvious disparagement. "He wants Cecilia as a drudge for some cousin's stepchildren, as I understand it."

"Oh, bloody, *bloody* hell, Grandmother! So all of this time we've been concealing a runaway with a false name? Grandmother," he rumbled on a rising note, facing the dowager squarely. "Just what, exactly, do you think you are about here?"

But Her Grace dismissed his hostility with an airy wave of her hand. "Pooh! Stephen. There's not the least difficulty, so there's no need for you to swear. Once her uncle arrives, I'm sure we can satisfy him that it is to everyone's advantage for her to stay with us. However, dear boy, I would like to know how you consider yourself concerned in all of this?" Her eyes were keen to detect his response.

Before he could reply, Cecilia spoke up from her seat on the sofa. She suddenly felt herself unable, wholly unable, to bear what Stephen might answer.

202

"Can it really make any difference?" she asked of no one in particular. She made herself to sit up straighter. Turning to her employer, she said with quiet firmness, "Ma'am, I shan't countenance your further involvement. It is not right." Prodding her pet with her slipper, she then rose from the cushions and studied each of the ladies by turns. "I have," she said softly, "entangled each of you in my lies, one by one. It's time and past to say 'no more.' I must beg your forgiveness, and do thank you all for trying to help, but when Uncle Andrew comes, I expect I shall go as he bids me." Giving His Grace a small, apologetic smile—she couldn't squeeze another word past the overlarge lump in her throat—she glided sedately from the room. A disgruntled Briard followed.

The duke stared after her for several seconds. Then he, too, stalked out, bearing a look of less-than-complete self-possession. He wondered if he had gone entirely mad. An hour earlier he had quite made up his mind to marry Cecilia, whatever was her background. Now he had to deal with the news that her name was not Langley, that she had a guardian who was a baronet, and that—at a scant nineteen years—she was sheltering in his home in violation of the law. It was unnerving. The door to his library was heard to slam shut moments later.

Her Grace, apparently unmoved, poured out generous shares of wine into three fresh glasses.

"Now, my dears," she said, passing the delicate crystals around, "you must tell me just what it is that you've been up to. And no running sly, mind."

CHAPTER SEVENTEEN

"His Grace, the Most Noble Duke of Kelthorpe, the Marquis of Trelwyn, the Baron Trelwyn, the Baron . . ."

The deep baritone announced the latest arrivals to the elevated company convened in Lady Smithers's lavishly prepared ballroom. In an opulent display, graceful loops of dark green foliage, sprinkled with hundreds of pristine white roses, decorated the walls, while a twelve-piece orchestra played softly from the dais. It was Friday night, and the privileged elite were gathered for an introduction to their hostess's goddaughter, Miss Emmeline Moorehead.

. . . Baron-this, Baron-that. It sounds like Stephen is a whole roomful *of people, all by himself,* Cecilia thought irreverently as the various titles rolled forth.

She had begged her employer to leave her at home, but the crusty old dowager had gotten on her high ropes, declaring that they must go out together one last time. They would not mention the matter of Cecilia's name, Her Grace had decreed, declaring that none need know of the amendment unless Cecilia reconsidered and stayed on at Kelthorpe House. Had the dowager any inkling of her grandson's imprudent proposal at the start of the day, Cecilia doubted the old lady would have been so insistent.

That rash marriage proposal, in fact, was the reason Cecilia was determined to leave London without cry for quarter. The young duke's suit stemmed from an unrelenting sense of duty. *Her* heart was given, but he didn't see it. Not that it mattered. Stephen had told her quite plainly that her emotions were of no moment. And now, with her lies uncovered and her circumstances revealed—he would never again trust her.

Now he would plight his troth before the Dumont. *She* would make him a proper duchess.

Funny that it should be the wife Cecilia had chosen. Something inside twisted painfully at the thought. Almost, she wished she had taken the opportunity to bind Stephen to her.

Cecilia concentrated on the present as they started into the ballroom. The guest of honor was not yet in evidence, it being the practice for a debutante to withhold her appearance until all the guests were assembled. From her position overlooking those gathered, Cecilia recognized golden-haired Janet Whitte with her newly intended, the Honorable Samuel Swanrow. She also glimpsed Lady Arabella in the crowd, strolling away from the doorway as though unaware her soon-to-be intended had just come. *Too, too ridiculous,* Cecilia considered. No one could miss hearing the stentorian tones heralding His Grace's arrival.

With no sign of the same disinterest, Major Lord Emberley was at that same time advancing eagerly toward them. He was easy to pick out from the more modestly garbed, since he had elected to wear full dress regimentals, complete with scarlet tunic, white inexpressibles, and thick cords of gold braid draped from one shoulder. Varicolored medals and honors were pinned to his chest below an elaborate cravat; only a very large man could carry such a gorgeous display without looking preposterous. And Vivian Emberley was just such a one.

"Oh, well met," he greeted them. "Your Grace . . . Miss Langley . . . Stephen!" He clasped each hand in turn and accepted their compliments on his choice of dress. "Have to do the thing up right!" he proclaimed. "Emm—Miss Moorehead, I mean, likes to see me in m'monkey suit, though I don't really care for it m'self. Just as she wishes, though. Lud, yes!"

After a few more such convivial exchanges, the dowager indicated that she was interested in moving on in search of her favorite acquaintances. She excused herself from the gentlemen's company and set off into the throng with Cecilia trailing in her wake.

A wisp of an approving whistle was heard to pass the earl's lips as his eyes followed their departure. Catching sight of Stephen's face, however, the earl met with a thunderous scowl. "What's toward, man?" he questioned, his fluffy yellow brows aloft. "Since when is it shocking that a prime beauty like that fails to pass unnoticed? She was first rank at your dinner party last night—goes without saying, but in the frock tonight—" His lips again pursed in appreciation.

The only reply to this sally was an increased darkening of His Grace's brow. Stephen was in the process of realizing that his friend wasn't the only gentleman to cast a lingering look after Miss "Langley." He had been so intent on the way she had turned his world upside down—and not just today, but every time they met—he had forgotten how attractive she was.

In a gown of silver-shot gray silk, Cecilia made a striking picture. Her height gave distinction to the cut of her dress, even as its muted color drew attention to her fiery curls. Black velvet piping crossed high between her breasts, then gathered into rosettes at the shoulder à la grecque; thus, classic lines displayed the fullness of her figure without bringing cause for censure. She gained the notice of everyone who hadn't yet had the privilege of meeting the dowager's companion. Of those who had, she was reassessed through newly opened eyes.

As she followed the dowager across the room, Stephen's eyes lingered on slim skirts, swirling provocatively against hip and rounded thigh. He brought his senses to order only when his fellow recalled him to his surroundings.

"Take hold, man!" Lord Emberley nudged him. "It won't do to be making black looks and stirring the gossips' porridge. If you have a bone to pick with Miss Langley, 'tisn't as if you should give it to the gabble mongers on a serving plate!"

One corner of Stephen's mouth pulled to the side in self-chastisement. The single eyebrow that had been steadily rising settled back to its accustomed place. "Sorry, Viv. My mind was somewhere else, I'm afraid."

He had been thinking of the letter from Dr. Fosgate that had finally answered his nagging questions, and of the odd coincidence that had brought a second communication to his hand today, as well.

Sergeant-Major Haskell had responded to his former colonel's request by submitting three names for admission to Pen House. The sergeant was so enthused by the project that he had even volunteered his own services after his tour of duty was up and he came of retirement age. The sergeant-major's organizational skills would be extremely useful. He and Sir John had been hoping to find just such a man to take charge of the day-to-day activities at the hospice.

But there was more to the sergeant's letter than that. Sergeant Haskell had also relayed the facts as he knew them concerning Miss Cecilia Linscombe, confirming what Stephen had already learned. And, just like Dr. Fosgate, the sergeant-major was unstinting in his praise. It was apparent that Cecilia had made a particular conquest of the gruff old soldier, for his recrossed letter detailed a fulsome chronicle of the young lady's many merits. Watching Cecilia thread her way through the crowd, Stephen couldn't decide if he was relieved or sorry to have learned this day's several truths.

He hated believing that Cecilia had purposely deceived him after he had proposed to make her his wife. Ever a man of action, this morning he had paid his addresses on the moment—and had been spurned just as quickly—but he couldn't stop himself from wondering what might have happened if he had stayed her in time to insist that she accept his offer.

And why ever had she not?

The bearlike earl threw an arm around his friend's broad shoulders, effectively breaking into these thoughts. "What you need is a drop of the wet," he decreed as Stephen's eyes continued on Cecilia. "Won't have a chance for something with any strength to it once the dancing starts, for my Emmeline says this is her night for champagne. Nasty stuff. Let's get ourselves to the board for something stronger before she comes down. What say you?"

Concluding that this was an excellent suggestion, Stephen agreed. They headed off to the refreshment table, Stephen's black thoughts more or less forgotten in returned camaraderie with the earl.

He was not to know that one spectator, far from dismissing the little episode, instead chose to view what she had seen as a juicy morsel that must be shared.

The baroness Carruthers had been witness to the duke's long, jealous look. Perhaps her recent bout with a similar, unpleasant emotion had pierced her self-important reserve, for she'd been nursing a pique ever since Lady Arabella had supplanted her as the leading contender for the ducal title. Now, armed with her observations, the baroness was pleased to be handed the means to cut up a rival. Ignoring all but the subject of her envy, she plotted a course through Lady Smithers's guests to where Lady Arabella Dumont stood in conversation.

"Baroness," Lady Arabella acknowledged the newcomer. She made room for Lady Carruthers to join the set of Fashionables with whom she was just chatting.

"The Duke of Kelthorpe has arrived," Lady Carruthers pronounced significantly.

"Yes, I may have heard the announcement," Lady Arabella replied. "I expect His Grace will soon seek me out. So flattering, don't you agree?" She pressed such a sticky-sweet smile on her would-be rival that the baroness could scarce hold her tongue to civility.

"Oh, indeed, his manners are everything conciliating!" Lady Carruthers trilled with a smile as confectionery as any. "Why, I daresay everyone bends to his charm. Not, of course, that we women should expect much more from him, not under the circumstances," she added portentously.

Never very quick in her understanding, some warning must nonetheless have managed to enter Lady Arabella's mind. She drew her informer over to one side, out of earshot of the others. "Pray, to what do you refer, Baroness? I don't quite comprehend you."

The baroness was pleased as Punch at the chance to enjoy someone else's discomfort. "Oh, I'm sure I tell you nothing that you don't know. I refer to His Grace's involvement with—what shall we call her?—his *convenient*, whom he brought with him tonight."

Lady Arabella looked mystified and not a little suspicious. "What are you saying, Baroness? If you refer to Miss Langley, you misunderstand her position. She is engaged as the dowager's companion, merely a genteel dowd in reduced circumstances." Then, with complaisance, "You must know that I expect His Grace to declare himself any day."

"Well, if that's the case, I should say nothing more. However—" The baroness sharpened her weapons and set herself to destroying a reputation. "*Dear* Lady Arabella, permit me to remind you that His Grace never went about when last he was in town, yet since his return, he goes everywhere, dancing attendance on Miss Langley. I'm surprised you didn't recognize their liaison sooner. Likely, the duke got her the position with the dowager in the first place."

Lady Arabella looked shocked. "Are you implying that there is something *between* His Grace and Miss Langley? But it was she who told me how His Grace held me in particular regard. I encouraged his attentions because she said he had already singled me out."

It was the baroness's turn to be shocked. "You say Miss Langley apprised you of the duke's partiality? How interesting, when she assured me that *I* stood high in His Grace's esteem. At the time, she excused his lack of forthcomingness because she said he was shy."

"No, no," Lady Arabella demurred. "Miss Langley confided the reason for the duke's failure to approach *me* as due to an injury suffered in the war."

"Bosh! No such thing." The baroness laughed unpleasantly. "If His Grace had suffered so much as a single scratch, you may be sure we would have heard of it. No, I think our Miss Langley wanted to inspire our interest so as to cover up her own scandalous deportment. Mark my words, His Grace knows just what she's about, too. See for yourself."

The baroness indicated the spot where Miss Langley sat with the dowager. The duke, a few steps away, had his eyes fixed on the young woman, an intent, almost hungry appreciation on his face.

"Oooh!" breathed Lady Arabella, uncertain whether to swoon or to scream.

But the baroness guided her vacillating thoughts toward more positive action. "Someone ought to enlighten Her Grace," she said with honeyed malice. "The dowager needs to be told before it becomes the subject of general gossip. Of course, since you assure me that you are all but affianced to her grandson, you should to be the one to see to it."

But even Lady Arabella's confidence was shaken by this enjoinder. She feared the old dowager would not take kindly to criticism of her house, and Her Grace's reputation for dispensing a sharp snubbing was well known. The Prince Regent himself trode lightly when crossing her path! "But do you consider that I really should?" Lady Arabella asked. "I mean, it isn't as if we had any particular evidence."

"Certainly, we do," Lady Carruthers maintained. "What about the dreadful Banbury tales Miss Langley has been telling? That alone convicts her!"

Lady Arabella, stung, was in full agreement with this. In spite of her earlier declaration, she had ofttimes found the duke deficient in the appropriate courtesies to herself. He didn't send her flowers or sweet verses of poetry like her other admirers—that nice Lord Hallstead, for example. And if His Grace weren't pained by a wound, for so she'd excused him these many lapses, why, it meant that he wasn't even a hero!

Lady Arabella was shaken to realize that the duke was in no wise worthy of her passionate concern. Like the baroness, she felt a strong need to retaliate. To have wasted her time on a man of crass nature was bad enough, but to have been cut out by the drab Miss Langley was beyond what someone of her refined sensibilities could countenance. A person of Miss Langley's stamp did not belong in their *monde élevé*.

Baroness Carruthers smiled in satisfaction, when, without another word, the dark beauty started over to where the dowager duchess sat with her companion.

Before Lady Arabella made it across the floor, however, Miss Emmeline Moorehead was introduced to the assembly. All conversation stopped as the *ton* paid homage to its newest member. Ethereal in a cloud of rarest floss silk, the debutante began her slow descent into the ballroom. Lady Arabella had to step lively to get to her destination before the first dance was announced.

While everyone's attention was drawn to the doorway, the old dowager glanced away in time to note the young peeress's movements. "Just you let me handle this," she advised her companion.

Cecilia, watching Miss Moorehead's entry and joining in with the applause of greeting for the debutante, at first didn't understand Her Grace's warning. She hadn't remarked the consultation between Lady Arabella and Baroness Carruthers—hadn't realized that this day required a further reckoning.

"Your Grace," Lady Arabella purred, sidling over. "I regret having to bring it to your notice, but I feel obliged to tell you that we have both been deceived in Miss Langley." Careful not to be heard above the clapping sounds, she continued. "Miss Langley has bandied it about that the duke, your grandson, was *épris* in certain directions; additionally, she gave me to understand that he had sustained an injury in the war, which I have since learned was untrue. I was misled in judging His Grace's nature because of her interference, although I must be glad to have learned the truth before my heart was quite, quite broken!" She said this last with a sob of emotion, quickly erased by a cool and spiteful look. "I believe we must examine her reasons for these inventions," she insisted.

Staccato raps of the dowager's cane put a stop to further complaints. "And *I* take leave to tell you that you've not had two thoughts to rub together since you were in swaddling clothes," Her Grace snarled. "The only misjudgment that's occurred here was in Cecilia's presuming that you had enough furniture in the upstairs to make a match of it with a duke. So, be off with you, gel, before I tell you precisely what I think of you. And where everyone can hear it!"

A scowl of such ferocity accompanied this denunciation that Lady Arabella couldn't doubt that the enraged old dowager meant what she said. None of the other guests, so far, had noticed, leaving Lady Arabella to seek succor among gentler souls than those of the House of Kelthorpe. Lord Hallstead came into her view, and she rushed to his side and took up his arm, holding to it as if glued.

For her part, Cecilia had all she could do to keep her mouth from hanging open. The dowager's sudden display of vitriol had sent her mind reeling, even as the implications of the skirmish doused hopes for a peaceful evening.

Nor had Her Grace finished venting her spleen. "As for you, my young miss—" The old lady turned and glared at her. "Did you think to please me by setting those hulver-headed gels on my grandson? I don't say I entirely understand what you thought you were about, but I will say that it was a very sly piece of work. Clever girl!" she approved.

Cecilia did open her mouth at this—and closed it—feeling very like a landed fish. She felt such a fool, so exposed! The old dowager didn't seem to mind what she had done, though, nor expect explanations. For that Cecilia could only be grateful.

After the opening dance ended, Cecilia's thoughts were cheered somewhat when she was introduced to the fair lady who had captured Major Lord Emberley's heart. Every bit as charming as her pretty face promised, Cecilia was pleased to exchange speech with Miss Emmeline Moorehead. Although the young lady had few minutes to call her own, their brief visit showed Miss Moorehead as possessed of an infectious gaiety which colored the evening for everyone.

And for Cecilia in particular.

Where normally she could consider herself an unobtrusive element in any assembly, and tonight had prayed for such neglect, instead, the very air seemed wont to glisten and shimmer with contagious enthusiasm. She was conscious that others felt it, too, since a number of gentlemen—one, then another—sought introduction to their party. Presently, Cecilia found herself awash in Bucks and Bloods, though Her Grace evidenced little interest. Most confounding of all was when Cecilia saw the Duke of Kelthorpe recruited into service.

The first time it happened, Stephen approached her rather warily with a young officer of the Guards at his side. He made her acquainted with the young captain, then turned on his heel and left. Thereafter, the duke was compelled to introduce other importuning young men, some of the military and some not, while his look underwent various changes until it became one of almost comical resignation. Finally, he elected to stay by her side for convenience' sake.

Cecilia was relieved when his presence proved some sort of deterrent. The crowd surrounding her thinned until she stood alone with His Grace. She offered him a look of commiseration, becoming flustered at his answer to her overture.

"Not exactly how we began the day, is it?" he said under his breath. "Behold, my chivalrous conceit." He made a brief motion toward the group of beaux who had collected a short distance away, all gazing at Cecilia with similar hopeful expressions. Stephen shook his head. "Can you believe this? We started off this morning with what I believe you termed a 'farce,' and have ended with a—dare I say it?—a farce." He raised one winged brow and gave her a touchingly lopsided smile.

Cecilia yearned to tell him that she hadn't meant this morning's bitter words in the garden at all. She wished she could reach back in time and begin the day anew, praying that if given a second chance, she would have the courage to tell him the truth without having been forced to it. She knew she should have had enough of admissions and confessions, but his opening decided her to make a clean breast of it before she had time to change her mind.

"There is, I fear, another thing you don't know of, something else I've done that you may not quite like."

"Hold line," he at once intervened. "Let it rest, Cecilia. We've had sufficient to deal with this day already, have we not?"

She thought she discerned a note of benediction

in his voice; it near broke her heart that this last confession would put an end to his compassion. "But you will need to know what I've done." She sighed and took a fortifying breath. "You see, it's about Miss Whitte and the baroness Carruthers—and, well, mostly about Lady Arabella."

"Did I not charge you to halt?" he quizzed her with a smile. "I know all about it, for Grandmother filled me in while you were busy with your entourage of admirers. The Dumont *was* too tiresome to be borne, I admit. And Grandmother also reminded me that, when she summoned me to London to find a wife, she had meant for me to choose one with at least a modicum of sense."

Cecilia fairly goggled at this. "What say you? Her Grace charged you to marry? But—but I thought it was you who wanted a wife!"

"Not in the beginning. It was Grandmother who recalled me to my duty and demanded that I look to my nursery. Why? Does it make a difference?"

"Nooo," she answered. "But when your letter came, you presented the matter as if it were *your* plan. It made me think you intended to banish your grandmother to some dismal dower house at the earliest opportunity." She refused to look away, holding her ground despite his obvious disgust. "It was because of what had happened to me—how Uncle Andrew decided that I was a burden, you see. That's why I encouraged my choices for your bride; I picked out those most apt to prefer living away from London, thinking to ensure Her Grace's continued residence at Kelthorpe House."

"You thought I could do such a thing?" Angrily, he perused a spot on the floor in front of him. After a few moments he seemed to relax and brought his gaze back to hers. He looked as though he would read her thoughts.

"Oh, we do make a habit of misjudging each other, don't we, Cecilia? Still, after the treatment you suffered at the hands of your family, I suppose it was logical for you to expect others to act the same way. I am truly sorry. I could have been quicker to realize what you were afraid of, instead of adding to your problems. You simply set yourself to helping someone you thought needed protection. Ah, yes," he murmured, "farce, indeed."

Rather than respond to the implied intimacy, Cecilia took refuge in a light rejoinder. "Well, I agree that this evening presents some kind of comedy. You would never credit the flattery that has come my way! And while it might be nice to pretend I deserve such adulation, my looking-glass shows me otherwise. Oh, the trim on this dress is by my own hand and not too badly done"—she touched a velvet rosette at her shoulder—"but I cannot attribute tonight's accolades to my stitchery. Oh! I say, do you suppose Miss Moorehead's champagne punch has made everyone noddy?"

Stephen stared at her in wonder. "Then, you don't think the gentlemen are drawn by your beauty, Cecilia?"

Sparkling laughter tumbled out. "Hardly that," she chortled. "Not unless red-haired giantesses have become all the rage." Struck by the thought, she beamed him a wide smile. "But that's the answer!" she insisted. "We're forever hearing about this or that absurd fashion—they seem to come and go for no reason at all. This latest piece of nonsense must be just another of Society's eccentricities. Of course!" She clapped her hands together, gleeful at having solved the puzzle.

"If that is what you believe, it would explain much," he said, a slight harshness coloring his tone. "Cecilia, do you not understand how captivating you are? Look about the room," he commanded with a gesture. "Look and see women clench their teeth in envy. And how many men have begged me tonight, yes, begged me! for an introduction to the most arresting young lady present. Your expressive dark eyes, with their enticing specks of gold, would cost a *saint* his virtue." Stephen studied her startled expression before continuing more gently,

"And even if you did believe me, even if you realized your power, you wouldn't care what these people thought, would you?"

What on earth was he getting at? She most certainly did care if he found her pleasing to look at. Why, there was nothing she wouldn't give to be thought alluring by this man. She drank in the sight of his cloud-soft eyes, aching to have him take her in his arms and into the warmth of his embrace.

Once again, without her having uttered a word, Stephen seemed to read something in her face. "So, that's the way of it," he said softly. "Indeed, I've been a bloody awful fool about this, haven't I?"

Such an enigmatic expression followed this bit of rhetoric that Cecilia was less than sure of his meaning. Before she could find a reply, however, he thought to ask the question which had stayed on his mind for weeks.

He held her eyes, his own face unreadable, and said, "There is one other thing I would know from you, since this seems to be our day for candor. Tell me, who was that fellow standing outside the hotel when your dog came in answer to my dinner invitation? And, yes, I surely saw him," he answered her appalled look.

Cecilia bit her lip. She scanned the area to be sure none stood within hearing. She whispered, "That was I."

"You?" he blurted out, unconcerned for any listeners. "But that can't be right. It was a young man I saw . . ."

She shook her head. "No, it wasn't. I have this apparel, you see. It's what you might even call a disguise. Anyway, it's what I wore when I took Marpessa out that night. I used the same ensemble when I left Linscombe Hall, for it made me less noticeable on the stage trip here to London. Miss Sheldon didn't approve," she added wryly, "but it seemed appropriate at the time."

Stephen was *completely* stupefied. He had never

thought that when the explanation came, it would be anything so simple—or so improbable.

A chuckle escaped him. Another soon followed. Then, before he knew it, he was laughing aloud and in real earnest, helplessly shouting in elation.

Lord Rutheven heard and was compelled to an answering grin. Gone was Stephen's usual sober air; he now made the picture of a man who was enjoying himself hugely. Others in hearing reacted with smiles and chuckles of pleasure, while Cecilia gurgled with happy laughter of her own. Before long, their half of the room had joined into the merrymaking, though few understood its source.

Her Grace's attention was caught by the scene. She considered the pair who had started the incident, then she eased over to where her grandson stood with Cecilia. "So," she said without preamble, "you're a man like your grandfather, after all, Stephen. Proximity was the answer *then*, and it's all that was needed now. My boy, I think it's time we took ourselves home!"

Before Cecilia could absorb what was happening, she found herself whisked away to their carriage, rolling homeward over the cobbled streets. She was sure that her behavior had somehow, much as had transpired so many times in her youth, given offense.

Claiming that her eyes were too tired to tolerate another flicker of light until the morrow, the old lady extinguished the inside lamps so that they traveled the short distance to Cavendish Square in darkness. No one spoke. Cecilia kept silent in courtesy to the dowager, who would not be able to "hear"; Stephen held his own private thoughts; and Her Grace . . . ? Well, Her Grace was silent for her own reasons.

CHAPTER EIGHTEEN

The ride home accomplished, they found Marpessa waiting in the front hallway. She greeted her mistress with glad little yips, then offered her ears for the duke's attentions, wriggling in idiotic ecstasy when he complied. While he extended this service, Cecilia hoped someone would explain.

Stephen's laughter tonight had all but made her heart burst from gladness, till the dowager had interfered. Had Her Grace learned about the duke's impetuous proposal, and was that why she had seemed so angry? If Her Grace knew of her grandson's folly, though, she must know how impossible it was that he would renew his suit. What harm if they parted friends?

But no explanation came. "Cecilia," the dowager ordered, "you will oblige me by remaining in your bedchamber tomorrow until I send for you. Ring for your breakfast to be brought when you wish, but stay in your room until you have word from me. Do you understand?" Both hands atop her cane, she frowned into her companion's uncomprehending face.

"As you like, ma'am," Cecilia managed to say. She stole a quick look at Stephen, but his attention was still on Marpessa. Cecilia swallowed her fears and questions and said, "The time will be useful for readying my belongings, ma'am, for my uncle is not a patient man. He will appreciate my being prepared for departure."

She had passed any hope of exoneration, better to play least-in-sight until her uncle came. What plans Uncle Andrew would have for her, she dared not speculate upon, but she didn't want to further upend Her Grace, who had, until then, been nothing but kindness itself.

Rising from his crouch beside the Briard, Stephen addressed his grandmother. "And shall you expect me to remain behind my doors as well?" he said in flat tones. "You need not bother, Grandmother, for I've business to see to and may not return before lunchtime." He held the dowager with a steady eye.

"Of course, you must do as you please, Stephen." She met his look. "I shall join you at lunch then; that is, if you've no objection."

He nodded acquiescence and, without so much as a glance in Cecilia's direction, took his grandmother's arm to guide her up the staircase. Cecilia hoped he would at least wish her farewell on the morrow.

The Briard led the way, going immediately to Cecilia's room. Iverson had kept the door to that chamber open, judging from the crumpled twist in the bedside carpet. Cecilia closed the door after her pet. Thoughtfully, she considered the position of the gilt-framed cheval glass mirror in the corner of her room.

Squaring her shoulders, Cecilia dragged the heavy looking-glass to a new location, its casters groaning in protest. She positioned the glass in the center of the room, then half lifted, half pulled her two bedside tables over to stand beside the mirror. Gathering up every candle she could find, she arranged them on the tables and lit each wick in turn. The room filled with light.

She stood in front of the glass. No shadows distorted her image. She began a thorough comparison between herself and the proclaimed beauties on the town, while half-forgotten memories of her father's compliments floated through her mind. Miss Sheldon's assurances, Mrs. Dockery and the dressmaker . . . Captivating? Not gawky? Not garish? A slow, easing smile lit her face. Yes. Definitely *cap-*

tivating. She twirled around in a circle, relishing the new feeling of self-awareness.

Stephen had wanted her to believe that she was lovely—and she was!

Satisfied, she extinguished all but one flame and returned the items of revelation to their places. Whatever sadness the morrow's partings might bring, she would take with her one item which no one could steal away. She would take with her the knowledge that Stephen Trelwyn had found her beautiful on one very special night.

When Cecilia awoke the next day, her little enameled timepiece informed her that she had slept past her regular hour. She jumped from her bed and snatched up her dressing gown before she remembered that the day held none of the usual duties. She dropped back down on the edge of the lace-trimmed coverlet.

Marpessa rose majestically and stretched to her length, shaking first one hind leg and then the other, and yawned. After which, she went to the door and looked back at her mistress with obvious intent.

Here was a to-do! Her dog wanted to make a visit to the gardens, while *she* was enjoined to stay in her room.

Cecilia began to dress. There was no sense in making her pet suffer, and it was unthinkable to let Marpessa roam the house unescorted—the outside doors might all be shut against her. Not that there was any danger that the Briard might "forget herself," but Cecilia decided that the dog should not be left uncomfortable because of her mistress's current state of disgrace.

Shrugging at her disobedience to the dowager's wishes, Cecilia marched down the front staircase, turned through the breakfast room, and exited through the conservatory. Unlikely as it might seem, each of these rooms was unoccupied, so none remarked her progress.

"Sit you down and be silent," Her Grace commanded.

"But, Your Grace, I only wanted to say that I—"

"I'll warrant that I understand you very well, sirrah. You imply that I do not know of Cecilia's tie with your house, but I take leave to tell you that such is not at all the case. On the contrary, your acres march not many miles from the lady Astemarle's—a friend of mine, by the bye—and I have long since written to tell her that Miss Cecilia Linscombe resides here with me and is my dearest companion. I can assure you that it will be thought most peculiar if you deny knowledge of what half of Sussex already knows—the Marchioness of Astemarle does so dearly love to gossip."

Dumbstruck, Sir Andrew sank into a brocaded chair cushion of light blue silk.

The baronet had arrived at Kelthorpe House just after nine, forgetting that town hours differed from those thought seemly in the country. Nonetheless, he had been led into the grandest room imaginable by a very proper, very dignified butler who, though saying nothing about it, had still managed to convey the impropriety of his having called so early of a morning. The baronet had been told to wait upon Her Grace's pleasure, then was left to cool his heels for an hour before the dowager duchess had been announced. Sir Andrew next had learned that not only was he expected, but that his niece's position and name were no news to anyone!

In a light, bellefleur pongee trimmed with narrow bands of organdied silk, the dowager duchess presented a powerful presence on Sir Andrew's shaken senses. He had come expecting to see Cecilia dismissed on the spot, never thinking to find himself under attack.

And he was, indeed, familiar with Lady Astemarle's reputation. Although the Linscombes had seldom obtained an invitation to the Astemarle marquisate, he knew that Lady Linscombe would never forgive him if things got so far out of hand that they found themselves shunned by local society. The dowager's uncompromising mien convinced him, too, that the white-haired *grande dame* meant every word.

"But in London my niece is known as 'Langley,'" he blustered. "How do you think to explain that, Your Grace?"

Had the dowager's hearing been in better order, she might have noted a mewling note in the baronet's tone. As it was, however, she had no need of sound to tell her that the portly man in the goslin-green superfine was well and truly beaten. "Tomorrow we go to Carlton House," she announced, delivering the *coup de grâce*. "There Cecilia will make her bow before His Royal Highness, the Prince Regent of England. After Prinny acknowledges Miss Cecilia Linscombe, think you any will dare to remark? My experience of our world says that all will be forgotten by those who may have 'misunderstood' the name."

The baronet was impressed. He bethought himself that a connection with noble Kelthorpe House was not to be despised! "I hadn't expected to visit Carlton House," he cried, overcome by the honor. "I'm not sure whether I've brought sufficient wardrobe for the occasion, but my London tailor will smarten me up in short order—Smerley & Alfinch, as you see." Fondly, he patted the fashionably wide lapels of his coat. "Oh, too bad Lady Linscombe cannot be here, eh? eh?"

"*Au contraire,*" the dowager barked with a crack of her cane. "You have been invited nowhere at all! And I will tell you further that neither you nor your wife will be allowed a foot inside *my* door in the future. If Cecilia desires to visit you in Sussex, she may do so at her convenience, but at Kelthorpe House"—she paused to let the effrontery of his assumption soak in—"we do not welcome you."

With the prescience of his calling, Iverson chose this moment to open the double-wide doors to the

Blue Drawing Room. A virtual parade of footmen followed him, all in one straight and silent line. In his hand Iverson bore the baronet's hat, held at a precise angle of readiness. The Kelthorpe butler awaited Her Grace's pleasure.

The dowager duchess stood and, in the chilliest of accents, said, "Good day to you, sirrah," as she left the room.

Sir Andrew gaped after her. Such insult had never before come his way. He was actually being given the *cut*.

"This way, sir," Iverson intoned, his eyes fixed some inches above the baronet's head.

Left no other option, Sir Andrew collected his stylish chapeau and quitted the house in defeat. He could only pray that no report of the dowager's snub reached ready ears in Hazelmere.

As the baronet stood outside, attempting to hail a hackney carriage to take him away, even upon the moment when he raised his hand to signal his need, another person was moving out of doors in like confusion and dread.

Cecilia was at the point of seating herself on her favorite bench in the rose arbor.

She stared down at her hands, empty and immobile in her lap. She was unaware of either the morning's visitor, or that Marpessa was busily sniffing out the gardens, inch over inch, at a ground-covering pace. When the dog trotted over to the double-tiered fountain near her mistress's seat to obtain a refreshing taste of London water, Cecilia at last looked up. The gurgling patter of the waterfall made a soothing sound in her ears.

It also disguised other sounds. Neither the Briard nor her mistress heard approaching footsteps.

"I've no ha'penny to offer you, but perhaps this will reveal your thoughts" came a deep voice at Cecilia's shoulder.

Cecilia gulped, her hands flying to cover cheeks rapidly staining pink. She chided herself and fought to regain her aplomb. "I know I'm not supposed to be out here, but 'Pessa needed to—she wanted to . . ."

Retrieving his extended and as yet unnoticed hand, Stephen sat down on the bench beside her. Ignoring her stumbling excuses, low-voiced, he said, "Now, why is it, I wonder, that I'm not surprised at finding you here? Whatever could make me suppose that you would do as directed? Naturally, if greater concerns call for your attention, you must do what is needful. I understand that much about you." He turned to where the Briard stood, noisily lapping up her drink. "So, I can appreciate that you felt your first duty was to allow Marpessa to, ah, assuage her impressive thirst."

Relieved of her immediate embarrassment, Cecilia raised her eyes as far as His Grace's neckcloth. However, her eyes shot up to his when his next words smote her ears.

"I encountered your uncle a few moments ago. No, no, dearest one," he soothed her. "There's no need for alarm, he was just leaving." Stephen laid an arm across her shoulders. "Grandmother sent him off with a flea in his ear; he won't return, never doubt it."

Stephen brought his other hand forward again. Using his thumb, he flicked the tiny brass latch to open a small velvet box. Nestled inside was a great bluish-green stone, surrounded by cut diamonds so icy-white that anyone could see that they were of the first water. Their brilliance enhanced the darker glow from the huge center stone; it was an utterly marvelous gem.

Emerald. Its transparent glow stood in timeless symbol of a true lover's faithfulness.

It took several seconds for Cecilia to realize that the item she beheld was a ring. Even so, the recognition failed to sink home. She sat in silence as he gently removed his arm from around her shoulders, taking up his gift to slide it onto the fourth finger of her left hand. She shivered as if chilled, despite the brightness of the sunshine.

Stephen replaced his arm about her, drawing her into the warmth of his wide chest. "I suppose I could fetch the half-penny; although, I admit, I had hoped that the Earthly Delights would tempt you to prefer a Flesh and Blood creature for your Company." One silky black eyebrow climbed to a quizzical peak.

Giving in to a long-denied impulse, Cecilia reached out to touch the furrow raised on his forehead. She stroked the warm skin back to unlined smoothness. She was not really conscious of her actions, neither did she give particular notice to the ring encircling her finger, being intent on the task she performed. But the lush green stone would not be ignored. A spark of green fire put the surrounding foliage to shame.

"Oh, my," she whispered as the jewel attracted her interest.

This caused the duke's brow to rise yet again. "Don't say you dislike the color, my love. I was sure this morning when I made my selection that it was perfect. Or, perhaps, you mean to tell me that you intend another refusal. Before you do that, though, consider that there rests in my pocket your uncle's signature on a document approving me as your husband. You see," he continued mildly, "I convinced Sir Andrew he should award me this favor."

"But—but you cannot mean we should marry," Cecilia squeaked. "I am naught but a fraud, a hoyden, a *liar*. I am hardly an acceptable wife for a duke. Stephen, you cannot have thought this through!"

She tried to pull away, but his grasp held firm as he took up the hand now bearing his ring. "Oh, my beautiful angel," he said gently. Smoke-gray eyes looked into hers, undisturbed. "If the lack, or so I thought, of proper antecedents couldn't deter me from offering you marriage yesterday, why should my learning of the expedients you've been put to concern me now? If we're to speak of truth, then the truth is in what I finally realized last night. A duchess"—he paused, his voice strengthening as he emphasized his words—"needs follow no one's pattern. She must, rather, be just what I now hold in my arms: a woman moved by her own judgment and one who, in honor, disregards outside opinion. She must also, and most important, be a woman who loves me—as I love her."

Cecilia's thoughts took a crazy tilt and spun madly. Her eyes blurred, then focused on his ardent look. She protested, "But Her Grace! She cannot want—"

Stephen forestalled her with a shake of his head and a handsome, carefree smile. "Grandmother? I thought something of the same thing when I braved her room early this morning, thinking to assert my privilege as head of my house, you understand. Instead, I learned that she, along with your two stalwart patronesses—Mrs. Dockery and Miss Sheldon, if you've not already caught on to them—had connived at our union almost from the first. It seems that all three of them conspired to throw us together. And, as happens so often with your sex," he said in self-mocking tones, "the ladies assessed your character far sooner than I. Oh, yes, I fear I've spent too many years in the company of males and only lately have learned to appreciate the canniness of the female."

Marpessa ambled over to sniff at His Grace's boot. Grateful for the intrusion, Cecilia said, "So I came here by design? Miss Sheldon and Mrs. Dockery expected us to meet?"

"Well, Grandmother implied as much, though she refused me the particulars. In any case, she entered into the scheme independently and with a winning hand." Stephen's face split into a happy grin, tiny creases fanning out from the corners of his eyes. "Older and wiser heads than ours have been at work here, Cecilia, so it behooves us to give in gracefully, don't you think?"

This time Cecilia didn't hesitate. She met his look, willingly moving toward the kiss that she knew awaited her. She surrendered her heart and her future to her bold, arrogant, most wonderful love.

Whispering words of devotion, both took advantage of the plotters' result.

EPILOGUE

High above crenelated ramparts of golden-gray stone, a kestrel hovered in the late summer air. In silence, the falcon peered down, then moved slowly away to the north, beyond a dark green lake. The kestrel made a lazy circle of the lake before languidly winging his way toward the surrounding hills.

"And how does James Carlisle like his home acres?" asked the gentleman who stretched out on the shore grass beside that same lake. His Schweitzer-made coat was casually draped over a nearby bush.

"Stephen, fie," admonished his young wife. "It's only this week that the doctor confirms my condition; anyway, just what makes you so sure of a boy?"

The Duke of Kelthorpe rolled onto his side and raised the lid of a picnic hamper to examine the remains. "Well," he replied, his eye on the food, "Mrs. Mullins sent us out with a whole chicken, four fruit tarts, half a round of cheese—and what else? Ah, yes. Bread, apples, and two large meat pies. Now, I recall eating less than half of what's missing from this basket, so . . ."

A small carriage-pillow was sent flying into his face. "Oh, what has that to say to anything? It was the long ride in the pony cart—it made me hungry, that's all."

"Possibly, possibly. But Grandmother tells me that I was ever known for my appetite, and I watched you devour the better part of our lunch with such relish that I thought my conclusion obvious." He passed his wife a smug look. "I may wish to name our first son for your father, but he will be a Trelwyn for all that."

Cecilia reached out to recover her pillow, tucking it comfortably under her neck. A smile lit her eyes as she lay back to view the puffs of cloud high above. "Her Grace is pleased, isn't she? Why, she told me only this morning that, from now on, she plans to spend every autumn with us here at the castle—*if* we promise ourselves to her in the spring. You would think that at her age an infant would be too much fuss for her, but no. I don't believe anyone could be more excited than she at our news."

One long, masculine arm extended to the pillow and tossed it aside. At the same time, Stephen inserted a thick forearm beneath Cecilia's head. Scarcely a cinnamon-colored curl was disturbed. His eyes fell to within inches of her own as he said, "But you shan't say that, my angel, for you are as delighted by the coming event as am I, and surely none could match our, um . . . excitement."

Cecilia blushed quite as prettily as any bride of sixteen weeks could and hid her face in his collar. "You know perfectly well that's not what I meant."

Drawing back slightly to better observe her expression, Stephen said, "Well, insofar as Grandmother's wishes go, we'll have to wait and see whether we can comply or not. Our child plans his or *her* first appearance sometime in May, I believe? Hmmm. Now that I consider it, Cecilia, I think I would prefer a daughter, a beautiful and independent-minded poppet, just like her mother. Yes, that should do me." He straightened up on his elbows and regarded his wife's sparkling eyes.

"More likely the middle of April," she corrected, giggling when a splash of color rose high in His Grace's cheeks. "Our wedding *was* the tenth day of July, Stephen." She then said dreamily, "And wasn't it truly the most beautiful day? I felt like a queen when I entered the castle's chapel and found the Dockerys and Miss Sheldon, the dear dowager, and even Iverson waiting for me. Then, when Mr. Dockery couldn't turn his head past his collar while he fumbled around trying to find my hand to pass it into yours—and your friend Vivian couldn't remember into which pocket he'd put the ring—!" She laughed with the memory.

"And your Marpessa in the pew with Miss Sheldon holding her paw, threatening to 'sing' with the village choir. Don't forget that part. How came I to allow a dog into our wedding party, anyway?"

"Oh, but it was all lovely." Cecilia sighed in contentment. "It is hard to imagine so much has happened and in such a short time."

"My special thanks go to Miss Sheldon," Stephen murmured into her ear. "Her agreement to stay half the year with Grandmother leaves us free to spend most of our time here. And did you remember to show her that slow, selective blink to indicate a speaker for Grandmother? A neat trick that."

"Yes, she knows of it. Miss Sheldon is thrilled to spend the time in London, too, and your grandmother is teaching her the fine points of piquet. B-but what—!" Cecilia raised herself up, nearly knocking heads with her spouse as she realized the import of his question. "Stephen!" she accused. "Do you mean to tell me that you knew all along that Her Grace was deaf?"

"I'm not such a nodcock as to miss a thing like that," he retorted with an air of injured pride. "I suspected something of the sort when I returned from the Peninsula, and subsequent occurrences confirmed the matter. Didn't you notice that I never spoke unless I had her full attention?"

Shamefaced at her oversight, particularly since she remembered that she had scarcely regarded anything much whenever Stephen was in the same room, Cecilia conceded her omission.

"Moreover," he stated firmly, "I've convinced Grandmother that while it may be unnecessary to announce the fact of her condition to all and sundry, it would be helpful if she informed everyone close to her about her difficulty."

"Quite right!" Cecilia returned. "I often thought that Lord Rutheven knew, and I did note that Iverson took pains to catch her eye." She stretched and settled her head back against Stephen's arm. "How I do love it here," she said after a space. "I think I fell in love with Castle Kelthorpe before ever we arrived."

"You're not sorry we forewent a bride-trip, then? Sheep and crops don't leave you discontent?" Gray eyes looked down upon the smooth oval of Cecilia's face. When her burnished curls shook in the negative, Stephen's lips parted in a slow smile. "Then, my most beautiful angel, since we've managed to elude Marpessa's company this afternoon, we would be remiss if we wasted the next hour . . . or two. What say you, my love?"

Provoking gold specks swam enticingly beneath his gaze. Correctly assessing the significance of this response, Stephen proceeded to use the time as desired.

More Romance
from Regency